Volume Three

AIRSHIP 27 PRODUCTIONS

Sinbad: The New Voyages Volume 3
"The Warriors of Forever"
© 2014 C.B. Harvey

Published by Airship 27 Productions
www.airship27.com
www.airship27hangar.com

Interior and cover illustrations © 2014 James Conahan

Editor: Ron Fortier
Associate Editor: Charles Saunders
Production and design: Rob Davis
Marketing and Promotions: Michael Vance

eBook Edition

"The Warriors of Forever"
C.B. Harvey

Chapter One

He gazed keenly out across the azure sea, green eyes rendered orange with the rising of the gigantic orb to the West. The creature sensed something, but did not possess the mind to comprehend what that something might be. It was danger, he knew that much. A pointed, slightly bitten ear twitched, in response to a shriek and then another, followed by an altogether more mighty, metallic scraping. He stretched forward on the prow, confident in his ability to balance without falling. Now he could see something bobbing on the water: a wooden vessel, akin to the one upon which he stood and which had lately become his home. Then two more of similar scale, but also many smaller vessels. And beyond them something else, something huge and horrific, striding through the water. Samson the cat let out a low hiss.

Now he was a blur of action, jumping down from the prow and onto the deck, then up again, into the rigging, racing ever skyward. Upon reaching its summit he leapt, with a gracefulness that belied his size, onto the figure of a snoring Haroun.

The youngster swiped the large cat away, turning on his side in the process. In return Samson batted Haroun insistently about the face, and Haroun's eyes flickered open in annoyance. Samson hissed again and Haroun mimicked, narrowing his eyes. Samson didn't see the joke, instead emitting an impatient yowl. Resigned, the wiry youth pulled himself to his feet and peered out at the rising sun, lifting a battered-looking spyglass to his eye. What he saw made his jaw swing open.

In his adventures aboard this ship Haroun had seen many things that he would never have imagined possible, often from far distances, and this was one such instance. He could see, or at least he *thought* he could see, a colossal metal dragon, as high as a mountain, wading through the sea. Ahead of the behemoth a flotilla of ships of all sizes, from dhows to tiny row boats and makeshift rafts. As he looked on the dragon crashed its humungous claws into the midst of the escaping craft, throwing up an extraordinary explosion of water, splintered wood and flailing people.

Haroun's holler went up loud and sustained. The unmistakable figure of his Captain appeared instantly on the deck far below. He cast a chiseled face up toward Haroun, fiercely intelligent eyes glittering in the emergent dawn. The Captain's name was Sinbad El Ari. Or, if you preferred, Sinbad the *Sailor*.

"What ho?" he demanded of Haroun. The rest of the crew was alive now, urgent gazes directed to the crow's nest.

"'Tis a monster the size of a god!" proclaimed Haroun, pointing.

The crew rushed to the side of the vessel. The silhouette of the giant was clear on the horizon against the rising sun, ahead of it the scattered flotilla.

"What manner of beast is it?" Henri Delacrois declared, shielding his eyes against the coming light.

"'Tis a monster, true enough," said Ralf Gunarson, the tremendous Viking beside him. "A dragon no less. Though unlike any I've ever clapped eyes upon."

"We can outrun it if we but tack eastwards," muttered Omar, Master of the Crew and Sinbad's First Mate.

"We will not run," riposted Sinbad. "We have bested worse monsters afore."

"This is no natural beast," protested Omar. "The dragon's skin glints in the new dawn. It is a thing of metal, animated by bestial sorcery."

"Aye, so it is," said Sinbad levelly. "Even so. We do not run from such terrors. Tack westward."

Omar knew better than to labor the point. He nodded, "Aye, Cap'n," then bellowed to the crew, "Westward as she goes, shipmates!" The crew obeyed without hesitation.

The mighty Blue Nymph, wrought from Ethiopian teakwood, its sole indigo sail rippling in the morning wind, began to sweep starboard. Its prow shaped like a comely mermaid, dipped and rose into the suddenly animated Aegean, the scale of the waves the result of the behemoth's approach rather than the modest wind. Sinbad had dashed for the aft of the ship and now stood at the tiller, his ebony, muscular chest tautly evident beneath a baggy white shirt and purple sash, face fixed in concentration.

"Master of the Crew!" he bellowed suddenly, in a deep, resonant voice that carried above the waves and the flapping of the sail.

"Aye, Cap'n?" called Omar. He had partially scaled the rigging to garner a better idea of what they were confronting.

"We need more speed, Omar," snapped Sinbad, sapphire eyes remaining fixed on the danger ahead of them. "This is the Blue Nymph, not a royal yacht!" Sinbad had been born of regal lineage and knew well the saturnine nature of such vessels.

"Aye, Cap'n," responded Omar. He understood his Captain well enough that no further elucidation was required. Omar turned to the crew and began barking instructions.

"Oarsmen!" he yelled, gesticulating. "Man the oars! To the oars with you!"

In their turn the crew immediately obeyed, skittering across the deck of the ship and jumping down into the belly of the vessel. Omar clenched and unclenched his fists impatiently, pivoting anxiously on the spot, waiting not only for the oarsmen to find their seats but for the oar master and drummer to commence. Only when the rhythmic beating had begun, and the oars were majestically descending and then rising in unison, did he allow himself a satisfied grimace. With each stroke the seventy-foot ship leapt forward, its low design enabling it to scythe through the waves with consummate ease.

Ahead of them the colossal dragon crashed its tremendous arms down once more so that another dhow was cracked in half. By now the screams of the poor souls caught beneath the creature's blows were easy to hear. Few of the noises that reached Sinbad's crew sounded like the shrieks of hardy sailors.

"Have you ever witnessed such a sight?" intoned Sinbad, aware of a diminutive but nonetheless reassuring figure beside him, though he kept his gaze fixed intently ahead. "Is it an automaton, such as we have encountered afore, only on a grand scale?"

"It might be a machine," replied a delicate, female voice, "yet I do not think so."

A look of puzzlement crossed Sinbad's features. "It stands and moves like a machine, and it seems made of metal, formed of nuts and bolts. Is that not an automaton, of the kind the Clockwork Sorcerer might artifice?"

"I have seen many automatons," said the woman, bowing ever so slightly, her small hands playing on the hilt of the ever-present katana at her side. "In my land tinkers construct tiny ones which give the appearance of life. Yet I do not think this is such."

"Because of its size?"

"No," said Tishimi, furrowing her forehead. "It possesses an aura."

"Sorcery then," said Sinbad, still without looking at her.

"Aye, Sinbad san," replied Tishimi. "The enchantments involved in animating inorganic objects are not overly difficult to master. It may even be that this object has been rendered larger than it might ordinarily be. Such spells are similarly straightforward to master if one is suitably persistent."

"Then how might we best it?"

"I do not know," said Tishimi. "Except that the aura circumscribes its body. If you were to somehow break the body asunder..."

"Aye," nodded Sinbad. "I understand. If I were to break it apart the enchantments would also be broken."

"That is my contention, Sinbad san," said Tishimi. "But how you might accomplish such a task, I do not know."

By now the Blue Nymph was traversing a sea strewn with timber and flotsam from the destroyed ships and boats. Sounds of survivors had not yet reached Sinbad's ears, but he knew anyway that they could do nothing for them until the titanic demon was dealt with. Sinbad instead concentrated on gauging the movements of the behemoth, which seemed to him hesitant and lacking in co-ordination. Fearsome it might be, but this creature was also an ungainly monster. He licked his lips thoughtfully, hoping that particular fact might afford some solution to the problem.

"Ralf Gunarson!" yelled Sinbad abruptly. "Where art thou, Viking?"

"Here!" responded the Nordic warrior, sliding deftly down the cantilevering deck to be at his Captain's side. "What is your bidding, O Sinbad?"

"Take the tiller," Sinbad instructed. "Steer us a course that skirts the edge of the colossus. As close as you can manage without imperiling the Blue Nymph."

"Aye, as you command, Cap'n," nodded Gunarson, assuming the tiller from Sinbad.

"Henri!" cried Sinbad, using the rigging to enable his progress back up the ship toward the prow. "I need your eyes, man!"

"I am with you, Capitaine," came Henri's distinct reply. "What is your plan?"

The Blue Nymph's unrelenting speed meant that they were now firmly in the midst of the unfolding calamity. Dhows full of drenched people struggled to evade both the monster and to negotiate a sea teeming with smaller boats, debris and bobbing figures. Towering above them all was the mammoth figure of the dragon, its every motion accompanied by shrieking metal. Its eyes, which from afar had appeared red and somehow alive in the dawn sunlight, were seemingly immense rubies. The creature crashed amongst the craft, its head swiveling as it searched for its next target. Behind, probably little more than ten miles distant, was a verdant island, presumably the point of origin for the ships and boats.

"Fetch me a keg of beer," said Sinbad rapidly to Byrne, a broad-shouldered, ruddy-faced Celt sporting numerous ornate tattoos, "the frothier the better." Byrne looked startled at the enquiry but swiftly checked himself and set about the task.

"Are we to carouse in the face of such peril?" yelled Gunarson with characteristic humor, struggling to pilot the Blue Nymph. Though he was intent on steering them a safe course, he clearly couldn't help but witness the exchange between Sinbad and Byrne.

Sinbad evinced a smile but otherwise did not respond. Instead he hoisted an iron harpoon from off the deck and handed it to Henri. The Gaul accepted the weapon with a look of intrigue.

"Mon ami," responded Henri, eyeing the harpoon's mighty blade, "this might pierce the skin of a whale but I cannot vouch for it against a hide like that." He gestured toward the giant.

"We will take that chance," replied Sinbad, uncurling the length of rope attached to the harpoon. "You must aim for the creature's neck and hope for purchase."

"*Capitaine*," said Henri urgently, "we might manage the monster's middriff if Gunarson can pilot us close enough. But I do not have the power to propel you much higher."

By now Byrne had returned with a large barrel of beer. "Observe, Henri. We will fight sorcery with science," said Sinbad. "Byrne, shake this barrel for all your worth."

Byrne looked at him incredulously, "Cap'n?"

"When I give you the word I want you to release the cap, you understand?"

"Aye, Cap'n," responded Byrne, though his face was one of confusion.

"Start shaking!" snapped Sinbad.

"Aye, Cap'n," replied Byrne. The Celt began to vibrate the keg. In moments it had begun to shudder with the building pressure.

"Quickly, Henri," intoned Sinbad urgently, securing the length of rope around his midriff. "Position the harpoon upon the barrel and aim at the creature's neck. You are the most accurate marksmen I have ever met; do not let me down!"

The Blue Nymph was now fifty or so feet from the extent of the dragon. Fortuitously for Sinbad's vessel the creature's attention had until now been taken up deciding on other targets. But now it saw the Blue Nymph skirting below it, and its ruby eyes seemed to gleam with hungry menace.

Henri struggled to aim the harpoon, the rumbling barrel of beer positioned immediately behind it.

"Now, Byrne, release the cap!" cried Sinbad.

Byrne unleashed the stopper on the rear of the barrel, the beer exploding forth with the bubbling pressure. At the same time Henri unleashed the harpoon. It thundered upwards in a graceful arc, carried far higher than it would ordinarily travel by the added momentum of the gushing ale, the rope snapping to and pulling Sinbad with it. The harpoon thumped into the shoulder of the dragon but the monster did not seem to notice. Sinbad meanwhile soared through the air as though suddenly gifted the power of flight. A second later he slammed into the monster's shoulder blade, immediately struggling to find handholds and footholds.

"A veritable hit!" yelled Gunarson jubilantly from the rear of the ship. "Though a shame for the wasted ale!"

"The least of our problems, Viking!" responded Rafi, a sage-like, elderly member of Sinbad's crew. He flung a trembling hand upwards. "Look to the beast, look to the beast!"

Gunarson craned his neck upward and the smile immediately vanished from his face. Realizing the creature was preparing to crash an enormous claw down on the Blue Nymph, the Norseman began pulling the tiller hard to for all his worth. "Portside!" he shouted, "Portside!" Hearing Gunarson's cries, Omar signaled to the relevant oarsmen, who immediately ceased rowing. Meanwhile the starboard oarsmen renewed their efforts, the Blue Nymph turning swiftly just as the dragon's clawed arm crashed down. Its limb narrowly missed the vessel but sent up a tremendous wave, tipping the Blue Nymph precariously on its side.

"Heave-ho, heave-ho!" bellowed Gunarson, remaining fast at the tiller despite the cascading water. In front of him crewmembers clung to the rigging in a desperate bid to avoid being washed overboard. The oarsmen below were drenched, their grizzled faces gasping for breath, straining to hear the continued beating of the drums.

Meanwhile, high above them, Sinbad reeled from the dragon's swipe at the Blue Nymph, struggling to hold on. He watched as his beloved vessel was buffeted by the resultant waves, then turned, determined to scale the creature's metal scales. Hands bloodied by the ascent, he eventually reached his destination, a mammoth bolt emerging from the monster's neck. Wind whipping around him, Sinbad used one of the creature's protruding metal scales to secure himself, then grabbed hold of the bolt as best he could and tried to turn it. The bolt, however, remained stubbornly inert. Sinbad chanced a look over his shoulder and saw the Blue Nymph trying to correct itself, but then felt a lurch as the dragon set off in pursuit.

Realizing the Blue Nymph would be unlikely to survive another onslaught, Sinbad turned back to the task in hand with renewed vigor. Gradually, every sinew in his body straining, the rust around the bolt began to crack and flake away, and then the bolt began to turn. Momentum achieved,

Sinbad succeeded in spinning the bolt around. Then with a tremendous effort he hefted the bolt away, letting it drop. He paused only momentarily to watch the bolt clatter against the exterior of the dragon before disappearing into the turbulent sea. Sinbad felt salt water stinging his hands, and looked down to see that the bolt had ripped apart his palms. He paid his injury no heed.

His first objective complete, Sinbad looked across at the harpoon, still embedded in the dragon's shoulder, its rope still connected to his midriff. He wondered how securely the harpoon was fixed, then discounted such concerns as meaningless in the circumstances. He must trust in the will of Allah. Sinbad unhooked himself from the scale he'd used to secure himself and then stood. He paused, and then with a grimace leapt from the creature's shoulder, swinging through the air, the rope bringing him around in a tight sweep.

He landed on the creature's other shoulder, just as his weight pulled the harpoon from its makeshift mooring. The heavy harpoon, now unattached, swung fitfully in the air, dragging Sinbad backwards as he struggled to grab a new pair of handholds. At the last moment he succeeded in grabbing hold of two scales. The rope had closed around his midriff, crunching his diaphragm, tightening with each swing of the harpoon. Gasping for breath, he began pulling himself up the creature's body.

Far below, still at the tiller, Gunarson turned to watch the monster bearing down on them. All around him, coughing and spluttering crewmen had taken to bailing out the water which continued to sloop around the poop deck and to continually douse the oarsmen beneath. The ship's path once again true, Omar had instructed both sets of oarsmen to resume rowing for all their worth. Though the creature's progress was plodding and haphazard its scale was so vast that Gunarson doubted even the mighty Blue Nymph and its muscular oarsmen would be able to outrun it. He had seen Sinbad's death-defying leap, watched as the Captain struggled to remain atop the creature. Gunarson allowed himself a short prayer to Odin that Sinbad's scheme would prove successful. He knew his Captain's mind well and had a good idea what his plan might involve.

Sinbad had reached the second bolt now, the swinging harpoon continuing to make the rope around his midriff tighten with every movement. Again the bolt proved unwilling to move and his lacerated hands rendered it slippery with his blood, making the task even harder. He frantically ripped a portion of his shirt, wrapping the torn material around his hands, then resumed his task.

Finally, with the aid of his makeshift bandages and accompanied by a great, echoing screech, the bolt began to revolve, slowly at first then gathering in pace. Sinbad span the bolt as fast he could, barely succeeding in removing it before the weight of the harpoon proved too much and he was pulled backwards, tumbling toward the sea. So high was his fall it took him seconds to descend, desperately hoping he didn't collide with the monster's body on the way down. Moments later Sinbad hit the waves. Though the water had slowed him he continued to fall, the harpoon dragging him ever downward, consciousness departing him.

The dragon continued its pursuit of the Blue Nymph, intent on its destruction. Gunarson saw Sinbad hitting the water. Then he watched, in astonishment, as the head of the dragon came free, and began to slide away.

"Steady yerselves!" screamed Rafi hoarsely, watching as the dragon's head crashed into the ocean, sending up an almighty explosion of water. As the head fell the rest of the dragon's body stumbled forward, then it too collapsed to one side. The impact of the two parts of the dragon produced two walls of water which rapidly combined and began travelling toward the Blue Nymph. The crew hastily sought to secure themselves, wrapping rope and rigging around their arms and legs.

They braced themselves, some thinking of loved ones, others their gods, some their next tankard of mead, or at least their *last* tankard of mead. Omar thought of his children, his many, many children. The elderly Rafi closed his eyes and thought of Allah, of the world yet to come, and his regret at having no children. Young Haroun thought of family long lost to illness, to war and to circumstance. Tishimi thought of her father and that fateful night when she found his body. Ralf Gunarson saw himself striding through the hall of Valhalla and taking his place alongside Odin and Thor and the other great warriors of his own clan. Henri Delacrois thought of women; but then they were never far from his mind.

The wall of water began to lift the Blue Nymph like a prize, high into the air, before eventually breaking around it, turning the vessel as it did, threatening either to capsize it or overwhelm it in its entirety, or both. But the Blue Nymph was an extraordinary ship, unlike any other to sail the world's oceans before or since. Some said the wood from which it had been wrought was somehow enchanted. Others said that Sinbad was personally defended by Allah and that as a consequence his beloved vessel, too, was protected by divine intervention. Whatever the reason, as the wave finally subsided and against the odds, the Blue Nymph came to rest on the turbulent sea.

Even the mighty Gunarson had been forced to his knees by the strength of the wave, though he had managed to cling to the tiller. Now he pulled himself up, hair matted and clothes drenched. He looked toward the crew, soaked and some moaning from cuts and bruises caused by flying debris, pulling themselves upright, most up to their ankles in sloshing seawater. But the Viking's jubilation at the Blue Nymph and her crew having survived the destruction of the monster largely intact suddenly dissipated. His gaze travelled up to the mast, the upper section of which stood at a precarious angle, supported only by the rigging. The tidal wave had evidently broken it in twain about two thirds of the way up its length, and the indigo sail flapped fitfully like some great swatted butterfly.

"The Blue Nymph is injured," Gunarson shouted to Omar, whose face had been lacerated by something. Omar staggered toward Gunarson, the wound glistening in the morning light, trickles of blood hazarding down his thick neck and onto his sodden clothes.

"Aye," acknowledged the grizzled First Mate, "but we've seen worse. We need a port."

"We need our Captain first," interjected Delacrois. "I saw him topple the beast but of his fate I have no clue!"

Rafi gestured, the old man struggling momentarily with a coughing fit. "In the briny. Make haste for the spot where he fell."

"The time it would take is too lengthy," replied Gunarson. "Rafi, take the tiller and follow us. Omar, if I do not return in good time I suggest you head for the island and make repairs."

"Follow you?" said Omar in surprise. "You don't seriously propose to swim?"

Gunarson towered over Omar. "Sinbad saved us all, and the lives of those fleeing people. I have no choice."

"I will join you, mon ami," intoned Delacrois. The Frenchman had been wringing out his shirt before realizing the futility of this. "After all, I cannot get any wetter."

"Good," said Gunarson, slapping the Gaul heartily on the back. "Let us not tarry here."

And with that the giant Norseman launched himself off the side of the vessel and into the rippling Aegean. Delacrois flashed an uncertain smile at his crewmates, before turning and following.

Chapter Two

The boy turned, surprised. Though the yashmak obscured her face, somehow he recognized her from the way she held herself, the manner in which she walked. That and her eyes. They were greenish-blue like the ocean, swirling; the black that encircled their irises struggling to contain a powerful intelligence. They fixed him coolly, perhaps even impudently, from across the room as she strode, head held high, the light blue of her yashmak replicated in her billowing robes. The girl bowed as decorum dictated, clasping her hands together in supplication, but even in this action there was a resistance, an unmistakable aura of subversion that couldn't help but pique his interest. When she straightened, he realized that she towered above him by several inches, despite the similarity in their ages.

"I know you," he said, trying hard to convey irritation in his voice, though in reality he was very pleased to see her indeed. "King Tirigan's daughter no less."

"Aye, but I am called Ashanti," she nodded.

"Ashanti," he repeated, pretending he had forgotten it. "It is a comely name."

"You are too kind." He could tell from her eyes that she was smiling mockingly beneath the yashmak. "And I know you. Sinbad El Ari. Sinbad the *prince*."

"We are to be wed," he observed, making an unconvincing attempt at nonchalance.

"Yes," she nodded again. "Our marriage will help unite our two nations."

"Aye, 'tis so. My father is very eager," said Sinbad. "And so is the Caliph."

"And you, Sinbad El Ari?" Ashanti responded, arching an eyebrow. "Are you eager?"

The young prince was taken aback. He went to speak but found his normally assured voice to be possessed of only a curious croaking noise. He cleared his throat in what he hoped was a regal way, before managing, "I, uh, understand your people produce much wheat. Is that correct?"

Ashanti had turned away from him, an action which was wholly improper given his status, not to mention his gender, but which intrigued him as much as her earlier insouciance. "Our land is verdant," she acknowledged, going to a table bedecked with food. She reached out a lithe hand and plucked a large purple grape, examining it with frowning curiosity. "Inshallah, our crop yields are always bountiful, our livestock always healthy. Spices too, such that you have never tasted."

"I have tasted many different flavors," he said indignantly. This time his annoyance was genuine, and it showed. He checked himself, trying hard not to sound quite so immature. "Spices from all across the world."

"You have travelled?" She'd stopped, seeming surprised, her eyes suddenly quizzical, searching.

"No," he admitted sheepishly, lowering his gaze, his eyebrows beetling. "But our merchants bring me gifts," he mumbled. "I have tasted delicacies from many different places, drunk wines and eaten all manner of things you would not…"

"I see," she said witheringly, and resumed her examination of the food and drink spread out on the table.

He felt deflated, a sensation he was far from used to, except perhaps in the presence of his disciplinarian father or the school-master and his cane. Yet the feeling did not last long, vanishing as he watched her measured, precise movements. Somehow he could feel her presence in every fiber of his body. It made his breathing shallow and his head throb. She was unlike anyone he had ever met.

"Our marriage is important to both our nations," suggested Sinbad uncertainly, trying desperately to assert his authority. He joined her at the table, electing to pour himself a goblet of water. "You will supply us food and drink and the, uh, spices of which you speak. And in return our ships will protect your waterways. You will have nothing to fear from the Visigoths, or from the Mongols."

She did not look at him now, but her tone was mocking. "That is good to know." He watched, enraptured, as she carefully lifted the veil a portion and proceeded to place the grape she had been holding in her slender mouth. This was again a considerable breach of etiquette, one which might have earned her a flogging if she had grown up in his royal household. In other contexts it might even have earned her a beheading. He didn't care though. Her action offered a fleeting glimpse of her lips, moist and sensuous.

At that moment the goblet of water slipped from his grasp and clanged mightily on the stone-flagged floor, the water exploding upwards. Sinbad stared down at the puddle he had created, at the clear liquid hazarding down cracks and crevices, separating, reforming, until it disappeared. Sinbad looked to her, to his fair Ashanti. She had turned towards him, her pupils dilating; her body trembling in what he realized must be quiet mirth. He couldn't help but smile and then laugh too, his embarrassment cracking like a turtle's carapace. She took this as permission to laugh properly, a deep felt, delightful noise that made her body quake. As their laughter subsided their eyes locked, and he felt his heartbeat race still faster. He reached out a careful, tentative hand, touched those long, delicate fingers, caressing them. She did not remove her hand, nor did she flinch, her eyes intent on his.

And then suddenly he felt a wetness in his hand. He looked down to see her fingers exploding into liquid, multiple droplets spinning out across the table. He looked up in horror to see Ashanti beginning to distort, her figure fuzzing, blurring. In front of his eyes her entire body transformed to water, spilling to the flagged floor in a pool of lightest blue.

He awoke with a start from the dream, only to find a nightmare. He was falling. Not through air, but through water. All around. He looked down, and through the murkiness saw the harpoon dangling from his body, its weight pulling him toward the seabed, toward sure and certain death. Bubbles of air issued from his nose and mouth as he struggled frantically to release the rope around his midriff. It was steadfast, though, and would not budge. He fought back mounting panic. Instead he searched about himself and, just as he had hoped, found a blade tucked into his sash, where previously there had been nothing.

Yet the tightness of the rope made it impossible to release the knife. Sinbad closed his eyes and *imagined*.

Abruptly the blade was in his grasp and he was sawing away at the rope. As he cut at the cord the knife throbbed and glowed in his hand, for this was no ordinary weapon. This was Grachene, a six-inch dagger gifted him by Persephone herself, the Goddess of the Underworld. It was wrought from a substance unknown to mortals, could not be broken and could penetrate any material. Not only that. The knife was *alive*, he knew it. A mischievous spirit that came and went as it liked, disappearing and reappearing at its own whim. But he had never known it to let him down.

This time was no different. The rope was severed. He saw the harpoon falling away from him, vanishing into the murk below. Black shapes, hopefully fish, darted amidst the blue gloom. He realized he must have fallen some considerable distance. He could sense consciousness wanting to desert him again, an overwhelming urge to give himself over to memories of yesteryear. After all, they were such beautiful, happy memories. Most of them. He squeezed his eyes tight, shaking his head, then abruptly opened them. He knew somehow he must stay awake, that he must propel himself upwards.

He began to swim but he was too far down. The depths of the sea were calling more insistently now, its currents desperate to drag him to the bottom, to caress him into a deep sleep that would never end. The ocean had swallowed the harpoon and now it wanted him. Come dream with me, it said, and you can be with Ashanti *forever...*

Suddenly, only half-aware, Sinbad felt huge hands grabbing him and his body being lifted. He saw, fitfully, first the familiar face of Gunarson and then that of Delacrois, both men wearing expressions of unwavering intent. As they swam with him the murk began to dissipate, the sea around him returning to the familiar, welcoming azure of the Aegean's upper reaches. In seconds they had emerged gasping into warm sunlight, the Blue Nymph bobbing some short distance away, a happy sight even with her broken mast.

"You should rest some more," counseled Rafi.

Sinbad patted the old man fondly on the shoulder, "The Blue Nymph needs me more than I need respite." Rafi bowed his head in acknowledgement. It had taken Sinbad little more than fifteen minutes to recover from his ordeal. Gunarson had quaffed a tot of rum on his return, but Sinbad did not feel like partaking. Instead he had sat upon the deck, observing the destruction wrought by the unexpected tidal wave. Now he moved around the ship, carefully inspecting the damage. He stopped, his gaze travelling upward to the splintered mast. "My poor beauty is wounded..." he said softly, laying a hand gently upon the mast.

"Aye, Cap'n," said Omar. "But she has been hurt afore and we have made her well again. So it will be this time."

Sinbad looked to his old friend and then back to the mast, nodding, "Aye, so we shall."

"We will make landfall soon enough," continued the First Mate. "There looks to be timber aplenty. Not Ethiopian teakwood to be sure, but good enough until we're next in Baghdad, Inshallah."

"Cap'n!" came a familiar voice. Haroun, bereft of his normal place in the crow's nest, had taken to standing on the prow, accompanied by Samson the cat. "A boat's approaching!"

"The islanders, come to thank us I'll warrant," said Omar confidently.

"Let 'em aboard," responded Sinbad. "I would speak with them. I have many questions."

"Aye, Cap'n," agreed Gunarson, downing a second tot of rum then gasping appreciatively. "Methinks we all do."

A long boat pulled alongside the Blue Nymph. Sinbad's crew reached down and with some effort helped a middle-aged, portly figure clamber on deck, his retinue following with considerably more decorum. The men wore brightly colored shirts and trousers decorated with ornate gold and silver braiding, similar to that Sinbad had seen in India. The women wore something akin to a sari, the colors equally bright, the trimming as elaborate as their male companions. Their skin was dark but not as dark as Sinbad's, and several sported tattoos of butterflies and birds. He noticed that some of the younger women chose to wrap or hold the upper portions of their saris to obscure their eyes from view, but that the older females, presumably the married ones, did not bother with this particular custom.

"I am Al-Bulcar, leader of the Xubanthali, and I offer you thanks and praise," declaimed the portly man, bowing. Sinbad noticed a shining piece of misshapen glass hanging from around the man's ample neck, suspended by a length of string. It created a rainbow of colors on the man's flabby chin each time the sun took it.

Sinbad stepped forward, "I am Sinbad El Ari and I am Captain of this vessel. Welcome aboard."

"The legendary Sinbad," nodded Al-Bulcar enthusiastically, "we supposed as much. No other mortal could have achieved what you achieved."

"You're famous, Captain," said Gunarson, flipping Sinbad a mischievous grin. A ripple of good-natured laughter broke out amongst the crew, which Sinbad chose to ignore.

"Aye, 'tis true," acknowledged Al-Bulcar. "News of your exploits has reached even here. You are a legend, honored Captain."

"And the creature our legendary Captain bested," said Gunarson. "What manner of monstrosity was it?"

"It was this," said a familiar voice. The party turned to see Delacrois, dripping with water but ecstatic nevertheless, approaching holding two dull metallic objects. Delacrois lifted the pieces up for all to see. It was a model of a dragon, cast from metal, something akin to platinum, perhaps, and little more than fifty inches in height. Its head, ordinarily fastened with bolts, had been removed, and its eyes were made from rubies.

"It is Xuba," said Al-Bulcar, eyes wide, inclining his head reverentially and touching his forehead, as did his companions. "Our god. Or, at least, a rendition of our god."

"How did it come to be so vast and to gain animation?" enquired Sinbad, eyes narrowing. "Who granted it such scale and such ability?"

"Our shaman," explained Al-Bulcar. "He rendered it vast and afforded it motion. When you removed its head, O Sinbad, you must have destroyed the spell."

Sinbad caught Tishimi's eye, though she betrayed no hint of triumph that her judgment had been proven wholly accurate. "Aye, that was our intention, Al-Bulcar."

"I found it toward the shallows," said Delacrois, proudly grinning. "Nothing escapes me!"

"Nothing with rubies," muttered Gunarson *sotto voce*.

"It is not yours to claim," said Sinbad curtly, nodding his head pointedly.

The dripping Delacrois looked in outrage to his Captain, but Sinbad returned his gaze with steely eyes. The Gaul snorted, then handed the object to Al-Bulcar, who nodded his gratitude before handing it to one of his retinue. Delacrois meanwhile squelched away, muttering under his breath, his grumbling eventually disappearing amidst the lapping waves.

"Why, Al-Bulcar?" demanded Sinbad. "Why did your shaman give life to this monster?"

Al-Bulcar clicked his dry mouth. "Because of what came to our island, Captain. Because of the creatures."

"What creatures?" interjected Omar, incredulous. "In the name of Allah and all that is holy, what creatures could possibly be worse than a giant metal dragon?"

Al-Bulcar shook his head and the members of his retinue seemed to collectively shudder. Some looked away, tearful, others once more touched their foreheads in silent prayer. "Demons," said Al-Bulcar, his piggy eyes wide with the terror of the memory. "Undead creatures. Ships full of 'em. Warriors, dressed in armor and sporting blades and cudgels and pikes. Such supernatural horror as you wouldn't countenance."

Sinbad slowly nodded, "And you thought you could use the statue of Xuba against them?"

The leader nodded, his jowls wobbling, "Our god always protects us. Our shaman recognized the creatures from legend and asked Xuba for help. Xuba answered our prayers. The metal model of Xuba grew and came to life."

"But you couldn't control it?" said Rafi.

"The Warriors," answered Al-Bulcar, "they weren't alone. There was a woman with them. A young woman with but one eye. They seemed to obey her will. Such sorcery..." He bowed his head, remembering. "Her magic

The Gaul...handed the object to Al-Bucar...

was far stronger than that of our shaman's. He fought her but he was not powerful enough. He lies, dying, on the island."

"Why?" said Sinbad. "What did these undead creatures want of you?"

"Your mast is broken," said the leader hurriedly, turning away abruptly to view the damage to the ship. "We will fix it for you."

Sinbad viewed him suspiciously. "Aye," he said quietly.

Haroun padded behind the main party, wide eyes blinking in the morning sun. He had learned via chatter from the other crewmembers that the island, in common with its inhabitants, was also called Xubanthali. He could see for himself that it was certainly as verdant as it had appeared from afar. Yet the palm trees gyrating in the increasingly insistent wind stood incongruous against a golden beach littered with the debris of battle. His eyes played across the shards of timber projecting from the sand, the ripped canvas of sails flapping fitfully. His mouth went dry. Amidst the flotsam struggled broken human bodies, many lacking limbs, others sporting huge lacerations from where debris had smashed into them. He was surprised not to see any dead, though. There must certainly be many, judging by the ferocity of the metal behemoth's attack that he and Samson had witnessed from on high, at least until their position in the crow's nest had become too precarious to maintain.

Haroun decided the Xubanthali bodies must already have been spirited away. He remembered that some of the disparate religions he had encountered in his adventures aboard the Blue Nymph would rapidly dispose of corpses, lest the body's soul escape and transform to that of ghost, condemned to wander the physical world in perpetuity. Most probably the Xubanthali also held to this belief. There were certainly plenty of Xubanthali on the shore to help with the injured. They were easily distinguishable from the Blue Nymph's crew because of their brightly colored clothing.

Another thing that struck him as odd was the lack of noise. Save for the roar of the ocean, the rustling of the trees and the conversations between members of the Blue Nymph's crew, there was little else to be heard. Though he was still a young man, Haroun had seen the aftermath of battle many times previously, frequently while travelling with Sinbad but also at home in his native Persia. He knew the air would ordinarily be rent with the noise of the injured people's moaning, but also with the shrieking of those that had lost loved ones. Perhaps the genial Xubanthali simply chose not to show their grief in public.

How different from his own people, who greeted the joy and sorrow life threw at them with equal noisy passion. Not for the first time Haroun found himself thinking about the similarities and differences between the many cultures that inhabited the globe. Once again he found himself thanking Allah for opening his eyes to the world, for letting him travel the globe with Captain Sinbad and his crew.

The Blue Nymph had docked with a makeshift jetty emerging from a rocky section of the headland. Sinbad and Al-Bulcar, still surrounded by the latter's retinue, had disembarked and were advancing down the jetty toward the shore. Meanwhile Al-Bulcar's men and women clustered around the ship, marveling at its low-slung design and prominent prow, and thanking Sinbad's crew for their actions in vanquishing the monstrous metal dragon. The ever-protective Omar stayed with the vessel, energetically explaining how the mast should be repaired. Haroun saw him waving his hands in expansive fashion, his face a look of frowning concentration, sometimes nodding emphatically at the Xubanthali, but more often shaking his head vigorously and re-explaining his point.

From behind Haroun watched the titanic figure of Gunarson and the lithe figure of Delacrois, ever alert to potential dangers. They too were engaged in vigorous conversation, although Gunarson would occasionally lapse into guffawing laughter, while Delacrois continued gamely smiling, having evidently delivered one of his trademark *bon mots*. After a moment Haroun realized, awkwardly, that he had accidentally fallen into step with the mysterious, beautiful Tishimi. The Japanese woman walked, head bowed, her footfalls purposeful, silks billowing in the wind and the familiar katana at her side. Though she was always kindly toward him, he found her otherness, not to mention her beauty, unnerving in the extreme.

"'Tis a mighty wind brewing," observed Haroun, feeling the need to make conversation.

Tishimi did not lift her head. "It is a howl of pain."

Haroun nodded slowly, "You think so?"

"I feel it," she responded quietly. "Something is wrong with this place. The island is mourning."

"Aye," said Haroun slowly, looking around himself, his nervousness around Tishimi suddenly forgotten, displaced by something altogether more substantial. "I feel it too. There *is* something missing. But what?"

"We are a peaceable people," Al-Bulcar was saying to a stoic Sinbad, his words booming for all to hear, "Xuba only knows why such a tragedy should be visited upon us."

"Peaceable peoples can still fight when they need to," Sinbad responded levelly. "Yet you and your people chose to flee?"

Al-Bulcar stopped abruptly, turning to the Captain. Behind him the rest of the party came to a faltering halt. Sinbad wondered whether he had offended the Xubanthali leader. He half-hoped he had, if it elicited a response that would somehow crack asunder the Xubanthalis' polite façade.

"Captain Sinbad," said Al-Bulcar, bowing. "I cannot sufficiently express our gratitude to you for defeating the dragon. Truly Xuba has blessed you. Yet forgive me now if I speak forcefully." Sinbad saw that the portly man's eyes were brimming, "The creatures that attacked us were like nothing in this Earthly realm. Their faces were naught but rotting, peeling skin, their eye sockets empty. In their skeletal hands they carried scythes and swords and clubs with which to slash and kill us. We tried to defend ourselves but to no avail..."

Sinbad had folded his arms. "Aye," he said at length, "if these creatures were as terrible as you describe, then I can understand why you and your people fled. I am merely surprised you did not put up more resistance, Al-Bulcar."

"Oh, we put up resistance," said Al-Bulcar, shaking his head. "Really we did. But as I say, these creatures were *demons*, truly."

"Perhaps you intended to regroup and fight again," suggested Sinbad generously, his gaze fixed on the Xubanthali leader.

"Alas, we were not speedy enough," opined the man, dipping his head in sorrow.

"What do you mean?"

Al-Bulcar sighed, "Let me show you."

They continued on, through the palm trees and along a winding path that demanded they should advance in single-file. As they walked a distinct odor reached Sinbad's keen senses. It was smoke, but not any kind of smoke. The aftermath of battle. It became thicker as the party emerged into a blackened clearing. A village, or at least the remnants of a village. Smoke wafted from the charred, broken debris of cane houses. Amongst the ash and straw and pots and pans lay the bodies of animals. He could see several cats, a dog, a few cattle and some sheep, all eviscerated. Sinbad noticed, too, huge piles of cloth of many and varied colors. He wondered whether the Xubanthali traded their clothes with other nearby islands. It would explain why they would need quite so much material.

"Only one of fifteen such villages," croaked Al-Bulcar, casting his hand at the devastated scene. "All destroyed." Sinbad noticed for the first time huge bales of straw, grouped together at one end of the village. Like the huge piles of cloth, these bales seem to have weathered the attack untouched. He thought it curious indeed.

The rest of the group had gathered around them. Sinbad studied the haunted expressions of the men and women who had survived the ghouls and then the attack of the dragon. Beyond their trauma something was missing, of that he was convinced. He wondered what it could be.

"What did they want?" asked Delacrois abruptly. "These demon soldiers that attacked you?"

"Can you not see?" said a woman, her face a patchwork of lacerations, recently stitched. "Can you not see what has gone?"

Delacrois scanned the devastation around him. Despite his eagle eyes he could not perceive what was missing. "I..." he said slowly. "I am confounded."

"The children," said a quiet voice beside them. It was Tishimi. She had made her way to the front of the group. "They came for the children."

He sat and watched, his intense, azure eyes lost in thought. He could see Omar beside the Blue Nymph, arms folded, occasionally barking instructions but otherwise seeming to approve of the determined efficiency with which the Xubanthali sought to fix the snapped mast in concert with the Blue Nymph's crew. Sinbad reflected that the islanders' attention to the task might emerge from their gratitude but from something else too: expectation. A hope that the brave crew who had somehow, against the odds, defeated the dragon monster and prevented multitudes of the islanders from perishing in the brine might now turn their efforts to finding and rescuing their children.

The children. As Al-Bulcar breathlessly told the story, the islanders had been preoccupied with preparations for the annual harvest celebration when word reached them of ships on the horizon. This was extraordinary indeed, as their position in the midst of Xuba's ocean meant that they seldom encountered seafaring vessels, and if they did they generally heralded from nearby islands, their pilots intent on trade. The Xubanthali had downed their tools and rushed to the shore. There the astonished islanders saw the silhouettes of all manner of ships, from single-masted dhows to what sounded to Sinbad's ear to be vessels of European design. At one point Gunarson grunted, recognizing a description of what would almost certainly have been some form of Viking long-boat, or at least something emulating its distinctive shape and size. When it became apparent that the fleet was not passing by but intended to land on the island, the Xubanthali convened a welcoming party to be led by Al-Bulcar. But then the Xubanthali's elderly shaman Corsepis emerged from his meditation in the woods, proclaiming the approaching fleet to be a thing of evil, and urging the Xubanthali to prepare for horrific and bloody battle.

By then, though, it was too late. The ships were near enough to the island that the true nature of their crews had become apparent. Though their shape and bearing was that of people, the crews' humanity had crumbled from their bodies along with their parched skin. They were monsters, their dull armor encasing rotting corpses and leering skulls, their swords raised, laughter gurgling in bony, cracked throats. These were undead soldiers, pustule-ridden, scabrous wretches whose murderous intent was beyond doubt.

As Al-Bulcar kept earnestly reiterating, his people were not fighters. In the millennia that followed their God Xuba according them life they had warred with neighboring islands but such interactions were little more than skirmishes and in these enlightened times uncommon. The Xubanthali did not possess an army and their weapons were limited. Despite this, the people armed themselves as best they could, grabbing tools that hours earlier had been used in the fruit harvest, taking hammers from their carpenters and cleavers from their butchers. When they could find no more they improvised weapons from bits of wood and rock. They watched in wide-eyed terror as the ghouls descended from their vessels into the waves and began an inexorable advance across the shore. The monsters let out low, hissing cries, swaying from side to side as they approached, then suddenly rushed, screeching, forward. Those defenders that did not turn to run were immediately carved to pieces in a blur of blades or bludgeoned into oblivion with clubs.

Al-Bulcar hid behind a rocky promontory with several of his wives and Corsepis the shaman. From here Al-Bulcar could see that the ghouls' efforts were seemingly orchestrated by a one-eyed woman, not more than twenty years of age, her flesh covered in ornate tattoos. She stood on a plinth at the centre of an extraordinary ship that seemed itself to have been carved from bone, shouting instructions to the monsters. A strangely shaped horn hung from around her slender neck.

With the monstrous hordes scything their way through what little defense the Xubanthali could offer, Al-Bulcar and his retinue ran for the wooded interior of the island. The monsters, though, were not far behind, slashing their merry way through the foliage in pursuit. When they arrived at the villages the ghouls fell upon the adults, their swords and cudgels a whirl of scarlet efficiency. Al-Bulcar and Corsepis again hid. When the ghouls had finished with those adults who stood their ground, they began advancing toward cowering groups of children, blades raised high. But then the one-eyed woman appeared, flanked by still more of the undead Warriors. She smiled at the children and directed her soldiers towards the quaking infants.

These ghouls carried nets which they flung over the youngsters. The children were then carried, too terrified to scream or struggle, so whimpering instead, back to the ships, the one-eyed woman laughing. As she turned to go she kicked over a metal effigy of their god Xuba. When they were able to emerge from their hideaway Al-Bulcar and others of his retinue pleaded with Corsepis to ask Xuba himself for help. The grim-faced Corsepis had picked up the effigy, then proceeded to perform a series of rites around it, assisted by his daughter Illia. With each rite the effigy grew in size until finally it was colossal. An exhausted Corsepis continued his ritual, dancing around the statue, muttering incantation after incantation, his elderly body racking with energy as he used his own life-force to animate the monster.

With a tremendous scraping the creature began to move. Corsepis, barely able to stand, thrust a quivering hand in the direction of the ghouls and the ships. The monster bowed, then turned and followed.

Al-Bulcar and his retinue had watched as Xuba had set about the ghouls, crushing them under its mighty metal claws, flinging the creatures to one side. The ghouls charged at Xuba but their cudgels and swords were no use against its impenetrable metal hide. For moments it looked like the tide of the battle would be turned and that the undead hordes would be vanquished. But then the furious one-eyed woman turned her attention to the creature. She blew a long, low note upon her horn and the giant dragon stopped in its tracks, tilting its head to one side. And then it twisted its tremendous skull toward the one-eyed woman, bowing, before transferring its intent to the Xubanthali who had emerged from the jungle to watch their adversaries overcome. Now it smashed toward them instead, flinging the terrified people to one side as though they were ragdolls. Corsepis, his power spent, could only watch in horror as his magic was turned against his own people.

The laughing one-eyed woman and the ghouls, still dragging the children in their nets, plunged back into the sea and made for their ships. Meanwhile the Xubanthali were heading for their own ships and boats, desperate to escape the gigantic effigy of Xuba. The ghouls' ships powered away from the island, the Xubanthali children locked in their holds, their perfidious mission evidently complete. Al-Bulcar was caught amidst the surviving Xubanthali adults as they struggled desperately to evade the clutches of the colossal metal dragon, crashing through the water toward the Xubanthali ships. Corsepis, though, could not join them. The effort of the spells had rendered him too weak, and Al-Bulcar watched as the elderly shaman was led away by his daughter Illia back into the interior of the island. Then the dragon smashed first one and then another of the escaping dhows. Al-Bulcar had caught sight of the Blue Nymph and its distinctive, fluttering sail, but by then rescue had seemed a forlorn hope.

At that point Al-Bulcar stopped his account, his wobbling, animated face abruptly inert, his small black eyes staring into the middle distance from beneath his knitting brow. The trauma was evidently too much for him to recount further details. At any rate, Sinbad had heard enough. He stood, pausing only briefly to rest a reassuring hand on the Xubanthali leader's shoulder, before making his way across the beach. Sinbad didn't need to look back to know that Al-Bulcar's glassy eyes were continuing to stare into nothingness, his face frozen in grief and despair.

Sinbad had found a place on the shore in order that he might watch the repairs to the Blue Nymph and ponder what he had been told. His thoughts, though, were quickly disturbed.

"We've found him, Captain," said a familiar voice, slicing through Sinbad's reverie. It was Gunarson, advancing toward him with immense strides. "We've found the shaman."

Chapter Three

"How does he fare?" he said as he approached. The girl gazed at him from beneath the shade of her brilliant white sari. It was only when she tilted her elfin face slightly that he saw her eyes were limpid pools, the lightest blue, framed by arched, dark eyebrows.

"My father is dying," said the girl flatly.

"I would speak with him," said Sinbad gently.

The girl looked like she might refuse, but then cast a glance to Al-Bulcar, who nodded his assent.

Sinbad knelt by the figure, who lay upon a makeshift bed of leaves. The daughter's assessment was inarguable. The man was a withered husk, his cheeks hollow, his aged skin like parchment. His beard was specked with blood, and the shallow rise and fall of his chest was barely perceptible. In Sinbad's judgment he would not likely survive the hour. Yet Sinbad could see movement behind his eyelids, and in that moment the old man's eyes flicked open and stared upward toward the rustling trees and cloudless sky. Sinbad saw that his eyes were the palest blue, like those of his daughter.

Various of the Xubanthali had gathered around the figure of the dying shaman, heads bowed reverently. It was clear these people did not blame Corsepis for the fact that his giant version of Xuba had turned against them and apparently killed so many of their number, though Sinbad had yet to see any corpses or graves. Sinbad guessed that the shaman had been a wise figure amongst these people throughout his lifetime. They saw that he had tried to save them, and could not blame him that his powers had been in-sufficient against the magic of the one-eyed witch. A scattering of Sinbad's own crew were also present, the ones he had dispatched to find the shaman.

"Corsepis," said Sinbad softly, "I am Sinbad El Ari."

"I know who you are," rasped the shaman, still staring upward, past him. "It is foretold."

Sinbad disguised his surprise. "What do you know of the creatures that attacked you?"

"The Warriors of Forever," said Corsepis. "They have returned."

"The Warriors of Forever," repeated Sinbad. "I have not heard of them, wise shaman. What are they?"

"A myth from the ancient times," said a more familiar voice. Sinbad looked up to see Rafi, his aged shipmate, approaching. "It is doubtful they ever really existed. On the contrary, it is more likely to be the product of a poet's imaginative invention, a fairytale to scare the children. At least, that is what I believe."

Sinbad saw a ripple of discomfort pass across the faces of the normally impassive Xubanthali in response to Rafi's unfortunate turn of phrase. Knowing Rafi as he did, Sinbad guessed it to be deliberate provocation on his part.

"No," riposted Corsepis, betraying anger despite his mortal condition. "It is them. The captured souls of dead soldiers. They have risen again."

Rafi viewed the dying man skeptically. Rafi placed truth and learning higher than anything and was unlikely to indulge even a dying soul's views if he considered them incorrect or misleading. "Let us for a moment pretend they did exist," he said delicately. "According to the myth they were imprisoned for eternity."

Corsepis coughed, more blood beading on his stubbly chin. "Aye," he murmured, "they *were* imprisoned. By the great sorcerer Al-Izrikel the Scarlet."

"But now they have risen again," said his daughter hotly. "And they have taken the children of the Xubanthali."

"Why?" said Sinbad, looking from daughter to father. "To what purpose?"

"We do not know," said Corsepis. "We can but speculate as to what nefarious end they seek such youthful vigor." Again the gathered Xubanthali shuddered, some turning away, others closing their eyes and muttering incantations to Xuba. On this subject, at least, their emotions were far less guarded.

"Whatever the precise intent of their scheme," said Rafi in measured tones, "it seems they must take the children somewhere else to accomplish it."

"Aye," agreed Corsepis, "so perhaps there is still time."

"Still time for what?" said Sinbad.

"To stop them, Sinbad," asserted Corsepis. "To find them, defeat them and rescue the children."

"This is not our fight," interposed Omar. "With respect to the dead and dying, Captain, we have rescued these people once. Allah would not ask us to do more."

"I would not dare to guess the mind of God, Omar," snapped Sinbad. Omar's cheeks flushed in response.

"Riches," hissed Corsepis. "Al-Izrikel amassed enormous wealth. If that's the reward you desire. If you can but find it."

"Pah!" cried Omar, waving his hand dismissively. "The flame is not worth the candle." One of the Xubanthali moaned low and pitifully in response and had to be comforted by one of her fellows. "I am sorry," added Omar sheepishly. "But no good can come of our intervention."

"Corsepis," said Sinbad gently, ignoring his First Mate. "How did Al-Izrikel defeat the Warriors of Forever?"

"I do not know," coughed Corsepis. "You must discover *his* legend. You must find the Scholars of Bethshea. Their archives contain more knowledge than any place in this Earthly realm. They will surely know how he did it."

"The Scholars of Bethshea are themselves a myth and so is their Library," asserted Rafi scornfully. "Myth upon myth."

Corsepis issued a sigh, "You do not have children, old man."

Rafi was taken aback, "Aye, you are perceptive even in death, shaman," he said momentarily. "My late wife and I were never gifted with offspring. What of it?"

Corsepis reached out an emaciated hand toward his daughter Illia. She went to clasp it, bringing it lovingly to her cheek and kissing it. Sinbad noticed for the first time an elaborate bracelet that travelled the extent of her arm from wrist to elbow, fashioned in the form of a snake. "We are simple people," said Corsepis. "We put much store in our families. For us, such relationships are more important than anything." He blinked slowly, "You understand me?"

Rafi looked down, "I understand. But the crew of the Blue Nymph are my family. I will protect them as best as I can."

Corsepis replied, "We Xubanthali believe human kind are all family. We believe that to let one part of it willfully perish damns us all. If there was another way I would tell thee. But Xuba tells me there is not."

Sinbad reached out and grasped the dying man's hand. "I vow we will do as you say. Peace be with you on your journey. 'Tis the *greatest* journey."

"And peace be with you, O Sinbad," gasped Corsepis.

And with that Sinbad straightened. "Respect this man's last moments," he instructed, and strode from the clearing. Sinbad's crew looked to one another, then dutifully followed suit. Only Rafi remained, gazing at the ground, deep in thought. Then he too turned and left.

"What do we do, O Sinbad?" Omar watched as his Captain helped load buckets of multicolored fruits and vegetables into the Blue Nymph's hold. Above them the newly repaired mast, the Blue Nymph's familiar sail curled and waiting like an animal.

"Our course is clear, Omar," responded Sinbad gruffly, continuing his work. "You heard the shaman: there is no other way."

"It was Xuba, Cap'n," answered Omar, shifting uneasily. "Not *our* god."

"And yet Allah beckons us also," said Sinbad, pausing momentarily in his task, gazing at Omar with his piercing blue eyes. "Can you not feel it?"

"Aye," interjected Gunarson as he passed by clutching two barrels of drinking water under his huge arms. "Odin urges us onward too."

"'Tis the children," came Delacrois' voice, from his where he was sitting some small way distant. The Gaul was examining the shaft of one of his arrows, one eye closed. "They are what urges you onward." He laughed, "Are you not as soft and pliable as dough, fearsome Viking?" All around the rest of the crew snickered as they continued their tasks of readying the Blue Nymph.

Gunarson bowed in exaggerated agreement, "Friends, 'tis true we are adventurers and that we crave treasure. But 'tis also true we abhor devilry, especially when young 'uns be involved." At this the rest of the crew nodded and grunted their assent. "Who says we cannot rescue the innocents and liberate the loot at the same time?"

"I suspect there will be neither children nor treasure in this world if we fail," mused Sinbad. "Think. The Warriors of Forever are ancient creatures. Perhaps they have a use for youthful energy. Perhaps that is why they have stolen these people's children. To *consume* them." He caught Tishimi's eyes and thought there to be a look of skepticism in them, but she said nothing.

"With respect, Captain," interjected Rafi, turning from his task securing the rigging. "To discover the means by which Al-Izrikel the Scarlet originally imprisoned the Warriors we must find the Scholars of Bethshea and their library. But as I said to the shaman, the Scholars of Bethshea are themselves the stuff of legend. No-one has ever found their Library, though many have searched. If the rumors are true, it contains all the stories of the world. Alexandria pales in comparison."

"The witches of the Moon Peninsula know their location," came a voice. It was Al-Bulcar, accompanied as ever by his retinue.

"Witches?" said Sinbad, turning in surprise. "Tell us."

"They are called the Arlegon," said Illia, Corsepis' daughter, as she stepped forward. She still wore the brilliant white sari. Sinbad wondered how it remained so clean. "They are a coven of powerful witches. They know the location of the Scholars of Bethshea."

"Why would they tell us?" blurted Haroun. He had been listening from up in the rigging, where he was securing knots.

"We'll convince them," said Sinbad as an aside. He concentrated on the young woman. "Your father..?"

Illia inclined her head and Al-Bulcar spoke for her, "Xuba has taken our wise shaman. He is not to be grieved. He lived a long and venerable life, using his gifts for the good of our people and our island, right up to the last. But we are fortunate," and with this he placed a gentle, pudgy hand on Illia's shoulder, "because his daughter shares his powers."

Delacrois' eyes widened, "You are a sorceress?"

Al-Bulcar placed a finger under the girl's chin and gently lifted her head so that her eyes were visible beneath the sari. Sinbad half-expected to see tears but there were none, just her pale, limpid eyes. "Aye," she said softly, wincing.

"You see she has the same pale eyes as her father," said Al-Bulcar. "In Xubanthali culture it is the sign of one gifted with magical powers. In time she will be able to do all the things her father could. Perceive the future, slow time, animate that which is inorganic."

"The sunlight hurts her eyes," observed Sinbad slowly.

"'Tis true, she cannot abide bright light," said Al-Bulcar, smiling gently. "'Tis the same with all Xubanthali sorcerers. We think it a small price for such gifts."

By now Illia had evidently tired of being the object of discussion. She pulled away from Al-Bulcar, scowling. "Will you help us? Will you find our children and return them to us?" she demanded of Sinbad, pulling the sari hood to cover her eyes.

"Aye," said Sinbad. "If you can show us the location of the Arlegon."

"I will accompany you," asserted Illia.

"Is that so?" responded Sinbad, raising an eyebrow.

"Many of us would like to come," interjected Al-Bulcar hurriedly. "We want to play our part in rescuing our offspring."

Omar suddenly replied, casting his arms expansively at the Blue Nymph, "With respect, Al-Bulcar, you perceive the size of our vessel. Large it may be, but we cannot carry many more than our crew."

"*Not if we want to carry zee treasure,*" observed Delacrois, exaggerating his Gallic accent. Despite the humor, this comment elicited some grunted acknowledgements from his fellows. Sinbad could tell they were immediately wary at the prospect of any Xubanthali travelling with them.

Al-Bulcar was nodding enthusiastically. "Aye, we understand. Any spoils of this mission should rightly be yours. But remember we had intended on leaving this island. It would take little preparation to render our ships ready for such a journey."

Sinbad considered this, his suspicious eyes searching Al-Bulcar's face. "So be it," he said eventually. "Let us finish taking on board supplies for the journey. Choose your finest people and we will sail afore sunset."

While Sinbad's crew took to singing shanties and joshing one another while they readied the Blue Nymph for the departure, the Xubanthali islanders worked with good-natured though largely silent diligence as they loaded the Blue Nymph with supplies. As well as extraordinary fish, meats, fruits and vegetables, Sinbad noted with interest that they also loaded some flat, circular objects constructed from wood and animal skin. Closer inspection confirmed what Sinbad had suspected, that these were drums. They were evidently made from the local trees in a fashion not dissimilar to that involved in the construction of a barrel, strung with an animal hide of some kind, most probably that of cattle, and adorned with all manner of luminescent, sparkling seashells. Though such objects might take up valuable space that might be better spent on food and fresh water, Sinbad recognized the importance of entertainment on long, often arduous sea journeys, and so did not present any opposition. He figured that the drums might also hold some religious significance for the Xubanthali.

Once these things had been loaded, the Xubanthali then moved on to the job of preparing their own ships with comparable fixity of purpose. After discussion Al-Bulcar had selected three dhows to accompany the Blue Nymph on its journey to the Moon Peninsula. Sinbad noted that Al-Bulcar had over-exaggerated the extent to which these vessels were ready for departure. In reality, when the gigantic, animated model of Xuba had turned upon the islanders the three vessels, along with the rest of the haphazard flotilla, had launched with virtually no preparation. Only the careful ministrations of the ships' captains in each case had kept the vessels from falling prey to the monster; that and the remarkably robust design of the ships.

Sinbad watched intently as the islanders worked. He judged that they were ordinarily a happy people, content with life upon their island paradise, satisfied with the nominal leadership of Al-Bulcar and with a god they clearly regarded as benevolent. Sinbad learned from Al-Bulcar that a religious tract existed in the form of some ancient papyrus but that only those anointed with the appropriate powers of insight were ever given access to it. Until his death this parchment had been the special care of Corsepis, and now it would pass to his daughter Illia, although Al-Bulcar was permitted to study it in certain circumstances.

Indeed, as Al-Bulcar expressed it, the tract asked little of the islanders beyond their deference to Xuba and to the natural world that was Xuba's expression in the mortal realm. In other words, animals, birds and plants were to be understood as Xuba's emissaries, and accorded appropriate respect. This didn't mean the Xubanthali couldn't kill or otherwise exploit the island's bounties and that of the sea around. Far from it. Rather, the tract stated that the Xubanthali should treat the living world humanely, but that they should also exploit only to the extent of their need, rather than the extent of their *want*. Beyond these strictures, and unlike many other deities Sinbad and his crew had encountered in their wide-ranging voyages, Xuba did not demand sacrifices nor place onerous expectations upon the island community beyond that they should not kill or steal from one another.

Excepting the rule of Xuba and aside from Al-Bulcar and the reverence accorded Corsepis and subsequently his daughter, there was little indication of any hierarchy. The more Sinbad got to know these people, the more he became convinced that they must be descendants of sailors from India from the far distant past. While visiting Calcutta he had heard speak of religious orders which had eschewed caste and even strictures of gender, and which had consequently been persecuted for their egalitarian stance. These orders had supposedly left India in search of territory where they could establish themselves according to their own beliefs, without fear of subjugation. The fact that Xubanthali male and female alike would, for instance, engage in tasks of lifting and carrying with little discrimination only confirmed him in his supposition. Sinbad also figured that such activity would normally elicit songs and laughter, but that their absent off-spring was the reason for the look of intense, mournful longing that played behind their eyes and kindly smiles.

Illia stood out, not just because her sari was white, but because her skin was much lighter, of a kind Sinbad had rarely encountered in this part of the globe. She exercised a key role directing others to tasks, assertive but kindhearted, and not afraid to get involved herself. Sinbad's crew had initially tried to assist in loading the other ships just as the Xubanthali had helped in both fixing and loading the Blue Nymph, but the islanders were insistent that these tasks were theirs alone to complete. Sinbad wondered whether they might, on some level, be chastising themselves for their inability to protect the island, or to prevent their children from being taken by the Warriors of Forever. Whatever the reason, as a result Sinbad's crew now sat on the shore watching, some engaged in games of cards or dice, others whittling, some playing lutes or other musical instruments, many just resting in the heat in expectation of the travails to come.

"A comely wench," observed Gunarson, following Sinbad's gaze to the figure of Illia. The Viking lowered himself next to Sinbad.

"Aye," murmured Sinbad distantly.

"This will be a difficult voyage," observed Gunarson. "And these people are not adventurers." He cast his huge hand around them, at the golden sand, toward the gentle, lapping waves and rustling palm trees. "They lead a gentle, nourishing life."

"Their children have been taken from them," responded Sinbad. "They will fight and suffer privations. They will endure in order that their younglings are returned to them."

"Aye," acknowledged Gunarson, nodding slowly. "They will have their treasure and we shall have ours, if Odin allows it."

"Aye," said Sinbad.

By now the loading had apparently been completed and the islanders were gathering on the shore adjacent to the jetty. They could see a large figure moving amongst the Xubanthali that they recognized as Al-Bulcar. As he walked through their midst he would occasionally place a hand upon the shoulder of an individual. The chosen individual would then detach from the group and begin walking up the jetty to one of the ships anchored alongside it.

"We should choose our own crew in similar fashion," remarked Gunarson, as he and Sinbad stood.

Sinbad did not reply, instead flashing the Norseman a rueful glance. Behind them the rest of Sinbad's crew had noticed the Captain's movement toward the Blue Nymph. The crew stood, dusting themselves down, and began heading towards the jetty. Some inspected their weapons, others swigged from bottles, relishing the last dregs.

Their journey was about to begin.

Seated in his crow's nest, Haroun watched the island recede into the distance, absently stroking Samson's gray fur, the cat nestled amidst the rags at his feet, apparently sleeping. Despite its undeniable beauty Haroun had felt a searing melancholy at the heart of the island and he was glad to be leaving it. In ripping the children from the place it was as though the undead warriors had taken the island's soul. He was glad to be back in his eyrie, the rapidly cooling air fresh on his face, only the cat and occasional wheeling seabird for company. Haroun looked out toward the two vessels on portside, and then across to the dhow at their starboard. Despite the undeniable, not to mention surprising, elegance of these vessels none were a match for the mighty Blue Nymph and its majestic, billowing indigo sail.

Haroun looked down at the lengthening shadow of his mast on the deck below, and saw Captain Sinbad standing on the prow, his face toward the vast orange sphere sinking slowly into the sea. It occurred to Haroun, not for the first time, that as a rule his Captain never looked back at where they had been, only ever ahead. And not for the first time, Haroun wondered why that might be.

"Captain Sinbad," said a fulsome voice.

Sinbad turned, surprised, to see the portly figure of Al-Bulcar approaching.

"Al-Bulcar," he acknowledged levelly, "you are not aboard one of your own vessels."

"Ah well," said Al-Bulcar languidly and with a smile, "I thought it better to join you on your vessel, at the head of the fleet as it were."

"There are no quarters for you," responded Sinbad flatly.

Al-Bulcar's porcine features broke into a frown and his bulbous cheeks reddened. "Oh dear. I thought a personage as, well, *renowned* as your good self would have access to quarters…"

Al-Bulcar's booming voice was such that it had reached the ears of assorted of the crew, among them Omar, Gunarson and Delacrois. The three men threw back their heads in raucous laughter.

"I have my own cabin," conceded Sinbad, eyes glittering with barely concealed amusement. "As do my must trusted crewmembers."

"I see," said Al-Bulcar, reading the Captain's expression. "But there is no space for me."

Sinbad inclined his head, "I fear not."

"Then there is no space for Illia either," said Al-Bulcar rapidly, in an effort to cover up his embarrassment, as the young woman appeared alongside him.

"I will sleep amongst the rest of the crew," announced Illia, her head tilted so that her eyes were hidden beneath the shade of the sari. The light of the setting sun was bright, so Sinbad could understand why she would use the sari's hood to shield herself from it, but this didn't diminish the discomfort he felt at not being able to see her eyes. He found it disconcerting to concentrate only on the lower portion of her face, though her mouth was undeniably sensuous to behold.

Al-Bulcar looked to Illia, one eyebrow raised querulously, his irritation with the young woman obvious. "Very well. I, however, must return to one of my vessels in order that I might be refreshed by sleep and sustenance."

Sinbad had folded his arms and shook his head, "The Blue Nymph will neither slow nor stop that you might board another of the vessels. Our journey has begun, and nothing will prevent us reaching our destination. You have made your decision and will travel with us for the duration."

"But..." Al-Bulcar began, trailing off as he read Sinbad's implacable expression. His alacrity transformed to a smile, and he bowed a little, reverently touching his forehead. "Of course, Captain Sinbad. As you wish."

"Omar!" called Sinbad. "Allocate our guests some hammocks. And perhaps find them some grog, and a slice of melon."

"Aye!" responded Omar, grabbing Al-Bulcar by his bulbous arm and escorting him away from the ship's prow.

"Captain Sinbad," acknowledged Illia, inclining her head and turning to follow Al-Bulcar and Omar.

"Wait," said Sinbad suddenly, touching the young woman's arm, accidentally encountering the elaborate snake bracelet. He noticed she flinched instinctively. "I wondered why you..."

"Why I have joined this vessel and not a ship belonging to my own people?" She gazed at him, her delicate lips curling into a smile. "To navigate you, Captain."

Sinbad could not help but bristle, and he found himself feeling like an outraged adolescent all over again. "We are seasoned sailors. We can find the Moon Peninsula, my lady, I assure you," he heard himself saying, immediately wincing at his own bombast.

"I do not doubt it," she replied carefully. "But the approach is beset by dagger-like rocks. They would easily slice a hull such as the Blue Nymph's."

Sinbad half-smiled, "Is that so? You have much knowledge of Ethiopian teakwood?"

"I am beginning my life as a mystic, Captain," she said. "Though my powers are in their infancy, I can help you if you will allow me."

"Aye," Sinbad said slowly. "Tell me more."

"…I have joined this vessel…to navigate you, Captain."

She continued, "The learned one amongst your crew…"

"Rafi," interrupted Sinbad.

"Yes, Rafi, he is skeptical about our mission. The woman Tishimi also. Rightly so. There is no guarantee we will find the Arlegon, or the Scholars of Bethshea, or discover how we might defeat the Warriors of Forever and rescue the children."

"Or that we will find the treasure," added Sinbad.

"Indeed, if that is what concerns you," she nodded. She added, after a moment's consideration, "But I do not think it does."

He smiled. "If you can read me so well, perhaps you can read our destiny?"

She inclined her head so that he could at last see the woman's eyes, yet they were closed from him. He watched as she rocked on her feet. The sun was dipping below the horizon, and darkness had begun to envelop the flotilla. Suddenly her eyes snapped open. Sinbad watched in astonishment as the color of the pale irises seemed to stir and shift.

"The future is only clouds and uncertainty," she said softly, then turned on her heel.

Sinbad watched her go, then turned his attention to the view and the adventure ahead.

Chapter four

Together the four dhows cut through the water like an arrow, the Blue Nymph at its tip. Sinbad had taken the decision to travel deliberately slower than he ordinarily would, lest the sleek Blue Nymph outrun the trio of Xubanthali vessels. Though the three Xubanthali craft were undoubtedly impressive to behold, their wide bellies were clearly intended to carry cargo, almost certainly the cloth Sinbad had noticed at the Xubanthali encampment, to other islands in the vicinity. As a result they were less agile at turning, and struggled to keep pace with the Blue Nymph.

One week and a half had elapsed since they had left the island. It had so far proven a largely uneventful journey, save for the occasional fleeting glimpse of a shoal of enormous ray that seemed to find some peculiar interest in tracking their progress. Haroun noted with amusement that Samson the cat returned these creatures' attentions with his own particular brand of curiosity. The young man guessed that he was probably fantasizing about transforming them into his evening meal, despite the fact that the monsters dwarfed the feline.

During the first few days seasickness emerged as a common problem amongst the Xubanthali stationed on the Blue Nymph. The sailors among them were hardy enough, but this probably only amounted to about four or five of the eighteen who had been assigned to the Blue Nymph. The island of Xubanthali was seemingly so fertile, so full of edible flora and fauna, that few of the others ever had cause to venture off dry land for more than the occasional invigorating swim, or to fish with nets in the shallows, which were apparently abundant with edible, easy-to-catch sea-life. Indeed, the Xubanthali were unsurprisingly adept at fishing, the piles of netted fish on the Blue Nymph's deck testimony to their proficiency and perseverance.

Ironically their leader Al-Bulcar seemed most prone to seasickness, but that might have more to do with the exorbitant quantities of food and drink he consumed throughout the day. Often times Sinbad would stir to the unedifying sound and spectacle of the Xubanthali leader's enormous blubbery bulk bent over the side of the Blue Nymph, retching and releasing the previous night's generous meal. One morning this regular occurrence was so protracted, so disgusting to behold, that Sinbad was moved to comment upon the waste of supplies such a routine constituted. However, it transpired that Omar, never one for diplomacy, had got there first, issuing a torrent of abuse at the man. The sight of the swarthy First Mate yelling up at the flabby Xubanthali elicited cheers of merriment from Sinbad's crew and looks of horror from Al-Bulcar's retinue, save for the figure of Illia, whom Sinbad noted remained characteristically unmoved by the incident.

Duly chastised, Al-Bulcar was notably more restrained in his consumption the following evening, though his newfound temperance did not prove particularly long-lasting. By the end of the following week he had pretty much reverted to his old ways, once again imbibing vast amounts of food and drink with zealous abandon. Fortunately for everyone else his stomach seemed to have benefitted greatly from the break and as a consequence proved far better able to cope with the motion of the sea.

Indeed, as the days progressed, the rest of the Xubanthali who were not already seasoned sailors gained their sea-legs, and a deal of camaraderie established itself between Sinbad's crew and that of the islanders, even if the reserved demeanor of the Xubanthali meant it was expressed very subtly. When the light fell of an evening Henri Delacrois would produce his lute and proceed to lilt a song of romance (or at least bawdy behavior) from his native Gaul, which the islanders would listen to with attentive, broad-faced smiles, despite the grief that played behind their eyes for their lost children. Byrne would afterward sing songs of battle from his native Highlands, only to be joined by Gunarson, as so many of the Celt's ballads were recognizable to the Norseman. Sinbad's crew, though, was overwhelmingly Persian in origin, and soon the evening would be dominated by beautiful, sonorous paeans of derring-do particular to their region and culture.

To the crew of the Blue Nymph such an evening's festivities was a familiar event. What was truly unexpected was the Xubanthalis' response. Moving wordlessly and deftly, the smiling islanders had brought out their drums. Following a sign from Al-Bulcar, a single drummer began beating a steady tune, only to be joined by another and then another, each more urgent than the last. Now the Xubanthali began to whoop and cheer, and to sing extraordinary notes, some high, some low, some involving the rapid clacking of the tongue. Ordinarily so keen to repress their emotions, the islanders erupted into lively, infectious songs of thanks to their revered Xuba, all the while hammering out increasingly complex rhythms.

As the song gathered in momentum, some of the Xubanthali women and men engaged in a gyrating, jerky dance, clapping their hands above their heads and rubbing their bodies against one another. Sinbad's crew found this impossible to emulate, though some of them tried with gusto. The grog the Blue Nymph already possessed had disappeared even more swiftly than was normally the case, at least for those whose adherence to religious stricture was suitably flexible. Fortunately further carousing was afforded by a fruity, pungent wine supplied by the islanders.

Sinbad watched the ribaldry unfolding with an arched, amused demeanor. He saw Tishimi on the opposite side of the deck, equally detached. This did not surprise him. Nor did the sight of Rafi, the aged, tall man gazing on, a bottle of grog clutched in one hand, his expression one of concentration, though he would laugh occasionally at the antics of Gunarson, Omar and Delacrois. Rafi's slightly removed persona was something the crew was familiar with and accepted as entirely normal. What Sinbad did find out of the ordinary, however, was Illia. Unlike her Xubanthali crewmates her demeanor was unchanged. She stood inert by the prow, head bowed as usual. Sinbad, with his renowned eyesight, was able to see her mouth moving, barely perceptibly, perhaps whispering a dedication to her late father, or a prayer to Xuba. He watched her throughout the night, returning intermittently and seeing that she had not moved from her location at the front of the vessel. Nor had her whispering come to an end.

The next morning was one of diametric opposites. While swathes of Sinbad's crew wandered the decks clutching their heads or voiding their stomachs over the edge and into the briny, the Xubanthali men and women had returned to their former disposition. They moved amongst Sinbad's crew offering sympathetic smiles or consolatory pats on the back, applying themselves to their tasks with characteristic good nature. For the Xubanthali it was as though the previous evening had not occurred. Yet when another evening of carousing burst forth several days later, the islanders threw themselves into the partying as enthusiastically, perhaps more so, as they had that first evening. The following day, they reverted to their standard mode of behavior wherein restraint and reticence were primary. Clearly, Sinbad, surmised, the dancing, singing and drumming were the ways in which the Xubanthali released the extremes of their emotions.

A further week passed with neither incident nor sighting of land or any other vessel. Like any good ship's captain, Sinbad spent much of his time keenly observing the sky, which had transformed from a deep blue to a paler shade, and then to white. He noted that several of his ordinarily hardy crew, men who normally carried out their tasks bare-chested, had taken to pulling shirts about themselves and even other items of thicker clothing. Sinbad had himself been monitoring the drop in temperature for some time. It was entirely conceivable, of course, that there was a squall coming. Yet somehow he didn't think so. This felt markedly different, in a way he struggled to discern.

"The weather is turning," said the elderly Rafi, gazing at his frowning Captain.

"Aye," said Sinbad, still watching the sky. "What think you of this voyage, wise Rafi?"

Sinbad's crewmate shrugged, "I meant what I said. I have no family. No blood family, leastways. You, the Viking, the Gaul. The boy Haroun. The woman Tishimi. Even Omar. You are family to me. I will do what I ought to protect you."

"Perhaps this undertaking *is* protecting us," observed Sinbad. "The Warriors of Forever have returned. Who knows for what purpose they want the Xubanthali children? What will the monsters do if they are not challenged? What horrors will they reap upon the world, upon all of us mortals?"

"Aye," offered Rafi, though there was little conviction in his voice.

"Aye," nodded Sinbad. As he looked upward he saw something falling. A beautiful, tiny object, spinning through the air, extraordinarily fragile and white. The object landed on the deck of the Blue Nymph and immediately disappeared. Other of the tiny objects were falling too.

"By Odin's blood, 'tis snowing," exclaimed Gunarson in astonishment. "Are we not in the midst of the Aegean? How can this be?"

"Sorcery," said a female voice. The group turned to see Illia approaching, pulling her sari around herself for warmth. They looked expectantly at the young woman. "Someone is manipulating the weather."

"To what end?" asked Sinbad.

"To that end," Illia responded, thrusting a quivering finger at the horizon. They followed her gaze to see an extraordinary vortex of snow and ice spinning toward them across the sea, its progress illuminated by repeated forks of lightning.

"For the love of Allah," muttered Omar. "Where is that boy Haroun? The idle cur! Why did he not alert us?"

"He did not have time," responded Illia curtly. "I tell you again, it is a thing most unnatural!"

"Port ho!" yelled Sinbad. "Signal to the other ships to follow our lead!"

The Blue Nymph began to turn and the other ships tacked their own sails, mirroring her maneuver. But the vortex was still moving inexorably toward them, following the vessels as they turned, tearing walls of spume in its wake. The sound of its advance had reached them now, a howling, unearthly cacophony of rushing water and wind. Its approach brought with it a biting gale and more of the billowing snow, rendering the deck treacherous to negotiate.

"We'll never outrun it!" yelled Omar, frantically pulling at the Blue Nymph's tiller, snow catching around his stubbly face and fulsome eyebrows.

By now the vortex had reached the last of the dhows in the fleet. The crew of the Blue Nymph watched, incredulously, as it passed along the length of the vessel, apparently coating the ship in ice as it progressed. People aboard the vessel who had previously been chasing hither and yon and were now caught in the vortex's path froze where they stood. Seeing the plight of their fellows, others of the crew desperately tried to avoid the vortex by rushing to the prow of the vessel, many jumping for their lives into the crashing sea. Even this, though, was not necessarily sufficient to avoid the onslaught of the vortex, since its path was transforming the sea immediately around the vessel to ice.

"What horror is this?" muttered Delacrois.

"A direst magic, Delacrois san," said a quiet Japanese voice beside him. Tishimi had tilted her head and was staring at the unfolding nightmare with a look of intense curiosity.

"You've seen it before?" said Delacrois, similarly unable to take his eyes away from the gruesome spectacle.

"I have seen similar," confirmed Tishimi, with a faint nod of her head.

"Then how might we defeat it?" pressed Delacrois, still fascinated.

Tishimi shook her head. "This wizardry is the work of many. Only a very powerful magician could repel its power."

Sinbad addressed Illia, his tone urgent, "Listen to me, sorceress. You must halt this abomination."

She turned to him abruptly. Though he could not see her eyes, he could tell she was glowering from beneath the rim of the sari. "I make no claims for myself, beyond that I am a seer. I told you before, my powers are young. They are naught compared to this…"

"Bah, you're not even a good seer," grumbled Gunarson, "for you did not predict this!" The Blue Nymph was rocking wildly in its efforts to evade the eddy, the vortex rapidly gaining on them and the other ships.

"But I will *try*," Illia snapped, turning on her heel. Sinbad watched as the woman padded swiftly along the length of the vessel, disappearing from view behind the sail.

The dhow the vortex had enveloped sat atop the ice plain, its sail petrified, everyone aboard frozen. The vortex, meanwhile, was tacking direction, evidently intent on consuming a second Xubanthali vessel. Sinbad ducked under the sail and followed Illia to the Blue Nymph's aft. He saw her standing, arms outstretched, muttering incantation after incantation.

"This is no good," Al-Bulcar was saying, "no good at all. Illia's powers are not yet grown. And even if they were, she is but a prophet..."

"Her father animated the statue of Xuba and rendered it gigantic," observed Delacrois. "Your magicians are more powerful than you give them credit."

"They *become* that," responded Al-Bulcar. "Illia's father lived a long life during which he acquired many powers, much experience and considerable wisdom." His relentlessly polite tone was severely strained. He continued, "Illia has barely begun her journey. Perhaps one day she will have such powers as those possessed by her late father, but such an eventuality is many decades distant."

"Such powers are not as great as you might believe," observed Tishimi with her customary softness of voice. "An acolyte could master the power of animating objects with but a little effort."

"I bow to your wisdom, madam," retorted Al-Bulcar crisply. "But I assure you once again that Illia's powers are in their infancy."

Rafi gestured to the dhow visited by the vortex. "Behold your comrades, Al-Bulcar," he said, his voice tipped with anger. "They are frozen by this thing. We cannot fight it with swords and arrows. Your young sorceress is our only chance. Indeed, it is your children's only chance, too." He added, *sotto voce*, "If you what you claim is true."

Sinbad watched as an extraordinary, fierce light began to arc around Illia's outstretched hands. Her incantations had meanwhile become louder, more urgent, a garbled litany of hisses and jagged words. Suddenly the arcing light coalesced into a single beam that blasted forth from the young woman's hands, sizzling across the sky and colliding with the vortex, moments before it engulfed the second dhow. The beam's contact with the vortex caused it to slew to a halt, the point of collision throwing up a series of tremendous explosions that sent daggers of ice flying in all directions. Illia's body strained under the effort involved in generating and manipulating the energy beam.

"She's stopped it!" yelled Delacrois triumphantly from his vantage point. "I told you, she is more powerful than you believe!"

"It is not enough, Delacrois san," responded Tishimi calmly. "As I say, the vortex has been conjured and manipulated by more than one person."

"The Arlegon Witches!" said Delacrois in sudden realization. "It must be them. They are alerted to our quest."

"Perhaps," nodded Tishimi. "But such knowledge is of little benefit. The woman Illia can fend off this devilry for only a limited amount of time."

"Then what do we do?" said Delacrois wildly. "There must be something!"

"We need more energy," said Tishimi, her words as rapid as her thoughts. "More power from some source."

"There are no more magicians aboard this vessel, nor either of the others," interjected Sinbad. "How can we conjure such power, Tishimi?"

"What you say is true, Sinbad san," nodded Tishimi. "But there might be another way." She whirled, her voice bellowing unexpectedly above the fearsome wind, "*Haroun! Haroun!*"

"Aye, Madam Tishimi," returned Haroun, lowering himself from the rigging and skittering across the wet deck. By now snow had begun to collect haphazardly, incongruously, across the Blue Nymph, gathering amidst the rigging, atop barrels, coating coils of rope with glistening white.

"What is it that fascinates the ship's cat so?" demanded Tishimi.

"Samson?" said Haroun, surprised. He turned his attention to where Tishimi was looking. Oblivious to everything occurring around him, the feline had once more located himself at the edge of the deck, looking down at the sea. Even the whirling snowflakes weren't enough to distract him, though they were rapidly covering his fur. Haroun grinned uncertainly, "He watches the shoal of rays, Madam Tishimi. He thinks he might acquire one for his dinner."

"Then you have your answer," said Tishimi, a trace of triumph evident in her otherwise unemotional tones. "Such rays carry about themselves a powerful charge. If we can but direct the school into the heart of the vortex, their combined power might prove sufficient to disrupt those controlling it."

"Aye, 'tis true," nodded Rafi, raising his voice above the gale. "I have heard that Greek apothecaries use such beasts to numb the pain of childbirth. Perhaps such force might also be used for *destructive* rather than *creative* purposes."

"But how will you direct such creatures toward the centre of the vortex?" said Al-Bulcar, boggling.

"Leave it to me," responded Sinbad. In a flash the Captain was running toward a pile of netting clustered to one side of the deck. He scooped up one of the Xubanthali nets, filled to capacity with annelids, snake eels, sea anemones and assorted crabs, and threw it over his back, before launching himself into the water. Grachene, the enchanted dagger, had appeared once more, and he clutched it in his mouth as he dove. Sinbad crashed beneath the tumultuous, icy waves, just ahead of the shoal of gigantic rays.

Illia, meanwhile, was struggling to control the beam emanating from her hands, the clashing of energies continuing to cause a succession of extraordinary explosions. Perspiration hazarded down her face. Allowed time to escape, the threatened Xubanthali dhow was now some way distant from the encroaching menace. It was clear, however, that the vortex would simply continue its attack if allowed to do so. The vortex carried on spinning fitfully above the sea, and Illia continued her efforts to prevent it from moving.

Sinbad cut beneath the waves, the net trailing behind him, assorted dead fish dancing in his wake. Behind him darted the shoal of surprised manta ray, their eyes bulbous, wings flapping gracefully, mouths opening and closing excitedly to receive the trail of unexpected food. Through the ocean's gloom Sinbad could make out a funnel of churning water and he quickly began to feel the force of the vortex as it span through the sea.

As he neared the vortex the warm Aegean seemed a million miles distant. Huge chunks of ice pivoted past him, sculpted into extraordinary shapes by the spinning heart of the vortex. Sinbad felt his body beginning to stiffen, his sinews straining to propel him onward through the thickening water. He struggled to look behind him, and saw that the manta rays were continuing their progress, evidently unencumbered by the freezing water. To his fascination he saw why this was. Whenever a lump of ice span into the ray's path it would burst in an explosion of energy, shattering into a million spinning fragments. He realized if they made contact with him a similar fate would be his, and that it would surely constitute an agonizing death.

His movements were becoming sluggish. He could feel his heart slowing, his lungs becoming solid and heavy. He knew without looking back that the rays would inevitably catch him. Sinbad instead concentrated on what was ahead of him. He could see the heart of the icy vortex and realized that it would soon begin to pull him in. In desperation Sinbad spun himself around, once, then twice, and then a third time, slashing with Grachene as he did so, ripping the net asunder. His frantic efforts released the haul of dead fish, crustaceans and eels into the perimeter of the vortex.

The shoal of rays veered at the last moment, chasing hungrily after the cloud of food. As they did so, though, the vortex took hold of each ray, sucking it into its rotating depths. When the first ray was captured an explosion erupted from the centre of the vortex, sending Sinbad hurtling through the water. Another conflagration followed in rapid succession as another ray was caught up in the eddy, and then more until Sinbad's body was being propelled helplessly through the sea and then up and out of the water.

Sinbad burst upward through the surface, arms and legs flailing, then plummeted back into the waves. He struggled with all his might to swim, despite his frozen limbs. Very quickly he felt hands clawing at him as he was pulled into a small row boat. The familiar face of Gunarson, his savior once again, grinned at him. Sinbad was bleeding from a cut to his temple, and his body trembled with cold and the beginnings of frost bite. Otherwise, though, he was miraculously unscathed. He scrambled to sit up and saw that the explosions were still occurring from beneath the centre of the vortex, sending up colossal spumes of water each time. The sustained attack was causing the vortex to sag, the whirlpool bending even as it continued to rage. Turning, Sinbad could see Illia still on the prow of the Blue Nymph, her body evidently wracked in agony, desperate to maintain the force of her energy beam.

Finally, like a mammoth clay urn collapsing on a potter's wheel, the vortex buckled in upon itself, and dissipated into the water around. The energy beam vanished and he saw Illia collapsing to her knees.

"It is clear, then, that they know we're coming," said Sinbad with certainty as he swigged from a tankard of fresh water.

"Will they try such a ruse as this again?" asked Al-Bulcar innocently. "The vortex, I mean?"

Following the vortex's collapse the white, snowy sky had gradually given way to a familiar Aegean blue and the temperature had begun to rise. Tishimi, who was attending to the exhausted Illia, shook her head.

"My conjecture is that those who conjured the tempest will need to rest," she said softly, dabbing Illia's forehead with a damp cloth. "Such was the power involved."

"So they *might* try again!" squawked Al-Bulcar, his hand fluttering to his face.

"We must reach them quickly, then," replied Sinbad firmly.

"It is my judgment that proximity played a crucial role in that particular spell," observed Rafi thoughtfully.

"What do you mean, old man?" replied Omar, flashing him a scornful frown.

"He means for the spell to work the Arlegon, presuming it was them, must be close by," said Sinbad.

"So we must be near the Moon Peninsula," said Delacrois.

"Land ahoy!" came Haroun's familiar cry.

"Nearer than you think," replied Gunarson, clapping the Frenchman heartily on the shoulder with a broad smile.

The crew dispersed to take up their individual tasks. Now the 'fleet' was formed from only three ships. Upon Sinbad's return the Blue Nymph and two remaining Xubanthali vessels had launched boats to inspect the ship attacked by the vortex. What they encountered was extraordinary and terrible, more so for the Xubanthali as their people were the ones who had perished. In addition Sinbad had observed that despite their encounter with the Warriors of Forever the islanders were unused to the horrors the supernatural could visit upon the mortal realm. Sinbad's crew, by comparison, had encountered bizarre, often gruesome magical phenomena across multiple adventures. They were consequently hard to shock.

The dhow itself had started to creak as the Blue Nymph crewmembers and Xubanthali representatives boarded. Sinbad and his crew decreed that they should all move rapidly in ascertaining that all aboard were dead but also in confirming that the ship's supplies were beyond salvaging. They were correct on both counts. Both the people aboard the ship and the bodies floating in the sea around it had been frozen beyond help, their faces caught in expressions of surprise and woe. Some had seen their fate approaching, and had lifted their clasped hands skyward in reaching supplication to Xuba. Others had been petrified in the midst of some or other task, unaware of what was about to befall them. In a couple of cases individuals had even been frozen mid-air, as they jumped from the vessel into what they unwittingly perceived to be the safety of the sea.

Sinbad instructed that the Xubanthali vessel and all aboard should be abandoned to the ocean, though he allowed time for the islanders to offer prayers to their deity. The requirements of the mission, though, meant that such mourning was necessarily short-lived, and Sinbad had ordered the boats hasten back to the ships from which they had originated, that they might continue their journey without further delay.

Tishimi patted at Illia's forehead with a cloth. "It is okay," said Illia suddenly, grabbing the Japanese woman's wrist. "I have recovered."

Tishimi stepped back. "That is not possible," she replied gently. "You halted the progress of the vortex for a considerable time. The energy involved…"

Illia had pulled herself to her feet. She struggled to straighten her sari, checking the hood once again shaded her eyes. "I have recovered, Madam Tishimi," she said firmly.

Tishimi bowed as the young woman strode away from her to the other side of the deck. Only after Tishimi deemed she had been deferential enough did she seek to lift her head and further observe Illia. The young woman was staring out at the approaching rocks, her sari flapping in the breeze, fingers playing absently upon the snake-shaped bracelet travelling the extent of her arm.

Chapter Five

"The Moon Peninsula," observed Rafi, arriving by Sinbad's side. The Captain was standing, hands on hips, scanning the trails of mist that had descended and which the Blue Nymph and the two Xubanthali ships would shortly traverse.

Sinbad rubbed his clipped beard ruminatively, "Aye." The two men watched as the black rock of the Peninsula emerged from the mists. Sinbad's keen eyes scanned the cliff. He saw, jutting from the water, a succession of lethal rocks like daggers. Amongst these rocks were shards of timber and a portion of mast, complete with flapping, bedraggled and torn sail: their predecessors on this journey.

Sinbad turned, abruptly, and hollered to Omar at the tiller: "Starboard ho!" The Blue Nymph peeled off in response, the other two ships copying.

"Aye, Cap'n!" acknowledged the First Mate. His rugged face was a scowl of concentration.

The cliff-face was evidently split in twain, allowing a narrow path through. There was no choice but for the Blue Nymph and the other ships to follow this route through the ravine. Omar knew this was Sinbad's desire without having to ask his Captain.

"Captain, we must approach carefully," observed Rafi quietly and urgently, rubbing his grizzled chin. "These witches, the Arlegon, know of our approach. If they have recovered suitably they will surely try again. We have already encountered their formidable magic."

"I understand that, wise Rafi," replied Sinbad patiently. "But we swore an oath of allegiance to help these people find their children. And we have bested plenty of warlocks and witches afore now."

"Aye," nodded Rafi slowly. "And I do not have the monopoly on wisdom. All I urge is caution."

"Aye," agreed Sinbad, placing a strong hand on the older man's shoulder and squeezing it. "I value your counsel as always, wise Rafi."

Shadow fell across the three ships as they made their way through the ravine. The rock around them was jet black and looked as though it dated from the origin of the world if not the beginning of Time itself. Sinbad's crew and the Xubanthali aboard the Blue Nymph and the other dhows fell immediately silent as darkness enveloped them. Even Haroun, once again atop the crow's nest, was shrouded in gloom, such was the extent of the towering cliff-faces. He saw Samson the cat peering intently ahead of them,

"Starboard!" Delacrois yelled.."

eyes huge, and followed the creature's gaze.

"Rocks ahead!" yelled Haroun suddenly, his voice reverberating against the cliff walls.

Omar responded from the tiller, "Aye, lad!"

"Henri," said Sinbad quickly, "get to the prow. Spy what you can!"

"Aye, Cap'n," answered the Gaul, disappearing under the rigging. His archer's keen eyes, aided by a hastily illuminated torch, picked through the darkness in search of obstacles. Suddenly, the torch's flame glittered upon something protruding from the water.

"Starboard!" Delacrois yelled abruptly, and Omar responded with an "Aye!" before tacking the tiller appropriately. The Blue Nymph gently eased around a collection of stalagmites like inverted fangs, easily capable of ripping even a hull made of Ethiopian teakwood, let alone those of the Xubanthali vessels following. The other dhow pursued the BlueBlue Nymph in its gentle negotiation of the lethal obstacle.

And so their path continued, at a frustratingly slow pace, Haroun and Delacrois searching the darkness for anything that might cause their untimely destruction, the other two ships mimicking the tiniest maneuver of the lead vessel, insofar as their captains were able to replicate the dexterity of the Blue Nymph. Eventually the ravine began to widen and the shadow to lift. Sinbad's crew and the Xubanthali blinked in the sudden sunlight. The cliff-faces widened before coming together to form an impenetrable wall, arcing around a narrow beach. Sinbad guessed that from above it must appear like a crescent moon. Hence the name of this particular peninsula.

"'Tis a dead end," murmured Omar.

"Our fate lies beyond," said Illia confidently.

"Then there must be a way through," said Gunarson. "A secret point of access we cannot perceive from here."

"Drop anchor!" instructed Sinbad.

"Aye, Cap'n!" came the answer from his crew. With characteristic efficiency the anchor was lowered into the waters surrounding the ship. The other two dhow came to a rest and copied the Blue Nymph. Sinbad selected a handful of his crewmembers—Omar, Gunarson, Delacrois and Tishimi—to join him in inspecting the wall of rock for an entrance, perhaps steps leading up the rock face. They were about to disembark when Al-Bulcar intercepted them.

"Captain," he said hesitantly. "Might we join you in searching for a way through the wall?"

Sinbad viewed him skeptically, "And by 'we' you mean..?"

"Al-Bulcar and myself," said Illia, stepping forward.

"Aye," said Sinbad momentarily, before commencing his descent via the Jacob's ladder into the shallows. "And twelve of your best people, six from each of the other two vessels," he added, as he began wading through the water. Al-Bulcar nodded emphatically, then proceeded to bark instructions to his retinue.

The various groups made their way forward from the three ships, splashing through the waist-deep, vigorously lapping water, coming together on the narrow strip of white sand. Sinbad, Gunarson, Omar, Tishimi and Delacrois immediately moved to inspect the wall of rock. The others rapidly joining them in their hunt.

"'Tis solid," said Gunarson perplexedly, his giant hands roving the surface of the wall in search of the slimmest opening.

"Aye," affirmed Delacrois, stepping back to take a broader view, using his hand to shield himself against the fierce sunlight. "Trust me, Captain, there is no way through this."

Sinbad nodded. "So be it." He, too, stood back, his gaze travelling up the extent of the cliff-face.

Omar's eyes widened, "Cap'n, you're not suggesting..?"

Sinbad's face broke into a wide grin, and he clapped his First Mate on the back. "Take some of the men and fetch some rope, Omar."

"Aye, Cap'n," said Omar, his swarthy features a mask of resignation.

Once the climbers were secured to one another, Sinbad was the first to begin the ascent, in parallel with teams led by Gunarson and Delacrois. In the past Gunarson's bulk had made climbing difficult for him, but practicing on the Blue Nymph's rigging had evidently paid off. He was certainly more enthusiastic about the proposition than the hesitant Delacrois. The Gaul continued to utter a series of curses in his native tongue as he searched for each evasive handhold, very slowly heaving himself upward, feet struggling to find an equivalent site of purchase. Around the three men's waists were ropes, connected to the person who shortly followed them. In this way the group struggled upward. Of those who had come ashore only the portly Al-Bulcar remained on the beach, Illia having insisted, with characteristic obduracy, that she join the others on the climb up the cliff.

Sinbad advanced as quickly as he could but the Xubanthali man immediately behind him made a quick ascent nigh on impossible. During those frequent moments when Sinbad was forced to stop completely because the man behind was struggling to find a purchase, Sinbad would take the opportunity to either look to his side to monitor the progress of the other two teams, or he would cast a glance downward to examine his own team's advance up the precipice. Owing to his own initial hesitance, Delacrois' team were somewhat behind the other two, but as he progressed Henri seemed to build in confidence, and by now his team's ascent was gathering some much needed momentum. Indeed, because the Xubanthali male immediately behind Sinbad was slowing his team to such an extent, it wasn't long before Delacrois' team were parallel with that of Sinbad's. Gunarson's team, in stark contrast, was some considerable distance above the two other teams, scaling the wall extremely rapidly, the Viking's muscular frame virtually carrying the rest of the team up with him.

Gunarson even felt suitably confident to holler to Delacrois, "Gaul, if I reach the summit first I think you owe me a draft of frothing Norse beer!"

"Gladly," Sinbad heard Delacrois muttering, "If I but survive this tribulation I'll drink a flagon of the horse piss myself."

It was during one of these pauses to enable his own team to catch up, that Sinbad first heard the shriek. It was some distance off; evidently carried by the echo of the ravine they had just traversed. He peered into the distance, and saw something large wheeling through the air. He would have guessed it a bird, had the creature's wing-span not been so enormous. Another shriek followed, and he saw the creature turning toward them, its colossal beak opening to show rows of serried teeth. It looked for all the world like a tremendous lizard, awarded the power of flight.

Sinbad looked down and saw that the man immediately behind him had also seen the monster. "Move!" called Sinbad, but the man was frozen to the spot, as though the vortex from earlier had somehow belatedly petrified him.

Sinbad looked above him and saw that Gunarson, too, had seen the creature. He and Gunarson caught each other's eyes, and the Viking knew what to do. With a Herculean effort, Gunarson resumed his climb, dragging the rest of his team behind him.

Delacrois, now some short distance above Sinbad on a parallel section of rock, looked down.

"Mon ami, what is that creature?" he said, gasping for breath.

"Methinks it's the Arlegon's guard," replied Sinbad grimly. "Keep climbing, Henri. We have to get out of its path."

"Aye, Captain," nodded Delacrois, and with an intake of breath restarted his ascent.

Sinbad looked down to see the Xubanthali male below him clutching at the rocks immediately in front of him, crying and still petrified. Sinbad clicked his tongue in irritation, knowing there was nothing else for it. With a grimace he began climbing back down, trying to remember the path he had recently taken. To the Xubanthali man's amazement Sinbad arrived next to him, grabbing the man's shoulder.

"Listen to me," whispered Sinbad. "There is a creature coming which means to kill you, me, all of us. You have to *climb*."

"I cannot," muttered the man, hardly able to look at Sinbad. There were tears in his eyes.

"You have children?" pressed Sinbad.

"Aye," acknowledged the man, "a boy and a girl. I think."

Sinbad stared at him incredulously. "You *think*?"

The man shook his head, "I'm sorry, I'm so scared. Aye, I have two children."

Sinbad narrowed his eyes, "And the Warriors took them?"

The man looked straight at Sinbad now, "Of course, yes, they took them. Just like they took all our children. That's what happened."

Sinbad appraised the man. He was shaking with fear. The various traumas, the Warriors of Forever, the disappearance of his off-spring, the vortex, had clearly corrupted his mind. "And you would do anything to save them?"

"Yes. Of course."

Sinbad squeezed the man's shoulder, "Then you must climb. Climb for them."

"Aye, Captain Sinbad. I know that. It's just I'm not sure I can."

"You *must*," insisted Sinbad. "For the sake of your children. Xuba decrees it."

"Aye," said the man, nodding, stifling a sob. "I will try."

"Good," replied Sinbad, recommencing his climb. Once he was high enough he stole a look down and saw that the man was climbing once again. Above him he saw Illia, the last of Gunarson's team, scrabbling over the edge of the cliff and disappearing from sight, the final stage of her ascent assisted by Omar. Delacrois' team was somewhat distant from the edge but still ascending with urgency. Another shriek brought Sinbad's attention back to the monstrous flying creature. Sinbad saw, with horror, that the creature was not alone, and that a flock of the beings had gathered and was heading toward them. As they neared each of the monsters began to caw, perhaps in anticipation of the coming meal. As they approached the creatures' echoes transformed to a terrifying cacophony.

Sinbad climbed for all his might, praying to Allah that the people in the chain beneath him would follow suit. Occasionally a section would give way under his efforts, crumbling in a stream of rock and dust. On such occasions he would curse his poor judgment, and renew the hunt for more secure hand and footholds.

A shadow fell across him and he looked up to see one of the creatures reaching the lowest of Delacrois' team of climbers. The man shrieked in terror, trying ineffectually to bat the creature away with his leg, but the monster hovered, gnashing with its mighty beak, until finally it made contact. The beast, snorting in what was clearly an expression of triumph, ripped furiously at the man's leg. Screaming in agony the man released his grip, the rope preventing him from falling. Still climbing, Sinbad watched in horror as the man's weight caused the rest of Delacrois' team to drop several feet, the various team members barely able to arrest their drop by grabbing frantically at the cliff-face.

Sinbad continued to climb until he reached level with the man. The monster was continuing to savage him, his flailing form crashing repeatedly against the rock-wall. The rest of the team struggled to resist but the man's swinging bulk was too much. Sinbad crabbed toward him, sufficient that he could reach him.

Sinbad looked into the man's bulging eyes and the man nodded his wordless understanding. Grachene was suddenly in Sinbad's hand, and with a mighty swing he slashed at the rope suspending the man.

The man plummeted backward, smashing into the monster and causing the pair of them to crash down the length of the cliff. Sinbad saw that in his flailing the Xubanthali man had managed to grab hold of the creature, clearly intent on taking it with him. Released from the man's swinging weight, the rest of Delacrois' team were able to climb once more.

Sinbad went to resume his own climb but was unable to. Looking down he saw that another of the reptile-birds was attacking the individual immediately below him, the man Sinbad had encouraged to continue climbing. Without hesitation Sinbad scrabbled the ten feet or so downward to where the man was being attacked. Grachene still in his hand, Sinbad began slashing at the monster. Furious, the creature screeched in pain, soaring away from them. Now Sinbad slashed at the rope connecting him to the man.

"Move!" he urged at the man. Thankfully the Xubanthali didn't need to be told twice, and rapidly began ascending the cliff-face, the rest of Sinbad's team in swift pursuit.

Sinbad, meanwhile, crabbed away from his team, the urgency of the situation causing him to miss the occasional foot or handhold, and to momentarily flounder against the rock surface before regaining his position. These creatures were clearly not dumb animals. He could see the flock massing, perhaps seven or eight of the monsters, squawking animatedly at one another. He knew what they were doing. They'd clearly identified him as the central problem, and therefore the one to be eliminated.

Suddenly they were on him, gnashing at him, the sweep of their huge wings alone almost blowing him off the cliff-face, their piercing screeches all but deafening him. Sinbad slashed with Grachene, ripping into one of the creature's wings and causing it to collide and become tangled with one of its fellows, simultaneously emitting an ear-splitting cry of pain. Immediately the creature was replaced by another one that grabbed Sinbad by his knife arm. Sinbad's blood spurted, Grachene dropping from his grip, Sinbad barely able to hold on to the rock-face with one hand. Another of the creatures ripped into his side, sending another torrent of blood outward in a scarlet spray. Through the pain and ongoing attack Sinbad saw Grachene clattering against the side of the cliff-face before vanishing from view.

At that moment something flashed through the air and the lizard-bird clamped around Sinbad's arm fell backward, a shaft protruding from its skull. There was another blur and the creature attacking his side also tumbled backward, an arrow likewise protruding from its elongated face. The remaining creatures flapped backward, screeching in terror. Despite his ripped arm Sinbad resumed his climb, looking upward. He could see the silhouette of a figure, clearly that of Delacrois, leaning over the edge of the cliff-face and firing a succession of arrows at the disorientated birds.

Without looking back Sinbad could hear the shrieks as more of the creatures fell prey to Delacrois' expert marksmanship. Finally Sinbad reached the top of the cliff, hauled over the edge by Gunarson and various members of the Xubanthali, including the man in Sinbad's team he had encouraged to continue climbing.

"Good work," said Sinbad to Delacrois, watching as the remaining lizard-birds wheeled away, cawing in outrage.

Delacrois had returned his bow to the strap around his back. "A pleasure, mon Captaine," he said with a smile.

"You're hurt," said a female voice. It was Illia, her eyes once more hidden from view.

"Aye," replied Sinbad, reaching for the cut on his arm.

"Let me help," continued Illia, in a voice he had not heard before, at least not directed at him. It was one of concern. The young woman tore a length of her sari and proceeded to wrap the cut. Sinbad watched Illia work, her hands expert and rapid. He wished he could see those delicate eyes again. When she had finished he nodded his thanks, before turning his attention to their whereabouts.

What greeted him was extraordinary and unexpected. The barren cliff-face rapidly gave way to a bright green grassy escarpment that clearly dropped before transforming into rolling meadows. Exotic butterflies danced between enormous red flowers, trees bearing vibrant-colored fruit waving enticingly in the bright sunshine.

"Welcome to the Moon Peninsula," rasped Omar, who had been sitting, nursing the stubby hands he had grazed during the ascent of the cliff.

"Be on your guard," said Sinbad, gently moving away from Illia's ministrations. His hand went involuntarily to his sash, to which the magical Grachene had somehow returned.

"Captain," said Gunarson reproachfully, gesturing to the enchanting vista, "surely there is nothing here that can harm us?"

"Our journey has been too easy," replied Sinbad.

"Too easy?" riposted Delacrois. "First the vortex and then those reptile-birds? Not to mention the actual cliff, zut alors!"

"Aye," said Sinbad. "Those obstacles were difficult but not insurmountable, as our arrival here testifies. Be on your guard, all of you."

As he spoke, a lilting, laughing voice reached them. Immediately Gunarson unsheathed his broadsword, Delacrois whipping his bow from across his back and dropping to one knee, arrow poised. They watched as a figure appeared at the height of the escarpment. It was a woman, buxom to behold, her skin like bleached porcelain, flaxen hair flowing in tresses. Behind her, another young woman had appeared, dark-skinned and also laughing. And then another, a red-headed woman, green eyes flashing as she saw them. More of the women appeared, coming to a breathless halt some short distance from the bedraggled party.

Sinbad stepped forward, his hand playing around the hilt of Grachene.

"We seek the Arlegon Witches," he said simply.

The flaxen-haired woman curtsied, "Why, Captain. You have found them."

Chapter Six

S inbad, along with his crew and their Xubanthali comrades, sat and stared in amazement. The crew of the Blue Nymph hadn't seen such a repast since they'd left Baghdad, even accounting for the bountiful meals prepared for them during their short stay on the Xubanthali island, and indeed the supplies they'd been furnished with for their journey. Their eyes roved the dishes that had been set before them, some of them having to wipe drool from their lips. Their hosts had brought forth multicolored fruits and vegetables of extraordinary size and shape, many of which were completely alien to them. Even the ones they recognized, such as kumquats, cherimoya and achiote, were delicacies inexplicably distant from their lands of origin. There were freshly baked breads too, along with mighty platters upon which sat all manner of succulent, glistening fish, and sweet cakes of a quality and quantity that would not have disgraced the Sultan of Brunei.

Suffice to say, this was not what they had expected of the Arlegon Witches, especially given the travails they had encountered on their journey to this place. Sinbad's crew had looked to him incredulously as the smiling women took them by their calloused hands and led them up the verdant, sprawling hill, down into the meadow and then by turns into a level clearing strewn with satin pillows and surrounded by trees that rustled gently in the pleasant breeze.

The Xubanthali were similarly entranced, even the females, as the Arlegon coaxed and cajoled them, looks of infinite understanding on their beautiful visages, as though they somehow knew the grief of these people in having their children stolen from them. The Arlegon lowered themselves onto the pillows and beckoned for their guests to join them. Both Sinbad's crew and the Xubanthali happily acquiesced, their former suspicions having apparently dissipated. Aside from Sinbad himself, the two notable exceptions were Illia and Tishimi, who seemed immune to the women's charms, the former's face cast in a perpetual scowl, the latter characteristically studied in her attitude. However, while Tishimi would never dare refuse such hospitality and selected to sit obligingly with her crewmates as decorum dictated, in marked contrast Illia chose to sit some distance apart from the main group. As usual the young sorceress bowed her head, and once again Sinbad noticed that she took to whispering silently to herself. Fortunately the Arlegon did not seem to take offence at this, nodding and smiling their acceptance and instead turning their attentions to Sinbad's crew and the Xubanthali.

Sinbad had tried to broach the matter of their mission with the flax-en-haired woman, whom seemed to exercise some authority over her fellows, but the woman had simply waved her hand, as though to indicate that such matters would be discussed in due course. Before Sinbad could press his point the food had abruptly appeared, more of the shimmering women bringing forth golden platters laden with aromatic dishes, still more clutching burnished jugs from which they poured rippling scarlet mead. The centre-piece was four gigantic roasted hogs, the smell of which reached Gunarson long before the eight women carrying them hove into view, laughing and smiling. A trio of Arlegon had meanwhile gathered beneath one of the gently waving trees, one clutching an ornate wooden instrument akin to a flute, another a stringed instrument that looked much like a lyre. When the pair struck up the third woman began to sing a lilting note that seemed to wend, dip and rise through the air.

The intoxicating music only added to Sinbad's sense of unreality. Their beautiful, generous hosts, the piles of food, some exotic, some oddly familiar, even the rustling trees, all seemed somehow peculiar, but in ways he struggled to identify. He realized with a jolt what the problem was: everything was just too exacting, too perfect. The scene before him, beautiful women furnishing hard-pressed adventurers with all manner of hospitality, was like something one of the Sultan's more unimaginative scribes would conjure forth and set to parchment. In Sinbad's experience, reality tended to be considerably more complex.

Sinbad's people and the Xubanthali tore into the food with gusto, to the obvious pleasure of the Arlegon. If their hosts hadn't partaken of the fare Sinbad would have stopped his crew and the Xubanthali but the Arlegon ate and drank too, slurping and laughing, their enjoyment obvious and, it seemed to Sinbad, genuine. Sinbad himself sat implacable, eyes narrowed, demurring when offered food or drink. Realizing the merriment and indulgence was liable to continue unabated for some time; Sinbad chose to steal away from his comrades, in order that he might contemplate their situation undisturbed.

He headed for the gently undulating trees and stood amongst them, reaching out a tentative hand toward their rough, vine-covered trunks. Like many other things in this place he felt a sense of unease around them that was evidently not shared by his fellows. It was as though he had seen these trees before, perhaps in a dream, so that they felt eerie and uncanny. While he was considering the strangeness of this sensation he caught sight of something fleeting amidst the wood. A figure, not much bigger than a child, emaciated and dressed in rags. When the creature turned, momentarily, he understood that it was not human. Its visage and upper portion of its body were covered in bandages, offering only partial glimpses of a hooked mouth and gimlet eyes.

The being emanated evil. Sinbad felt Grachene suddenly in the palm of his hand, the blade vibrating. He went toward the apparition, but as he approached discovered only shadow, the creature's form evidently conjured by the twisting branches within the wood's interior. His imagination playing tricks on him. Unless…

A hand on his shoulder made him start and turn about, Grachene ready to strike. Sinbad lowered it upon seeing it was the flaxen-haired woman who had greeted them upon their arrival.

"Are you happy, sir? Will you not partake of the feast?" She cocked her head inquiringly.

He shook his head. "I cannot, madam," he replied simply. "Because I do not understand the why of it."

The woman fixed him with a quizzical gaze which rapidly resolved itself into understanding. "You are confused by our hospitality," she said with deliberation. "After your arduous experiences you find such conviviality to be a perplexing state of affairs. You expected monsters and horrors to greet you upon your arrival. But instead you found us." She gestured toward the feast, smiling pleasantly.

Sinbad eyed her skeptically. The precision of her insight made him wonder whether she had the power to enter minds, to determine meaning amongst the mist of men's thoughts. "Your conclusion is sound," he said at length. "As we approached here a powerful, freezing tempest rose up and engulfed one of our fleet. All hands were lost."

The flaxen-haired woman inclined her head. "I am sorry," she said.

"We lost more people when we scaled the cliff," Sinbad continued.

"It is a perilous climb," conceded the woman.

"We were attacked by flying serpents."

The woman sighed. "Zantra," she explained. "Their eyrie is some short distance. Still, you were unlucky to encounter them."

"They were brought to us," said another voice. Delicate, precise and unmistakable. Tishimi had appeared through the trees, picking her way through the undergrowth with tiny, methodical steps. "Just as the freezing vortex was conjured in order to consume us. Such magic is extremely powerful."

The flaxen-haired woman's smile looked suddenly more strained.

"I am Lonkra," she said, bowing.

"I am Captain Sinbad and this is Tishimi," said Sinbad, gesturing. "But the question remains. *Why?*"

"Myth has told you what to think of us." She cast her hand toward the festivities, toward the laughing, happy people. The music reached them on the breeze. "You see the reality is a little different."

"Reality," brooded Sinbad. "Is this really reality?"

"You are a good Captain," said Lonkra. "A good Captain asks questions. But sometimes it is better, I think, to simply accept what is."

"I disagree," replied Sinbad, his eyes flashing. "Allah gave us a voice to ask questions. Indeed, I have many for you. But one above all else. We seek..."

"I know what you seek," said Lonkra sharply. "But it is not time yet. Be patient."

With this she smiled and turned on her heel, heading back toward the carousing.

"This isn't reality," said Sinbad, watching her go.

"No, it is not, Sinbad san," replied Tishimi.

"Everything seems so familiar and yet somehow so strange. As though someone is conjuring it for our pleasure."

"Aye, Sinbad san. And yet their artifice falls short. In its very perfection it has become imperfect."

Sinbad motioned to his crewmembers, to the Xubanthali. "It is enough to convince our fellows."

"After an arduous journey they desire to be convinced," explained Tishimi, following his gaze. "In their heart of hearts they, too, know this place to be founded on lies."

"Aye, perhaps," Sinbad nodded. "It is as though there is a veil over this place. It confounds our senses."

"I believe so," nodded Tishimi. "It conceals the fact that something is *missing*."

"Missing?" Sinbad rubbed his chin. "Yes, you're right. Of course. It's not what is here, it's what is absent."

"Just as it was on the island of Xubanthali," continued Tishimi.

"I saw an apparition," said Sinbad, turning his attention back to the shadow of the woods. "It must have been conjured by the shapes within the woods. And yet..."

"And yet, Sinbad san?"

"And yet it looked so real. More real than many other things I see here."

"Might I ask what form it took?"

Sinbad considered. "It was like a child, covered in soiled bandages. One might have pitied had it not emanated such palpable evil."

Tishimi paused in thought. "Perhaps," she said presently, "the apparition you saw is the single true thing about this place."

By now the remnants of the feast had been carried jauntily away by the Argelon women. The lilting music had been displaced by drums, a cluster of the Argelon enthusiastically beating out a rapid tempo on curious-shaped wooden pans strung from their necks. The Xubanthali, ready to demonstrate their own passion for drumming, eagerly accepted wooden pans proffered to them by other of the women. The air filled with the sounds of rhythmic beating.

Most of Sinbad's crew and the Xubanthali were on their feet, many swaying, perhaps in time to the music, perhaps because of the copious amounts of wine they had supped. Sinbad saw Gunarson dancing a jig with two brunettes, perhaps twins, from time to time reaching down to lift them up and swing them laughingly around. Delacrois held a goblet in one hand, slapping his knee with mirth, just as he too was led into a dance by a beautiful dark-skinned woman. Even the elderly Rafi was caught up in the festivities, evidently trying to demonstrate a formal dance to a trio of nodding Arlegon females. Sinbad saw that only Illia stood alone, propped against a tree, her head lowered in contemplation. Occasionally one of the Argelon would go to her, evidently imploring her to join them, but Illia declined, head still bowed. Some of Sinbad's crew even attempted the same, to be similarly rebuffed.

Sinbad and Tishimi continued to watch as a wooden pole about a quarter the size of the Blue Nymph's repaired mast was carried to a place demarcated by a carpet of dainty, luminescent flowers. Long multicolored ropes hung from the pole. As they looked on, about twelve of the Argelon women stepped forward, each grabbing one of the lengths of rope. The drum music, which had continued unabated, suddenly ceased, but for a few seconds only, beginning again with vehemence. On this signal the dozen Argelon women began to dance and to whoop, chasing in and out of one another with rhythmic precision. As they did so the multicolored ropes began to wind around the top of the pole, creating an intricate pattern that sometimes unwove and then rewove in response to the dancers' movements.

Though his own body was free of alcohol or any other kind of external stimulation, Sinbad could sense the euphoria that accompanied the women's dance. In actual fact, it was impossible to resist the energy they gave out. As he looked on he felt the hair on his skin pricking, and a tingle buzzing in his extremities. It was as though the energy was coursing through his veins, and there was nothing he could do to resist it. He felt short of breath, and his heart had begun to pound in time with the women's rhythmic beating. The drums beat louder, the women danced faster, and the ropes wound and unwound, and suddenly it felt like those ropes were tugging at his very soul. His crew and the Xubanthali cheered and sang and laughed, their faces cracked wide with joy. To his astonishment he saw that even Tishimi had started to make her way towards the festivities, her face joyful, her hands clapping. He had never before seen her exhibit such an absolute extreme of emotion, even when angry or happy. With a growing sense of horror, Sinbad realized it was beyond their control, and that the dance was reaching some unfathomable, inevitable crescendo.

He saw above them that the previously azure sky had begun to roil with thunderous black clouds, and felt the wind whipping up around him. He looked to the horizon, to the far off cliff face and beyond that the gray sea, but his vision was blurred. A shifting haze had descended, rendering the world that had so recently been verdant, colorful and appealing, washed out and dull. As he wheeled around the whole world shimmered, as though the veil had begun to fall away. In the midst of it was a figure. The apparition he thought he'd imagined earlier was all too real, its dirty bandages flapping in the wind. Abruptly the creature lifted his emaciated limbs skyward, and Sinbad caught sight of a leering, misshapen smile. The creature was evidently jubilant. Whatever the being's scheme, it was clearly coming to fruition. Sinbad felt a wave of evil flood out from the figure, greater even than when he glimpsed it amidst the trees.

Suddenly everything changed.

From all around came gurgling, inhuman cries. Now the world not only shimmered, it shook as well. The Argelon's drumming had been supplanted by a cacophonous roar: the sound of galloping. Sinbad pivoted toward the source of the noise and saw an area of space, mid-air, that was bulging, as if something was trying to break through. The air itself shook then seemed to tear, and a jet black horse carrying an armored figure burst through the elongated hole. The figure was followed by another black horse also carrying a baying, chain-mailed rider, and then by a succession of such beasts and their riders. Though their shrieking visages were hidden behind ornate helmets, the weapons clasped in their gauntleted hands rendered their intentions clear. They swung at the Arlegon with maces and swords, sending the women screaming in horror amid a torrent of spinning blood, tissue and bone. Sinbad's crew and the Xubanthali could only reel in surprise, their minds and bodies, as though one were distinct from the other, seemingly left incapable.

Grachene leapt to Sinbad's hand and he found himself running toward the attackers, bellowing a war cry. His yell had the desired effect, stirring his crew from their torpor, the Xubanthali taking notice as well. Sinbad saw Gunarson pulling one of the riders from its horse and dashing the armored figure to the ground with a Viking snarl. Elsewhere, Byrne thrust his broad sword between the shoulder plates of one of the assailants, seeking out a weak spot, the Celt's grizzled face rapt with pleasure. Tishimi whirled her katana, bringing it expertly across the neck of a dismounted rider, sending its head spinning through the air, the severed neck spurting forth a fountain of crimson as the body pitched forward.

Sinbad's crew, and even the Xubanthali, fought with customary skill and commitment, but something was amiss. Sinbad was aware, peripherally, that each time his crew dispatched one of the riders there was an explosion of light elsewhere on the battlefield. When he saw Delacrois loosing an arrow that arced through the air before impacting in the slit on the helmet of the one of the knights he finally understood what was occurring. Delacrois' target slipped from its mount, clearly mortally wounded. As the figure fell, an Arlegon woman burst into spinning fragments that dispersed outward and upward in an explosion of light before disappearing. Sinbad saw that this was true each time one of the knights were dispatched, with one of the Witches screaming in pain before erupting into fragments and vanishing.

By now Sinbad had reached his target, a rider who held their ground, constantly reining in their mount, a mace in one hand, evidently intent on orchestrating the attack rather than engaging in it. His approach unnoticed, Sinbad leapt onto the back of the rider's steed, plunging Grachene into the knight's torso, into the space between the layers of armor. The magical blade easily pierced the chainmail beneath, blood spurting outward from the wound. Though its voice was muffled by the helmet, Sinbad heard the figure shriek in agony, the rider struggling vainly to retaliate with its mace, but its efforts causing it to slide from the horse. Sinbad leapt down and began approaching the prostrate figure, Grachene dripping a trail of scarlet in his wake.

Sinbad had to shout above the roar of the battle.

"Who are you?" he demanded. "What do you mean by this attack?"

The figure pointed a shaking, gauntleted hand toward the humanoid creature dressed in rags. Sinbad turned. The monstrous entity stood in the midst of the melee, its malformed, bandaged face unmistakably one of fury. Whatever his intentions had been, he had clearly been thwarted. Sinbad watched as the creature pivoted. Illia was approaching him, steadily, like a wild cat stalking a prey, her hands clenching and unclenching. A movement behind him made Sinbad whirl back around. The armored figure was on its feet, running from him, clutching its side from where Grachene had punctured it. Sinbad had to instantaneously make a choice as to whether to give chase or go to help Illia.

He chose to run after the knight he had wounded on the basis that it was clearly a leader of sorts, but he was too late. Another mounted rider swept past, gathering the figure up and onto its own steed. Sinbad continued his pursuit, his face creasing with frustration as he saw what the horse was galloping toward.

The rip in the world was still there, in the mid-air just ahead of them. A slit that contracted and expanded, warping the air around it, offering up only fleeting gray shapes and darkness beyond that continually shifted and bled into one another.

As Sinbad ran, he became aware of the other steeds passing him. The attack was over, and the assailants were evidently intent on making their escape. He noticed that injured riders had been hauled astride mounts and that they carried bodies and bits of bodies too, as though they were intent on leaving no trace whatsoever of what had occurred. Sinbad saw the first of the mounts leap and disappear through the tear, then watched as others followed its lead. A last, rider-less horse thundered past him, vanishing through the slit moments later. The slit was diminishing rapidly now and Sinbad redoubled his efforts, arms and legs furiously pumping.

He leapt, for all his worth, through the gap in reality.

Sinbad landed heavily, rolling into a crouch, coming up with Grachene poised. He looked around himself in amazement. He was in exactly the same place. There was the meadow and the rolling hill, there was the clearing, there were the gently rustling trees. He could hear the sea and knew they were not far from the cliff-face he and his people had scaled. And yet... This world was grayer, cast in shadow and shade, and he tasted smoke and

"Lonkra," he breathed. "How?"

ashes in the cold air. There were no signs of battle, and no evidence whatsoever of either his crew or the Xubanthali. He could, however, hear sounds of urgent conversation, of clinking armor, of horses neighing.

He walked toward the noise, Grachene still raised, his breathing tense. As he rounded the tree line he saw ahead of him an encampment. The black steeds had been led into a fenced area and a number had their heads bent low, drinking from troughs of water or scoffing from buckets of oats. Nearby a group of figures stood and sat, most in the process of removing their armor. He saw that one individual was surrounded by others who seemed to be tending to a wound in the individual's side, and realized this must be the soldier he had stabbed with Grachene. Bodies lay, including a decapitated figure and several with missing limbs, in a row some short distance away.

As Sinbad approached, and as their heated voices reached him on the breeze, something became apparent. All of them were female.

"You," said a voice suddenly. The group surrounding the injured soldier broke away, allowing the woman to push forward. She lurched toward him. Her hand, now free of the gauntlet, clutched at her exposed side with a bloodied rag. He recognized the flaxen hair whipping in the breeze.

"Lonkra," he breathed. "How?"

"You came through the rip," she replied icily. "You must know how, Captain Sinbad. Or, at least, you must be able to guess."

His eyes played on the faces of the other women. He recognized all of them as the Arlegon. "The women that greeted us. They are illusions."

"They are us," corrected one of the other women. "Or at least, projections of us. Ghosts of the living if you like."

Sinbad exhaled, "I think I understand. You are the real Arlegon. A part of you has been divided."

"Aye," replied the woman who had spoken before. "Divided and conquered."

"Not conquered, Sharlvel," riposted Lonkra angrily to her fellow. "Not yet."

"That is why the Arlegon we first encountered, the ones that fed us and were so friendly, that is why they exploded into fragments of light when one of you were killed," said Sinbad.

"Aye," nodded Lonkra. "Our ghosts vanish when we our destroyed. You cannot have one without the other."

Sinbad eyed them suspiciously, "But to what end? Why has this happened to you?"

"The ghosts you met are controlled by a force," explained Lonkra, "a creature of evil."

"You saw him," said the woman called Sharlvel, clanking towards him, her bottom half still encased in armor. "Surely you saw him."

"Aye, an abominable creature," nodded Sinbad. "Its face wrapped in bandages, it emanated pure evil."

"Marlek the Necrotist," spat Lonkra. "A more cunning, deceptive purveyor of the Black Arts you could not hope to find. Marlek is a demon who stole the body of a young child many years ago. But he cannot sustain the body. Each time he undertakes some nefarious scheme, the body ages, withers. Its bones snap and sores open up. Hence his decrepit appearance. But do not be misled, he is extremely powerful."

"He came to us across the waves, as everyone does," said Sharlvel.

"What did he want?" asked Sinbad.

"In the end everyone who comes to us wants the same," continued Sharlvel. "They might say they want knowledge, or insight, or even love." Her eyes flashed, "But in the end it is all the same."

Sinbad half-smiled, "What do you mean?"

"Power," interjected Lonkra. "In the end, everyone who comes to us wants power."

"Power?" said Sinbad wonderingly. "Aye, perhaps."

"'Tis true," said Lonkra. "Whether it be power over a nation, the world, or simply an individual. Perhaps they simply want power over themselves."

"At least," said the other woman reflectively, "Marlek was honest."

Lonkra nodded, "Yes. Sharlvel is right. Marlek never pretended anything else. He came to defeat us and steal our secret, that he might become the single most powerful magician to ever live, more powerful than Sokurah or Prince Koura or even Al-Izrikel the Scarlet. He rose above the cliff, bolts of lightning issuing from his hands. The Zantra devil birds were no match for him. Nor were we, at first. Many Arlegon died instantaneously, others slowly and painfully from hideous wounds."

"Pray, what is your secret?" said Sinbad. "What does Marlek want from you?"

Lonkra shook her head, "You know what our secret is, Sinbad."

Sinbad gazed at her, realization crossing his features. "The Scholars of Bethshea. You know their location. That is your secret."

Lonkra smiled, "Aye. You, your crew and the Xubanthali are not the only ones who seek the Scholars and their Library. Far from it. Imagine what such knowledge *means*. Imagine what a demon like Marlek would do with it."

"But you," said Sinbad. "You're witches. Great, powerful witches. How did Marlek best you?"

Lonkra laughed hollowly and the other Arlegon shook their heads in disgust. "Believe us, Sinbad. As soon as we understood the nature of the threat we called upon powers we had not used in millennia. Ancient, unstable spells. A mighty battle ensued, one that shook the dead in their graves. Still he fought us. Until, somehow, our combined might overwhelmed him."

"Then why this?" said Sinbad, wide-eyed, gesturing at the world around them. "Why this world of shades and darkness? Why the ghosts of yourselves that do Marlek's bidding?"

Lonkra's eyes narrowed with fury, "Because we made a mistake. We thought we were victorious. Marlek lay, bloodied, emaciated, seemingly dying in front of us. He begged for mercy. We paused, only momentarily, to consider his words when we should simply have smote him. He seized his opportunity. In that moment of mercy he uttered his own ancient incantation. He cleaved us in twain."

Sinbad shook his head in horror, "He cut you in half, each of you, and cut your world in half too." The wind had begun to whip around him.

Lonkra sighed, "Aye. The women you encountered are but echoes. Fantasies, manipulated by Marlek, and so is the world they inhabit. We are the real Arlegon, weakened and imprisoned in this parallel world. Marlek knows he cannot destroy us, but he can at least keep us captive. Fortunately we retain some of our powers. Sometimes we can break through, if there is sufficient necessity to do so."

Sinbad nodded in realization, "The freezing vortex. The flying lizards that attacked us on the cliff. You were trying to stop us coming to the Moon Peninsula. Why?"

"Because Marlek plans to feed upon your people," explained Lonkra. "If he performs the necessary ritual he can capture their energy, their life force. With that power he might finally overcome us and force us to reveal what we know."

Sinbad assented, "The dance. Yes, I see now. The world had begun to shimmer, to change."

"Yes, the dance," said the woman called Sharlvel. "That is why we entered the parallel world and disrupted the ritual. If we had not, then you and your people would have been consumed, their wills turned to energy for Marlek's purpose."

"And Marlek would have discovered the location of the Scholars," observed Sinbad.

"Aye," smiled Lonkra.

Sinbad hesitated, lost in thought. "Marlek will try again. When?"

"Soon," shrugged Sharlvel. "A few hours, perhaps."

"My people saw what happened. They will not be so easily beguiled this time."

"Perhaps," acknowledged Lonkra. "But our ghosts can be very persuasive. Marlek will make sure of that."

"Wait," said Sharlvel abruptly. She was staring at the ground, her face a mask of consternation. The horses were braying, and the wind had begun to whip around them.

Sinbad felt a dull tremble beneath his feet.

"What is it?" he demanded.

When Sharlvel looked up her eyes were swirling with ethereal colors: red, oranges and yellows that spiraled and cascaded into one another. "Marlek," she whispered. "Something is different…"

Lonkra had closed her eyes in concentration, "You're correct, sister. I feel it too."

All of the women had turned their attention to the sky above them, and Sinbad looked too. The gray clouds had darkened and as he watched they began to morph into recognizable shapes. A misshapen brow, a hideous nose, a deformed, crooked mouth. And the most terrible, gimlet eyes, peering out from a bandaged face. It was Marlek.

"Arlegon," said the image, a leer etched into his features, its voice croaking. "Hear me, Arlegon. The game has changed. Tell me your secret, share your knowledge. Tell me where they are! Tell me the location of the Scholars!"

"Never!" spat Lonkra. "We will die before we tell you!"

Marlek let out a low growling hiss that transformed into a great rumble of thunder. "So be it," he bellowed, as his features boiled away into the sky. The earth below them shook again, more violently this time. Fissures began to open up all around them.

Sharlvel looked to Lonkra in horror, "He means to destroy this world, to destroy us."

"How can this be?" said Lonkra wonderingly. "Such an outcome is beyond even his powers, otherwise he would have done such a thing afore now..!"

"He must have found some other source of energy," said Sharlvel. "The young woman." She whirled around to confront Sinbad. "*The sorceress!*"

"Illia," whispered Sinbad.

Chapter Seven

"Quickly." Lonkra turned to Sinbad, her eyes burning. "It is not simple," she admonished. "Each time we cross over we are diminished. You must be patient." She and the other Arlegon were gathered in a circle, each uttering incantations, their eyes transformed by the magic.

The ground shook once more, the horses rearing up in response, and a crack of lighting rent the sky. "Marlek's already powerful enough," replied Sinbad urgently. "He's destroying this reality. And us along with it!"

"He has co-opted your woman's powers," said Sharlvel. "She must be mighty indeed."

"She is not my woman," responded Sinbad. "And she is little more than an acolyte."

"No," said Sharlvel, shaking her head. "You are wrong, Sinbad. She *is* mighty indeed."

"But not mighty enough to fight off Marlek," riposted Lonkra. "*Concentrate, sisters!*"

Sinbad stepped back, watching keenly as the Arlegon lifted their arms skyward, their individual mantras entwining, becoming one. Ahead of them, some short distance away, he saw the air beginning to ripple and warp; a slither of shifting gray at its heart.

"We have pierced a hole separating realities," exclaimed Sharlvel. "Though 'tis barely anything at all!"

"It's not enough!" replied Lonkra. "Marlek must be stopping us!"

"Enough for me," muttered Sinbad. He was already running, Grachene at his side.

"Sinbad, no!" yelled Lonkra. "You'll never make it!"

"The gap is not wide enough! It will rip you apart!" shrieked Sharlvel.

The opening was slight, wobbling, contracting even as he sprinted toward it. Sinbad prayed to Allah that the women would continue their chanting long enough. The fissure was crackling now, its edge sparking with glowing green flame and wisps of smoke, presumably the result of Marlek trying to close the gap. He could hear the Argelon's chanting in his ears, louder now as they tried to resist Marlek's powers. As their chanting reached a bellowing climax Sinbad leapt, diving through the tear just as it fizzled out of existence.

He landed with a terrific thump in the midst of the familiar verdant clearing, his breath temporarily knocked from him. He lifted his head to see his crew and the Xubanthali backing away from an extraordinary, hideous spectacle. As he watched the Arlegon, or rather the 'ghosts' of the real ones he'd just encountered in the parallel reality, were transforming. Their skulls were elongating, fangs bursting through flesh, limbs distending and becoming clawed, spines arching, ripping upward. Sinbad pulled himself to his feet, his hand tracing the reassuring contours of Grachene's ornate, bejeweled hilt.

Sinbad whirled around, his keen eyes searching the chaotic vista. Amidst the mayhem he found what he sought. There was Marlek, his mutilated visage full of glee, clutching Illia to himself, one of his snake-like, emaciated arms wrapped around her lifeless body. Sinbad watched a steady flow of brilliant light emerge from Illia's body and enter the demon's, and saw the sores on his face beginning to heal, his posture gradually beginning to straighten as he sucked the energy from her.

Now Sinbad was running again, his breath coming to him in short, sharp bursts, Grachene raised high, a snarling war cry on his lips.

Marlek turned toward him, his face cracking with fury, his free hand whirling fluidly like the player of an invisible musical instrument, bursts of lightning cracking from his splayed palm. Now he saw the reason for the transformation of the fake Arlegon into hideous monsters. Each of Marlek's lightning blasts smashed into four of the Arlegon women, changing them from women into towering monstrosities, their distended jaws clattering, their beauty but an incomprehensible memory. The quartet lumbered toward him. Sinbad necessarily slewed to a halt, his path blocked by Marlek's monsters. He was surrounded by the behemoths, their slavering faces broken apart by yawning, lunatic grins, their dresses and straggles of hair the only clues as to their former appearance.

Sinbad went to dodge around one, but the creature capered into his way, guffawing like a hyena as she did so. The others joined in, pointing to the small human creature in their midst, as though he were an object of considerable merriment. Sinbad in his turn couldn't help but grimace in disgust at their monstrous appearance. Suddenly he was a flash and a whirl, Grachene ripping and slicing and plunging. The monsters fell back in surprise, their reptilian skin flapping, blood and tissue cascading outward, their shrieks renting the air. They stood panting, yellow eyes narrowed.

Sinbad bellowed, "Come you foul demons! Let me have at you!" Beyond him he could see that his crew were following his example and engaging the creatures in enthusiastic battle. The Xubanthali, too, had been shaken out of their terror and were making their own, admittedly haphazard, attempts at harrying the creatures.

"You," said a sudden grating voice.

Sinbad turned to see Marlek making his way toward him, Illia's limp body still clutched to his breast. "You're but a puny mortal. You really think you and your people could stop me? Such arrogance." His creatures watched passively as Marlek approached, clutching at the various wounds Sinbad had inflicted and occasionally whimpering.

"Let her go, demon," intoned Sinbad calmly. "Let her go and I will spare your life."

Marlek's emaciated form began to shake. Sinbad came to realize the magician was laughing at him. "Sinbad El Ari of Baghad. Thank you for what you have given me." With one hand he raised Illia's body into the air as though she were little more than a rag-doll, his body fizzing with energy. "I will use this girl to destroy the Arlegon forever unless they tell me what I want to know."

"And what would that be?" replied Sinbad, playing for time.

Marlek smiled slyly, "You know what I want. I seek the same as you."

Sinbad nodded, "Aye. The location of the Scholars of Bethshea. But tell me *why?*"

"Do you not see? We are the same, you and I," breathed Marlek. "The Arlegon are the key to the Scholars and their knowledge. If we work together..."

"The Warriors of Forever," said Sinbad, eyes narrowing. "Why do you seek them?"

Marlek cocked his head to one side, examining Sinbad with a quizzical air. "Oh, Sinbad. Let that not concern us. For now, our aims coincide. Let us agree to a truce. I can use your woman's power to hold the Arlegon to account. I promise she will be unharmed. Your crew, too, will be allowed to leave this place without fear of injury or harm."

"And the Arlegon?"

Marlek shrugged, "They are witches, exponents of the direst magic. I will squash their world until they reveal what they know. You will never discover the location of the Scholars and their Library unless I do."

"Never," said Sinbad, without hesitation. He had stepped forward, brandishing Grachene. "The Arlegon shall not suffer for your aims."

Marlek's tone changed, becoming deeper, more resonant. "I have heard of you, Sinbad. Tales of your deeds sing on the wind. But perhaps those stories have suffered in the telling. For they speak of a wise man, not a fool."

"I cannot claim to be a wise man," responded Sinbad, "but I try to be a good one. If that makes me a fool, well, perhaps I'll have the last laugh."

"Very well," said Marlek, nodding. "Then you and your people will suffer too." Immediately the demon fell into a low chant, uttering words Sinbad could not decipher. Sinbad watched incredulously as Marlek pulled his hand away from the prostrate form of Illia, which continued to hover in the air without his support, her body glowing with the ethereal light. Marlek had lifted his hands again, the chant increasing in intensity, as he strode away from her. Crackling beams of light arched out and upward from his hands, each bolt striking one of his creatures, the fake Arlegon.

"Cap'n!" came a familiar yell. It was Omar. The portly man was some way off, pointing to a cluster of the monsters. It was clear what was happening. Each of them had begun to swell to immense proportions, perhaps five times the size of an ordinary man. Sinbad whirled around to see the same thing happening to the monsters around him, the wounds he had inflicted with Grachene seemingly dissipating as they grew. He noticed, too, that they were licking their lips, their hideous visages carved with a renewed determination.

They were upon him now, talons ripping, jaws slavering. Sinbad fought desperately, Grachene glowing brilliantly in his grasp, sprays of blood and cartilage filling the air. But the creatures were now too big, too dogged, to be fought off. They ripped into his flesh, smashed into his skull, pulled him between them like a ragdoll. In the midst of it all he could hear the cries of his crew and that of the brave Xubanthali, and he caught fleeting glimpses of bodies being tossed and crushed. Marlek's monsters had overwhelmed all of them, of that there was no doubt. Sinbad and his crew, and the Xubanthali along with them, were doomed. In his head he heard Marlek's words, the product of the wizard's unholy magic: "*One last chance... Give me the word and this will stop, Sinbad. I promise you.*"

"Never," whispered Sinbad, as the monsters pulled him asunder.

And then it stopped. Abruptly, and for no apparent reason, the monsters froze. Bewildered, Sinbad pulled himself from their midst, his body covered in glistening lacerations and swellings. He limped away from the group, staring up at them. It was as though they had transformed to stone. He cast his bloody gaze toward the rest of the battlefield, and saw the same phenomenon occurring. Each of the monsters had frozen to the spot. Sinbad's people staggered toward him from their midst: Delacrois, reeling from a head wound, Tishimi clutching what looked to a badly broken arm. Even the mighty Gunarson stumbled as he walked, blood flowing from a wound to his temple. The surviving Xubanthali, too, crashed haphazardly toward him, supporting each other, though none wept or even moaned. Even Marlek was frozen to the spot, his gimlet eyes lifeless and staring amidst the tattered bandages that encircled his head.

"What new madness is this?" bellowed Gunarson.

"Not madness," said a voice Sinbad recognized. He turned to see the air warping and a fissure opening up. Lonkra stepped out and onto the ground, clad in her armor, Sharlvel and the other Arlegon, the *real* Arlegon, close behind. "But an *end* to madness."

Though bloodied and exhausted, Sinbad's crew was ready to do battle once more, and the Captain had to lift his hand emphatically to signal them to hold back.

"Wait," he said simply to his crew, then turned on Lonkra and the other Arlegon. "This is your doing," he said. "All of it. You have manipulated us."

Lonkra smiled, "Yes, Sinbad. It is so. And I am sorry. But for good reason." She abruptly wheeled around, sparks of glittering light emanating from her fingertips. Sinbad saw Illia's body lower gently to the ground, then watched as Marlek's form began to crumble, his emaciated arms and bandaged head collapsing in upon itself in a cloud of dust. The same thing was happening to the fake Arlegon, their distorted visages and distended bodies cascading into tiny particles that the breeze caught and blew away.

Sinbad looked down at his arms and watched as the lacerations faded. When he looked up it was to see the wounds of his crew and that of the Xubanthali similarly vanishing, and those that had fallen struggling to their feet, bewildered but otherwise unhurt.

"Extraordinary," acknowledged Sinbad. "But why?"

"You seek a piece of information from us," said Lonkra, her smile fading to a trace. "We had to be sure of your motivations."

"So you conjured all this," said Delacrois, eyes wide in disbelief. "The feast, the beautiful women that became monsters."

"Marlek himself," added Sinbad. "The parallel world I crossed into."

"Yes, all of it," nodded Sharlvel. "We had to be sure."

"We fought to come here," protested Gunarson. "We fought against an icy vortex, we scaled a cliff-face and battled terrible serpents. Could you still have doubted our motives?"

"Oh, we knew you were committed to your course of action," nodded Lonkra. "But we had to be certain you would not use our knowledge for evil means."

"So you invented Marlek and his army of demon creatures," said Tishimi, gathering her robes about her. "Ingenious."

"And we needed Sinbad to renounce him, even when Marlek offered him a pact, even when he promised to safeguard his crew and Illia," explained Sharlvel.

"Yes," nodded Lonkra, her eyes playing on Sinbad. "You could have betrayed us. As far as you knew you would have obtained the information you desired and your crew would have left here unharmed. But you chose not to. You are a hero, Sinbad. A man of pure heart. And it is that heart that has saved you all."

Sinbad nodded thoughtfully, "Will you tell us? Where will we find the Scholars of Bethshea?"

Sharlvel glanced at Lonkra, who nodded her agreement. "The Scholars constantly seek after knowledge," explained Sharlvel, "so their realm is not fixed."

Delacrois stared at her in amazement, "So they move around? Sacre bleu, how are we meant to locate them?"

Sharlvel smiled slightly at the Gaul's impudence. "We will give you a map."

"A map is no good if they keep moving," protested Delacrois. "They could be anywhere."

"This map is different to any you will have encountered," said Lonkra patiently. "Sinbad, we require a volunteer from among your crew. They will become the map."

"They will *become* the map?" echoed Sinbad. "Forgive me, wise Arlegon. You have already manipulated us quite effectively. How are we to know this is not part of some greater ruse?"

"Our sophistry was necessary. Now we speak the truth," said Lonkra, gazing at him levelly. "You know it."

Sinbad met her gaze. "Aye," he replied momentarily.

"The map must inhabit a living person because it is a living map," explained Sharlvel. "Only this can lead you to the Scholars. It will find them wherever they might be."

"Very well," nodded Sinbad slowly. "Who amongst us would you choose?"

"We cannot choose for you," said Lonkra.

"I will do it," said a gruff voice. It was Rafi. The old man stepped forward, his face resolute.

"You're sure?" said Tishimi gently. "This is powerful magic. Perhaps someone younger, Rafi san…"

"My life has been forever concerned with the pursuit of knowledge," replied Rafi. "I desire this more than anything. Let me become the map, let me lead us to the Scholars of Bethshea."

"Very well," said Sinbad.

"Sisters, join with me," instructed Lonkra. The other Arlegon wordlessly obeyed, surrounding Rafi, each placing a single hand on the old man. The rest of the crew and the Xubanthali stood back, fascinated.

This time there was no chanting. The witches simply stood, eyes closed, brows furrowed in concentration. As the others looked on multicolored, glowing tendrils the width of cotton began to emerge from the bodies of the women and to creep through the air towards Rafi. The elderly man shuddered as the tendrils touched him, winding their way around his arms, climbing up his face. In seconds more he was completely covered by the tendrils, which continued to glow as they sank into his skin, apparently merging with the blood vessels in Rafi's body. On an unspoken cue from Lonkra the Arlegon stepped back and Rafi staggered once, having to be supported by Gunarson and Delacrois. He pushed them away irritably, and stood unaided, though swaying slightly.

"I am fine," said Rafi croakily.

"The map will subside when its purpose is at an end," explained Lonkra. "No harm will befall your friend if this happens in good time."

"What if we are delayed?" demanded Delacrois. "What then?"

"You must hasten to the Library," riposted Sharlvel.

Delacrois looked liable to protest further, but Sinbad shot him a warning glance. "You have helped us mightily," he acknowledged, bowing.

"Aye," nodded Lonkra. "And your time with the Arlegon is at an end. We will give you food and drink and bid you a safe journey."

Sinbad and the others bowed their gratitude, and the remainder of Sinbad's crew and the dazed Xubanthali set about preparations for the climb back down the cliff towards their ship. The Arlegon were as good as their word, using magic to lower supplies down the cliff-face, much to Al-Bulcar's delight, the Xubanthali leader having been left waiting hungrily on the shoreline at the base of the cliff. During all this Illia had rested upon a rock, her face wan and exhausted, refusing the ministrations of the concerned Arlegon. Sinbad watched her thoughtfully.

"We wove a web of lies that we might elicit the truth of you," said a voice close beside him. It was Lonkra. "For that I humbly apologize, Captain Sinbad."

"You did what you needed to," replied Sinbad. "And in the gift of the map and these safe tidings you have more than made up for it."

Lonkra assented her agreement with a nod, "That is generous of you, Captain. I expected nothing less. But I have one more gift for you."

Sinbad turned, intrigued. "And what is that?"

The beautiful woman leant toward him and he thought, momentarily, that she might kiss him, but instead she moved close to his ear. "The girl Illia," she said with urgency. "It was true what I said. She is more powerful than you suspect. Perhaps, even, than she suspects."

Sinbad nodded wordlessly as the woman left his side. He turned and saw Illia watching, head tilted so that her pale eyes were visible. He wondered whether she had heard Lonkra's words to Sinbad. He and Illia exchanged looks for a long moment more, before Corsepis' daughter turned away from him and headed toward the cliff-face, away from this enchanted place.

Chapter Eight

"By the grace of Allah, how do you fare?" Sinbad had placed a gentle hand on Rafi's shoulder. He half-expected Rafi to jump with surprise but the old man continued gazing intently at the horizon, unflinching, brow furrowed in concentration. The spidery veins in his forehead, across his face and hands glowed with a translucent, shifting red. At points the veins collected together, indicating islands or other objects along their route. Very occasionally the blood vessels shifted in relation to one another, as their target presumably changed its own location.

"I feel extraordinary, Sinbad," said Rafi quietly, his breath coming to him in short, sharp bursts. His mottled fingers clasped the side of the ship, knuckles white with the intensity with which he clung to the Blue Nymph, as though he somehow hoped to propel it single-handedly through the waves. "I am a living map. I can see such things, Sinbad, as you would never conceive. Such astonishing things."

"Tell me," said Sinbad gently.

"I can see distances, such vast distances," Rafi murmured. "Through space, yes, but time too."

"But what do you see?" urged Sinbad.

"I see us, here, and I see our destination. And I see all possible points to our destination."

Sinbad leant forward, "What else?"

"I see you, Sinbad."

"Me?"

"Yes," whispered the old man. "I see you aboard different ships, in different seas. You look different, but it is always you."

"Parallel worlds," nodded Sinbad. "I have recently visited one as part of the Arlegon's deceit. What am I doing, wise Rafi, in these other realms?"

This brought forth a smile. "You are *adventuring*, Sinbad. You are always adventuring, no matter where and when you are."

"Perhaps we would do as well to concentrate on *this* particular adventure," said a familiar voice. It was Omar, who had come to join them at the prow. "'Cos I ain't never navigated using a human map afore, Rafi." As he said this Omar glared meaningfully at his Captain. Sailors tended to be characteristically hesitant around sorcery, and Omar was no different. Indeed, his adventures with Sinbad had taught him that magic was almost always to be distrusted at best and rallied against at worst. "If you don't know where we're going, Rafi, then Allah help us. We're liable to starve or full to scurvy. Or worse."

"You'll have to trust him, Omar," said Sinbad icily. "The Arlegon have imbued him with considerable powers. You yourself observed that a traditional map would be no use."

"But this…" said Omar despairingly, gesturing at Rafi's glowing form. "Cap'n, with due respect, the Arlegon misled us mightily. They sent that icy vortex to destroy us, and those devil birds to knock us from the cliff-face. Then they created a demon and all his monsters to destroy us. But it was all a lie, it was all their doing. Why should we trust them in this?"

"You know why the Witches did those things," intoned Sinbad. "They wanted to test our virtuosity. Fortunately we were not found wanting."

"Be that as it may, I say again, venerable Sinbad," riposted Omar. "Why should we should we trust them in this?"

"Because we have no choice," said Sinbad quietly, struggling to control his building anger with his First Mate. "The Scholars are constantly moving. We know that. We will never find them otherwise."

"Pah!" exclaimed Omar angrily, stalking away.

He stopped short when he saw Rafi suddenly thrust a finger toward the horizon. "They are many, many leagues from here. If we go to the very centre of the ocean we will find them."

"How can that be?" protested Omar. "How can they be where there is nothing? *Why* would they be there?"

Rafi turned now, the veins on his face throbbing ferociously. He cocked his head and cast a puzzled look at his shipmate. "They are Scholars, Omar. They crave knowledge, both of this world and worlds beyond. Who knows what new knowledge they have discovered?"

"'Tis a foolish thing," riposted Omar. "That we should be guided by such devilry."

"Enough!" snapped Sinbad furiously, causing everyone aboard to turn and look. It was unlike the calm, collected Sinbad to so thoroughly lose his temper. "Enough," he said again, more measured this time, patting Omar on the shoulder. "Continue to plot the course determined by Rafi. I command it."

"Aye," said Omar with a small sigh. His respect, love, indeed, for his Captain meant that he would argue this point no longer. The surrounding crew returned to their tasks. Sinbad saw Illia looking toward them, though her eyes were hidden by shade as per normal. He thought he saw a touch of red chasing the visible lower half of her face. This time she didn't hold his look.

Haroun sat atop his eyrie and watched the land of the Arlegon diminish into the distance, back into the mists of legend. Samson the cat nestled against his legs. The feline's appetite had recently been sated by a flatfish the cat had discovered amongst the haul of supplies the Witches had gifted the Blue Nymph and the two remaining Xubanthali ships. Haroun half-wondered whether the fish might have been enchanted, but Samson didn't seem to mind. But then he was easily pleased, much like Haroun himself. The boy craned his neck over the edge of the crow's nest to observe the comings and goings on the deck below.

Gunarson stood on the prow, blond pony tail whipping as the Blue Nymph gathered momentum, clad in vest and pants, his mammoth hands clasping the hilt of his broad sword. Elsewhere a group of sailors were clustered around an up-ended barrel, intent on a game of Knucklebones, Delacrois in their midst, Al-Bulcar watching with smiling interest. The woman Tishimi sat some little way distant, engrossed in one of her books, looking up occasionally with an expression of furrowed concentration on her beautiful, delicate features. Irascible but fundamentally good-natured Omar moved from sailor to sailor, checking they were engaged in their tasks with suitable focus and not distracted by their fellows, or indeed the more voluptuous Xubanthali women, who would occasionally cast them coquettish looks from beneath their veils. At the prow stood wise old Rafi, unmoving, the glow of the iridescent blood vessels that now roved his skin visible even from this distance.

And there at the aft of the vessel, his hand clutching the tiller, stood Sinbad the Sailor. Haroun could only guess why a noble such as Sinbad, a prince no less, should have taken to the seas when he could surely have stayed at home and, in due course, ruled a mighty kingdom. On occasion Omar, when plied with copious amounts of alcohol, had spoken of Sinbad's past, how as a young man he gambled and drank away his inheritance until he had no option but to sign aboard a Persian merchant ship. According to Omar, Sinbad had fallen in with the renowned Sindhi Sailors, learning the arts of navigation, of geography, and many foreign tongues to boot. No

"Then you are my responsibility now."

longer the spoilt royal personage, Sinbad set out on a continuing quest of adventure, gathering about him the most extraordinary array of people.

Plus a young boy from the back streets of Persia. Haroun had been named for the great Abbasid Caliph Haroun-al-Rashid himself, but unlike Sinbad that was as far as his royal connections stretched. Haroun's father had been a noted soldier, famed for an extraordinary scimitar he had forged at his own expense, its handle that of ivory. He had been killed defending Baghdad from marauders when Haroun was but a tiny child. Destiny, or more precisely, tuberculosis, took his mother little more than a year later, just as it had taken two of his siblings. When the tiny stone house where they lived was seized by a jubilant, conniving uncle, the remnants of the family, Haroun and his two elder brothers, were forced on to the streets. They lived, or rather *survived*, by pick-pocketing.

In fact, that was how Haroun met Sinbad. Haroun had been hanging around a souk looking for likely marks when he encountered an altercation between a market stall-holder and a young, impoverished-looking woman. The former was apparently accusing the latter of stealing trinkets from his stall when a tall black man, dressed in a majestic purple shirt and turban, intervened. The stranger seemed to know of the stall-holder and his reputation for accusing innocents of shop-lifting, particularly young women. Though he remained polite throughout their exchange, the stranger clearly believed the stall-holder to be perpetrating a ruse in order that he might procure the sexual attentions of the falsely accused female.

Haroun was impressed, as he knew the stranger's assertion to be correct, that this was indeed a scam the stall-owner regularly perpetrated. The stall-holder, a muscular, bullish man feared by everyone else in the souk, begged the stranger's forgiveness, trying to force any number of valuable trinkets on his person. The stranger demurred, instead insisting that the stall-owner hand the trinkets over to the young girl, which he reluctantly did.

It had been during this exchange that the eagle-eyed Haroun had caught sight of the money pouch hanging from the stranger's belt. Driven by a desperation borne of hunger, Haroun seized his chance and nabbed the pouch, darting away into the teeming crowd. Only when he was well away and ensconced in a dark side alley did he dare unclasp his hand to examine his prize. It was at exactly this point that he looked up to see the imposing figure of the stranger barring his exit from the alleyway.

"You know who I am?" the man had said.

"A sailor," Haroun had responded, for that much was obvious from his attire.

"They call me Sinbad," the stranger had said.

"*Sinbad*," Haroun had whispered the name in awe.

"Aye, 'tis so." He lowered himself so that he was half-kneeling, in order that he might be level with the boy. "What do they call you?"

"When I had a name it was Haroun," the boy had hesitantly replied. "Now it is just as likely to be Guttersnipe. Or worse."

The man called Sinbad had looked quizzical. "Why would a boy named for a Caliph resort to stealing? Do you have no reverence for your betters?"

"As Allah is my judge, I have no choice, sir," he had said, bowing his head.

Sinbad had nodded, "Your father and mother?"

Haroun continued looking down. "Gone, sir. To be with Allah. My father died defending the city. My mother died of illness."

"I am sorry for you," said Sinbad. "You live on the street?"

"Aye, Captain Sinbad. With my two brothers."

"Then you are my responsibility now," Sinbad had said, shifting position so as to better examine the boy. He had gently lifted Haroun's chin with his hand and fixed him with his mesmerizing blue eyes, that swirled like the sea. At least until Allah calls one or other of us to join your parents."

"Sir?" asked Haroun, eyes wide.

"You have good eyesight, don't you, Haroun? To see my pouch from where you were standing?"

"You saw me, sir?"

"I have good eyesight too. Answer the question." Though the statement was irritable there was a trace of a sympathetic smile on Sinbad's lips.

"Yes, sir. My father said I have the eyes of a hawk."

"Aye, Haroun the Hawk," nodded Sinbad. "Or perhaps a crow with its own nest. I cannot always be on watch, young Haroun. I need you to be my eyes, to scan the sea in search of danger and opportunity. Do you think you could do that?" he asked warmly.

"Yes, sir."

"Good." Sinbad took the pouch from his grasp, pulling out two burnished coins. "We steal from monsters, villains and tyrants, and only when I say. You understand?"

Haroun nodded his head vigorously. "Yes, sir."

Sinbad proffered the two coins. "These are for your brothers. Tell them if they are wise they will purchase a cow and a shed with this money. They can live in the shed and sell the milk the cow yields. In time, if they are clever and turn sufficient profit, they might buy a farm. You understand?"

Haroun, eyes still wide and disbelieving, took the coins from him and nodded woodenly.

"The Blue Nymph leaves at first light." And with this Sinbad the Sailor, straightened, wheeled about and disappeared around the corner and back into the whirling masses of the souk.

Haroun had run with all his might to the underside of the bridge that he and his brothers had decreed home in the absence of any other vaguely safe place. He found them there, disbelieving as he handed over the two coins, and explained Sinbad's advice about the cow and the shed. Then he embraced and kissed each of them, before turning and running to the dock, hours before first light. It never occurred to him, not for one moment, that he could have stayed with his brothers and used the coins Sinbad had given him to live a comfortable life.

He had never regretted that decision. In the four years that had followed, his young eyes had beheld such wonders, such opportunities and dangers, as would fill any man's lifetime. He prayed to Allah that his brothers had done as Sinbad had advised, and that they lived happy lives. Oft times, Haroun would wonder whether his heroic soldier father would have been proud of all that his youngest son had accomplished.

Haroun was started from his reverie by the familiar voice of Sinbad. He looked down to see his Captain peering up at him.

Sinbad grinned and pointed two fingers to his own eyes, before turning the two fingers on Haroun.

"Aye, Cap'n," acknowledged Haroun, Sinbad's intention clear. The boy in the crow's nest turned his eyes expectantly to the horizon.

The trio of ships thrust onward, the two remaining Xubanthali vessels struggling to match the pace of the mighty Blue Nymph. Sinbad had instructed Omar to let the the Blue Nymph travel at a speed it was more used to, trusting that the increasingly confident Xubanthali sailors would manage to keep up. As days translated to weeks the Blue Nymph maintained its velocity, even through buffeting winds and tumultuous storms, slowing only when it looked like its fellow vessels might lose sight of it completely. Through it all Rafi remained transfixed on the horizon, breaking away only to gesture or shout emphatically at Omar when the Blue Nymph looked to be straying from the course he indicated. Fortuitously this was a reasonably rare occurrence, happening only when Rafi's pulsating form showed some sizeable detour was in order.

Sinbad reflected that the Xubanthali continued to remain in high spirits. None of the travails associated with encountering the Arlegon and eliciting the necessary information regarding the location of the Scholars seemed to dint their optimism. Sinbad's encounters with the Xubanthali were uniformly upbeat, even despite the nature of life aboard ship, which tended to be tedious in the extreme. They would cook hearty meals for the rest of the crew, and in the evenings bang out their joy on their extraordinary drums.

He had begun to realize that what he had initially taken to be a brave stance in the face of adversity, namely the loss of their beloved off-spring to the forces of darkness, was in actual fact an approach to life hard-wired into their very souls. The Xubanthali could not behave in a downcast fashion because they did not know how to. Clearly they believed in their god Xuba, and in its ability to affect the world by using good people as its instruments. The most virtuous way to interact with the world, therefore, was in a spirit of continued equanimity, even despite the horrors that had befallen them. He now viewed them as extraordinary people, of a character he had not often encountered in his many adventures across the Seven Seas.

With one exception of course. Since their encounter with the Arlegon, Illia had given Sinbad a wide berth, or at least as wide a berth as is possible aboard a ship, even a reasonably large ship such as the Blue Nymph. He figured that she was probably embarrassed at the ease with which the Arlegon had used her to enact their 'test' as to the virtue of Sinbad and his crew's intentions.

Most of the time she stood, wrapped in her white sari, her eyes obscured by the shade of the hood, perhaps gazing out at the crashing waves, perhaps meditating, or perhaps ruminating on exploits or conjecturing possibilities. As an afterthought it occurred to Sinbad that she might also, of course, be mourning the loss of her father. He supposed that events had unfolded so rapidly that there had been little time for such reflection.

However, on one occasion since their departure from the Moon Peninsula, probably a month into this particular leg of their journey, the duo was forced into an unexpected interaction. The weather had lately turned extremely hot, forcing both Sinbad's crew and the Xubanthali to strip down to as little as modesty would allow. Illia, unsurprisingly, continued to wear the full-length sari, though this was presumably highly effective in keeping her cool, especially given its brilliant white color, which somehow remained unblemished despite their adventures.

Al-Bulcar, because of his size, took to lounging on a mat on the upper reaches of the deck wearing only a highly revealing improvised toga, much to the disgust of Sinbad's crew. He reminded Sinbad of a gigantic beached sea-lion he and his crew had once encountered on a beach on the Adriatic, and which, with some carefully constructed harnesses, they had managed to eventually drag back out to sea. Beyond plopping grapes into his mouth, courtesy of the Arlegon's plentiful supplies, the oppressive heat meant Al-Bulcar was apparently only capable of reading an ancient piece of papyrus he had brought with him. Sinbad surmised it must be the religious tract Al-Bulcar had previously alluded to.

Al-Bulcar's eyesight being somewhat problematic, the portly Xuban-thali leader utilized the piece of misshapen glass Sinbad had noticed hanging from his neck when he had first met him, using it to enlarge the spidery text. Several of the crew were impressed with the magnifying glass, their intrigue overwhelming the sight of Al-Bulcar's undulating, exposed flesh. Delacrois, who knew something of lenses and grinding, had asked to inspect the object. Al-Bulcar, keen to be of some use, obligingly handed the object over. He explained that he had inherited the lens from one of his ancestors, which suggested to Sinbad that the object heralded originally from India, further supporting his contention that the Xubanthali had emigrated from the sub-continent to the island he and his crew had first encountered them on.

Delacrois demonstrated the lens' use by running it across his own hand and that of a portion of the rigging, explaining it was akin to the spyglass employed by Haroun. Sinbad's crew expressed their amazement as the glass magnified everything in its path, and Al-Bulcar nodded enthusiastically as it was passed among them. Only Omar's grumpy appearance, wondering loudly why no-one appeared to be at their station or attending to their tasks, put an end to the excited discussion. As the men returned to their roles, a skeptical Omar handed the object back to a smiling Al-Bulcar, muttering that he considered such a device the work of Satan and that there was quite enough malignant sorcery aboard the Blue Nymph as it was, at which point he looked meaningfully toward the inert figure of Rafi at the prow. Al-Bulcar protested otherwise, but by this point Omar had stalked off, grumbling.

Several hours later, Sinbad was deep in conversation with Tishimi concerning the nature of the Arlegon magic inhabiting Rafi, when a sudden squawking caught his attention. To his and Tishimi's amazement Al-Bulcar fled past them, flames billowing from his makeshift toga. Behind him raced Byrne, clutching a wooden bucket full of slopping water, shouting for Al-Bulcar to stop. Sinbad grabbed Byrne by the arm as he passed, being careful so as not to make him drop the bucket.

"It's drinking water," hissed Sinbad.

The wide-eyed Celt, realizing his error, returned the bucket carefully to its place of safety, all the while grunting an apology to his Captain. Meantime, Al-Bulcar continued to race around the deck, his pace surprisingly rapid despite his considerable bulk, flames and smoke whipping from the remnants of his toga. For a moment it even looked to Sinbad as though his actual body was on fire, but Sinbad dismissed this as a trick of the light and a product of the confusion on deck. The air was full of shouts and shrieks from both Sinbad's crew and the Xubanthali, urging him to remove the garment.

Sinbad knew that if the flames were not quickly doused then the Blue Nymph would be in grave danger of catching alight. He caught sight of Illia, head bowed, and felt anger fuel in his gut. He wondered why she, with her extraordinary powers, did not simply intervene and extinguish the fire that threatened to consume her leader and possibly everyone else aboard the ship.

Sinbad realized Illia was not about to do anything and that he himself would have to act, when a gigantic figure emerged from below deck. It was Gunarson. He had evidently been taking some well-earned rest, and emerged stretching and yawning. Despite his sleepiness he appraised the situation with characteristic quick-mindedness, and immediately seized hold of Al-Bulcar as he shot past, lifting the enormous man effortlessly off the deck and over the edge of the ship. Al-Bulcar let out a terrific squeal as Gunarson let him drop into the roiling briny. A tremendous splash went up, as the Blue Nymph's crew and the Xubanthali rushed to see the fate of their comrade.

Al-Bulcar was splashing frantically in the water. He had become ensnared in one of the many fishing nets strung from the length of the Blue Nymph. Given that he clearly couldn't swim particularly well and that the swells were particularly unforgiving, Sinbad mused that this outcome was fortuitous indeed, and that Al-Bulcar should offer thanks to his god as soon as possible. Whether the now naked Al-Bulcar thought this as he was winched aboard amidst a writhing morass of flat-fish, eels and squid was another matter. Gunarson and the others, including Byrne, clearly eager to make up for his earlier mistake with the bucket of drinking water, lowered the net to the deck, letting its contents topple out, including the fat Xubanthali. Al-Bulcar cascaded across the deck, yelping as the fish flapped and snapped against all parts of his glistening, humongous body. His Xubanthali retinue rushed to protect the man's modesty as best they could given the circumstances, though by this stage it was largely futile.

It was some time later, when his Xubanthali fellows had fashioned him a new, altogether more secure toga, that Al-Bulcar revealed to Sinbad what had caused the fire. Al-Bulcar had apparently been examining his scroll with the lens when he had dozed off. The magnifying glass, he had concluded, must have caused the scroll to burst into flames, which in turn had engulfed his toga. He held up the charred remnants of papyrus as evidence. Sinbad half-considered confiscating the lens from the man, which he noticed had returned to its position on a piece of string around Al-Bulcar's bulbous neck, but thought better of further humiliating the Xubanthali leader in front of his people. Sinbad figured that the smell of fish and the associated mocking from the Blue Nymph's crew would prove a suitable deterrent to future carelessness of this sort.

By now night was falling. As he watched Al-Bulcar waddling away, Sinbad's gaze again fell upon Illia, her back toward him. He wondered why, when she could have helped, the mysterious sorceress chose not to.

Chapter Nine

When Haroun finally succeeding in opening his eyes, he couldn't see anything. The world around him was only mist, a freezing tissue of shifting vapor obscuring the night-time darkness, illuminated by a vague white light that could only be the moon. The boy looked down to see Samson on the floor of the crow's nest, hissing his distress, his terror, at what was happening. Haroun reached down a trembling hand to try and comfort the creature but felt only the cat's iced, pointed fur. In desperation he tried to call out to his shipmates down below, to his Captain, but his words emerged rasping and incomprehensible.

Was this Death? Had the clawing, relentless tuberculosis that had consumed his mother and two of his younger siblings finally come to take him? Or perhaps, just perhaps, it was a dream; a febrile fantasy brought about by the day's blistering sun. His breath was short and sharp, and he wondered whether each painful intake of air would solidify his lungs.

This was no dream.

Suddenly a familiar, determined face lurched at him through the mist. He felt Sinbad's firm grip around his waist; fleetingly saw Samson the cat leaping upon onto his Captain's shoulder. Barely clinging to consciousness, he sensed the mild vibration of Sinbad's nimble, dexterous footfalls as he scaled down the rigging and deposited Haroun amidst some hessian rugs, where he was cuddled up by clucking Xubanthali women as though he were one of their missing sons.

"What is happening to us, Captain?" said a voice, close and urgent, in Sinbad's ear. Sinbad turned to see Delacrois. It was unusual for him to look so concerned. The Gaul's neatly trimmed mustache was speckled with ice. It would have rendered his normally handsome visage comical in the extreme, were the situation Sinbad and his crew found themselves in not quite so bizarre.

"Rafi," Gunarson whispered, gathering his great cloak about him. "Look to the old man."

Sinbad followed Gunarson's pointing arm to the figure of Rafi. The elderly man still stood at the prow of the vessel, just as he had for untold weeks, his body shivering with cold, though his blood vessels still pulsated a translucent scarlet. But something was different. Rather than staring ahead he now looked to the sky, his attitude fixed.

As Sinbad neared, his crew and that of the Xubanthali breaking around him, he saw more clearly what had changed. The veins on Rafi's body no longer indicated a complex route across the oceans. In fact, they no longer pointed horizontally in any direction. Now the glowing veins pointed only one way, and it was *upward*.

The mist was all around them now, rendering it difficult for Sinbad to see the people crowding around him. He could hear Omar shouting, and it was toward this familiar noise that Sinbad necessarily orientated himself.

"What is it, Omar?" he demanded.

"Rafi is right, Cap'n," burbled Omar, pointing over the side of the vessel. "We're going *up*."

Without replying Sinbad strained to see over the side of the ship, through the enveloping fog. Far below them, its surface rippling with the dappling reflection of the moon was the sea. Omar was correct. The Blue Nymph was flying!

"Find the other two vessels," snapped Sinbad. "Check the same is true of them."

"Aye, Cap'n," responded the Master, before disappearing into the mist.

"What new sorcery is this?" Sinbad ruminated, more to himself than anyone else. To his surprise, he received an answer.

"Rafi has done as he promised," said Tishimi's soft, measured tones. "He has brought us to the centre of the ocean."

"The centre," echoed Sinbad, searching the mist for a sight of Tishimi's features. "And yet we are being dragged into the sky itself. Why?"

She stepped forward, placing a reassuring hand on his arm. "If the legends are to be believed, that is the nature of the Scholars of Bethshea. They search for knowledge. On the ground, in the sea..."

"In the air itself."

"So it would seem," nodded Tishimi.

"'Tis true, Cap'n," said Omar's sudden, gruff voice. "The two Xubanthali vessels float with us, up into the clouds 'emselves."

"The vapor is clearing," said another, unmistakable voice. Gunarson strode towards them, trails of mist dancing in his wake. "I believe we have surfaced above the cloud cover." Sinbad looked past him to the dissipating clouds and saw a sweep of stars.

"Oui," said Delacrois, following him. "And it grows palpably warmer again." It was true: Sinbad's damp shirt was already drying with the return of the balmy night.

Sinbad's keen eyes had picked something out but a league distant. A patch of sky from which stars were weirdly absent. As he looked the reason why became gradually clear. In the space where the stars were lacking, something was pivoting.

"Omar," Sinbad said abruptly, motioning. "You see?"

"Aye, Cap'n," nodded the Master, following Sinbad's train of sight. "'Tis curious indeed. I do not like it."

Sinbad directed his attention to the Blue Nymph's fulsome sail. "Be that as it may, Omar. That is where we need to go." As if to bear this out Rafi had appeared, the first time in weeks he had left his position at the prow. The glowing lines on his body were becoming thicker still, more insistent, as they strained upward.

"We are here," wheezed Rafi, the exertion of speaking almost too much for him. "We have found the Scholars of Bethshea." The elderly man staggered where he stood, looking as though he might faint.

While Gunarson and Delacrois went to support their aged comrade, Sinbad patted him affectionately on the shoulder. "Thank you, wise Rafi. Now you must rest. Afore long this sorcery will abate and your true nature will reassert itself."

Rafi nodded wordlessly, as Gunarson and Delacrois helped him below deck. Sinbad turned his attention to Omar.

"Take us in, First Mate."

"Aye, Cap'n," acknowledged Omar, his uncertainty disappearing. Such seafaring commands were familiar and could be acted upon, even if the Blue Nymph's own position was unnatural indeed. Omar would simply assume they were still in the ocean, even if this was palpably not the case. "Port ho!" the First Mate bellowed. "To the oars, bring us about!"

The cloud having now completely vanished below them, it was easy to discern the crew running hither and yon in their endeavors to carry out Omar's instructions, the oar master and drummer jumping into position. The rhythmic beating began, and very gradually the Blue Nymph began to pitch to the left, and the object to which they were headed began to transform into a more tangible shape. Hanging over the edge, Sinbad saw the cloud cover below them, now obscuring the ocean far below. He turned and saw that the accompanying Xubanthali vessels were accomplishing the same maneuver, if somewhat less gracefully, their far less experienced sailors struggling to tack their sails with comparable speed. Sinbad returned his attention to the object slowly pivoting in the sky.

Abruptly he detached himself from his position at the side of the Blue Nymph and raced to the prow of the vessel that he might better discern the size and scale of the object. In truth, even he could not conceal his astonishment. He had witnessed many extraordinary sights in his adventures across the globe, from fantastical beasts to stupendous natural spectacles. He had endured experiences that would have driven many to madness. Yet this thing they were now approaching, in a ship of the sea which was somehow magically suspended miles above the ocean, was a sight like no other.

It was a pyramid, far, far vaster than any found in Egypt, including the mighty Giza Necropolis. It hung in space, rotating in saturnine fashion, as if it were somehow glorying in its own majestic impossibility. Only now, as the Blue Nymph continued its gradual approach, did Sinbad and his crew begin to understand the colossal scale of the object. It was more akin to a city, albeit one suspended in the sky. The nearer they got, the more it became possible to perceive figures standing along several of the edges, some moving, many still, all clad in cloaks and cowls of dark gray and brown. A welcoming committee.

At least, that was what he hoped.

Now his eyes caught sight of something else, a movement through the sky. Something was snaking towards them. In fact, several somethings, like sentient tendrils, reaching out for the Blue Nymph.

Sinbad heard Omar's incredulous voice behind him, at the tiller of the Blue Nymph. "What in the name of Allah and all that's holy are those things?"

As Sinbad turned to Omar he saw several more of the crew, widemouthed at the approach of the tendrils.

"Should we repel 'em, Cap'n?"

"No, Omar," came Sinbad's thoughtful reply, shouted so as to ensure the entire crew heard him. "I'll wager they merely mean to bring us toward them without damage to themselves or to us. Trust in Allah."

Sinbad was correct. Very quickly the tendrils, in actual fact mooring ropes afforded the power of animation by some clever sorcery, gently wrapped themselves around key elements of the Blue Nymph's architecture, that they might gradually draw the vessel toward the pyramid. Turning about, Sinbad saw that a similar process was occurring to the two Xubanthali vessels. Fortunately the crews of these two ships were evidently taking their cue from the Blue Nymph, and no attempt was made to resist the ropes.

Sure enough the ropes began to drag the Blue Nymph very carefully toward the pyramid. With nothing to do except watch, Sinbad's crew and the Xubanthali aboard the ship rushed to the starboard side to witness proceedings more clearly.

"Such sorcery would not embarrass Odin himself," mused Gunarson.

Within ten minutes or so the Blue Nymph had been brought alongside the pyramid. Sinbad and his crew watched in silence as a group of hooded figures extended a plank of wood toward the Blue Nymph. Further along Sinbad could see a similar process happening with one of the Xubanthali ships; the third ship was still being tethered by the reaching magical ropes.

Sinbad, as Captain, was the first to disembark the Blue Nymph, treading with confident footfalls toward the pyramid and the waiting clutch of figures. Before he could say anything, one of the figures stepped forward, pulling back his cowl to reveal a kindly, lined face and intense, intelligent green eyes.

"Greetings, Sinbad El Ari of Baghad," said the figure. "I am Scholar Ik Numari. Welcome, one and all, to the Library of Bethshea."

"You knew we were coming," said Sinbad as they proceeded along the corridor. The pyramid, it had transpired, was formed from varying kinds of limestone, just like the pyramids Sinbad had encountered in Egypt. Somehow, perversely, this made the edifice's ability to hang in the air many miles above the sea even more peculiar, even though Sinbad knew of no earthly substance which would have made this particular feat any less miraculous.

Sinbad had ordered that all able-bodied crew should come aboard the pyramid that they might stretch their legs. So it was that he and his crew, together with the Xubanthali from the Blue Nymph and the other two ships, had entered via a vaunting doorway in the exterior of the building. Each and every one of them were treated like honored guests, a fact which seemed to mildly annoy Al-Bulcar as he evidently considered he should be afforded more pomp and ritual than anyone else. Excepting Sinbad, of course.

"The Arlegon are our gate-keepers," affirmed Ik Numari. "They decide who is worthy enough that they might learn the location of our Library."

"They tested us mightily," agreed Sinbad.

"Yes. That is their purpose. But the very fact of your presence here shows you were not found wanting." They had arrived at an enormous archway, which opened out into an extraordinary, massive atrium lit by manifold stuttering torches. The chamber contained aisle upon aisle of towering shelves that disappeared amidst the darkness of the ceiling high above.

These shelves contained books, parchments and scrolls that must have numbered in the millions, probably more. Amid the shelves moved more of the hooded Scholars, some bent double at reading desks, others earnestly inspecting the unfurled scrolls, still others carrying piles of books. All of the Scholars conducted themselves with a studied reverence for their texts, heads lowered so that their faces were shrouded in the shadow of their cowls.

"An extraordinary place," observed Al-Bulcar.

Ik Numari cocked his head smilingly to one side. "Quite so. The Library is the greatest repository of knowledge ever amassed. It is the work of millennia. This is but one archive."

Al-Bulcar nodded enthusiastically, "Your knowledge of sorcery must be impressive indeed." He gestured around them, "To enable such a wonder as this immense pyramid to fly."

Ik Numari smiled, "'Tis true. Such knowledge allows us to travel into the sky, under the waves. Even beneath the earth itself."

Al-Bulcar bowed deeply, "Truly, your works are wonders, sir."

"We too seek knowledge, Scholar," said Sinbad, unable to hide his impatience. "We wish to know how Al-Izrikel the Scarlet imprisoned the Warriors of Forever."

Ik Numari came to a stuttering halt. Surprise traced across the aged Scholar's features. "The Warriors were fearsome creatures, their transformation into undead monsters accomplished by the most potent, direst magic. They walk the Earth again?"

"Aye," nodded Sinbad.

The Scholar looked grave indeed. "How did they escape their prison?"

Sinbad could not help but smile, even given the dire nature of the situation. "We do not know, Scholar. That is why we came to you."

The Scholar nodded. "Quite so. The Warriors cannot be destroyed but Al-Izrikel did indeed imprison them. But the knowledge of how this most powerful of wizards achieved this act is arcane indeed."

"But you possess it?" asked Sinbad doggedly.

"Perhaps. But we will need to look. It will take some small time."

Sinbad's reply was low and urgent, "Time is of the essence, Ik Numari. They have taken the children of these people, the Xubanthali. We believe that if they consume the youngsters' souls that they will be as powerful as ever they were. They will be a blight upon this world, just as they were a thousand years previously. Darkness will fall and it will not be easily lifted."

Ik Numari inclined his head, "Yes, Captain Sinbad. I understand the urgency. But there is a cost."

"A cost?" said Al-Bulcar, looking alarmed. "What do you mean? Our children may already have been consumed!"

Ik Numari shook his head, "You would know if they had been, Al-Bulcar. We all would."

Sinbad's hand was playing involuntarily on the hilt of Grachene. He could feel the magical blade trembling, ever so slightly. "What is this cost you speak of, Scholar?"

"Do not fret," said Ik Numari hurriedly, holding up his hands. "It is quite simply our creed. Knowledge for knowledge. Come, I will show you."

Ik Numari saw to it that most of Sinbad's crew and the Xubanthali were led away in order that the Scholars might offer them sustenance after their arduous sea voyage. Since most of the Arlegon's generous supplies had dwindled to little more than crumbs and dregs, this decision was greeted with unsurprising enthusiasm. Sinbad made sure everyone knew that they were to do as the Scholars instructed, but that Omar would be in charge of them, a fact which delighted the First Mate. Sinbad also tasked him with looking after Rafi, who seemed more dazed than ever, the veins on his body pulsating as insistently as ever.

So it was that once the bulk of the group had disappeared, Sinbad, along with Al-Bulcar, Gunarson, Delacrois and Tishimi were led down a series of winding staircases. Sinbad, despite being at the head of the group alongside Ik Numari, noticed that Illia had elected to join with them rather than the majority of the Xubanthali. She followed the body of the group, head bowed as usual.

"Here is the sacred heart of our Library," said Ik Numari as he led Sinbad and the others into an antechamber. The walls were bedecked with mammoth sigils, some carved from gold, others from silver, while others were wrought from altogether less precious substances, like iron and wood. Still more sigils were carved from substances Sinbad had never before encountered.

Beneath each of the sigils sat a Scholar, cross-legged and impassive atop a voluminous pillow. Sinbad saw that these Scholars wore markedly different cloaks to that of their comrades, composed of a far darker material, and that there was a rendering of each of the appropriate sigils sewn into the hoods of their outfits. In common with their fellows, their faces remained hidden in shadow beneath their cowls. Each Scholar clutched a magnificent quill, and before each of them lay an enormous, leather-bound book.

Ik Numari turned and addressed Sinbad and his companions. "Many millennia ago," he announced, "Our home of Bethshea was attacked, ravaged indeed, by forces of darkness who sought to commandeer the libraries and archives our ancestors had painstakingly created. They thought to grab for themselves the knowledge of direst sorcery that they might conquer the world." As he spoke the air rippled above them, and three-dimensional images appeared, depicting the events he recounted. Sinbad and the others stared upward in amazement at the animated illustration of terrible, demonic-looking hordes attacking the Library's pyramid, the very building in which they now stood.

Ik Numari continued with his solemn explanation. "Rather than let such knowledge fall into their hands, the original Scholars of Bethshea decided to use that knowledge to escape, and to begin a never-ending quest to discover, and record for posterity, all knowledge." Sinbad watched as the images blurred to show the pyramid beginning to rotate and then to levitate above the hordes that sought to destroy them, cascades of fire bursting from its base. The demonic armies roared and twisted in agony amidst the flames. Then the pyramid shot into the sky, leaving the surviving hordes cursing far below.

"Our ancestors swore we would never again let our knowledge be vulnerable to such attacks. As you know we tasked the Arlegon with determining who were and who were not worthy of accessing our Library." An image of Lonkra, Sharlvel and the other witches of the Moon Peninsula morphed fleetingly into view before disappearing to be replaced by images of Sinbad and his crew. "Only the virtuous may visit us and discover our secrets. You are such." With a wave of Ik Numari's hand, the images promptly vanished.

"Respected Scholar," began Al-Bulcar, "this place and your generosity toward us is extraordinary. Please let us know what we might give you in exchange for the information we, uh, desire."

Ik Numari smiled kindly, gesturing toward piles of satin cushions opposite each of the Scholars bearing the sigil. "Please, sit."

Sinbad's crew exchanged wary glances but took their lead from Illia, who sat without hesitation. Each of Sinbad's people positioned themselves opposite a Scholar, the mighty Gunarson struggling to pull his legs into a cross-legged position, the flabby Al-Bulcar experiencing comparable difficulties maneuvering his considerable bulk into the required pose. Sinbad saw that the Scholar opposite him had pulled out a gigantic tome and a quill, but that the pages of the book were empty.

"The process is simple," said Ik Numari, prowling the room as though he were giving a lecture. "We want from you your memories, your experiences. Perhaps you will tell us a story of derring-do. Perhaps you will tell us a story of joy, of sadness or longing." He had stopped walking and cocked his head as he stared at Sinbad. "Perhaps it will be a story of love. Or of loss."

"Sir, I fear the knowledge I might impart might be considered... *indelicate*," said Delacrois, exchanging a cheeky glance with Gunarson. The Viking guffawed in response.

Ik Numari chuckled, unconvincingly. "I should perhaps have said. We tend to find the most powerful knowledge is buried deep within the psyche. Such information is not readily accessed. We will have to..." he frowned as he searched for the apposite word "...*dig* for it." As he spoke Sinbad noticed that his own Scholar and the others in the room suddenly moved to open the mammoth leather bound books laid before them. Their white, empty pages looked to him suddenly hungry.

Ik Numari's words seemed to trigger something inside Gunarson. "You would root in my mind without my control?" roared the Viking. "I think not, cur!" And with that this Gunarson tried to stand, but found he could not. The Scholar in front of him, the individual's face but a patch of limitless darkness, had begun to write feverishly, though no words were apparent on the page.

"Do not concern yourselves," said Ik Numari, smiling benevolently down at them. "The process is painless. We simply desire knowledge for knowledge."

In horror Sinbad tried to stand but he could not either. None of them could.

"What will this process do to us?" demanded Sinbad. His speech sounded muffled to his own ears, as though he were submersed in water.

"The most wonderful thing," replied Ik Numari, his measured tones equally distorted. "It will grant you a place in our archives. In perpetuity. And when it is done, well, your bodies will be empty husks. But I assure you, we will furnish your colleagues with the information you came for. Knowledge for knowledge, that is our promise."

Sinbad looked to the Scholar ahead of him. The figure had begun to write with the quill, frantically, on the pages of the open book, though as with the others no actual words were evident on the page. Indeed, the room was alive with the sound of scribbling.

Involuntarily Sinbad reached out to grab the wrist of the Scholar, but as he did so he caught sight of his own hand. He saw with horror that the skin on the tips of his fingers had begun to transform into words. As he watched these words began to trail through the air toward the Scholar's fast-moving pen, and to situate themselves in the book, following the line of the Scholar's writing. Sinbad looked up at the face of the Scholar opposite him, and as he peered into the void where a face should have been, consciousness began to desert him. Sinbad struggled to stay awake, but the effort was too much.

As he looked the shadow in the cowl began to take form, to twist and to turn into something very, very familiar. A nose, a mouth, a pair of dark blue eyes, skin the color of coffee. A mustache and neatly trimmed beard. Sinbad's own face stared at him from within the depths of the cowl...

Chapter Ten

The air was alive with a thousand spinning fragments. The impact blew Sinbad off his feet, and it was all he could do to grab Ashanti from out of the path of a toppling, pulverized pillar. He pulled himself upward, head throbbing from the power of the blast. Blood coursed down his face from where a shard of spinning ceramic had ripped the side of his brow. He staggered, forcing his dizziness into abeyance.

The watching crowd had erupted into a panicking mass, audience members shrieking in terror as they struggled to exit the arena. They clambered over one another, tore at one another's clothes, pulled down marquees and trampled the young and the elderly in their desperate efforts to spill into the narrow alleyways leading off the area.

Head still ringing, Sinbad looked up to see another fireball scudding through the sky in a graceful arc, only to come smashing down on a podium full of dignitaries. Many were immediately killed, limbs and bodily organs dispersed in a fountain of gore that rained down on those below. Screaming men and women, their finery alight, collided fitfully with each other, some managing to scale the city wall and plunge themselves into the rocky sea below, others rolling on the cracked floor in a desperate attempt to extinguish the flames. Amidst the mayhem Sinbad saw the city guard ushering the Sultan and their parents to safety, and he issued a silent prayer of gratitude to Allah.

Sinbad helped a wobbling Ashanti as she struggled to her feet, her pale blue wedding dress ripped and flapping in the breeze. They had to step over the body of the priest, splayed awkwardly in front of them, his skull mashed by a dislodged section of masonry that fell when the pillar collapsed. The screaming of the crowd increased in intensity. Rounding a corner into the midst of the melee strode a vast figure, its upper torso that of a ravening wolf, its body that of a muscular man. City guards rushed toward the creature with spears and swords, but the behemoth simply dashed them to the ground or flung them out of its path.

Sinbad whirled around to face Ashanti, pulling her bridal veil away that he might look upon her beautiful face. "You must hide yourself," he told her.

"Sinbad," she replied urgently, her eyes full of tears. "My love." Her hand played on the jagged wound on his forehead. "I am so sorry."

"It is but a cut..." he began.

...another fireball...smashing down on a podium...

"You don't understand, my love. This is my doing. I knew of this. This is my fault."

Sinbad looked at her incredulously, "What is? What do you mean?"

She thrust a trembling hand at the monstrosity striding towards them, her words coming rapidly and breathlessly. "When I was but a child I almost died. My parents prayed to the powerful demon Ecrasis that he might come and save my life. And so he did. In exchange for saving me, Ecrasis made my parents solemnly promise my hand in marriage…" Tears hazarded down her beautiful face. "I thought it was a forgotten myth, but it is not!"

"No, fair maiden!" shrieked Ecrasis. It paused in its approach, pulling back its head, then spat another gobbet of fire into the air. This one tore through the city wall, flinging armored soldiers in multiple directions and leaving a tremendous, smoking hole in the wall. "You are mine!" roared the creature. "You were promised to me!"

"A contract with a demon is no contract at all!" yelled Sinbad. "Ashanti is betrothed to me!" He had pulled his ceremonial sword from his scabbard.

"Puny youth!" responded the creature. "You think you can slay me? Heroes greater than you have tried and failed!"

"I will try," said Sinbad. "But only if you show some honor, vile cur! We shall fight with swords, not sorcery! Do you agree?"

"Honor?" scoffed the creature. It wiped a trail of bubbling drool from its leering mouth. "Very well. I will spit no fire." The monster pulled a huge saber from off his back, batting its yellow eyes malevolently, "But I will cleave you in twain, callow youth, and scoop out what little brains you must surely possess!"

Sinbad felt the weight of his sword in his hands. It was an awkward weapon, not really intended for battle. "Aye, we shall see!" he cried, his throat dry.

"And the victor will marry this fair maiden." The creature bared its teeth at Sinbad, in what was presumably intended as a grin.

"Agreed," said Sinbad solemnly. He embraced Ashanti, felt her dark tresses against his face, and whispered. "Hide yourself. I will fight this creature and I will try to slay it. But if I do not, then you must run…"

"I want you as my husband," Ashanti replied. "You will defeat him, I know you will. All of Baghdad knows you will."

"Go," he urged. And with that she turned and ran, gathering her torn blue wedding dress about her, disappearing amidst the last stragglers who had yet to escape the city square.

"The blushing bride runs!" exclaimed Ecrasis, watching her departure.

"I promise I will find you, my love!" A low, growling laugh issued from within its slavering jaws.

By now the city grounds had largely cleared of people, save for those who had been injured by the monster or by the stampede, and the bodies of those unlucky enough to be consumed by Ecrasis' fireballs.

Sinbad leapt down from the wedding podium, blade secure in his right hand, all the time measuring its weight, his eyes roving the creature in search of possible weaknesses.

But Ecrasis spent no time on deliberation. Instead he launched himself up and forward, swiping downward with the blade as he landed. Sinbad leapt out of his opponent's path, using the post of an abandoned market stall as leverage so he could hurtle up and behind the creature. As soon as he hit the ground he brought his own sword along Ecrasis' back, pulling it smartly across its protruding, hairy spine so that a fine, jetting spray of blood shot up and outwards.

Ecrasis roared with pain and fury, wheeling around with surprising agility, so that he was able to smack Sinbad with one of his huge, clawed hands. Sinbad flailed backward, his sword spun from his grasp, visible on the tiled floor about five meters distant. Before he had time to scrabble for it Ecrasis was upon him, smashing his saber downward. Using his elbows and feet, Sinbad propelled himself backward, evading each of the creature's subsequent lumbering assaults with the sword. The floor cracked with each missed blow, sending up explosions of debris and dust. As he careered backward Sinbad wondered how long he could keep evading Ecrasis' blows, wishing for a weapon that would spring readily to his hand. Abruptly he felt something hard beneath his left elbow. It was his own sword, which he snatched up and proceeded to block the monster's next strike with, pulling himself to his feet in the process.

Sparks cascaded as Sinbad continued to parry, still reeling backward on the defensive. Out of the corner of his eye he spotted a spit, upon which someone had been roasting a celebratory hog prior to Ecrasis' untimely arrival. Sinbad pulled the spit over, which crashed into Ecrasis, sending glowing coals into the creature's exposed flesh.

Again the monster bellowed, but he had lost the initiative. Sinbad squatted to avoid another downward sweep of Ecrasis' sword, then shoved his own blade into the monster's gut, turning it brutally as he did so. He had plunged it with such venom that it was a struggle for Sinbad to release his sword.

This time Ecrasis didn't roar, but instead looked down at Sinbad's handiwork, at the guts spilling out of the slice in his side. Then the creature looked up, its wolverine features contorted with fury.

"You will die for that, Prince," snarled Ecrasis.

"If I do, it'll have been worth it!" riposted Sinbad, grinning broadly at the abomination.

The man and the monster lifted their swords in readiness, then joined battle again, their blades a furious blur. When they eventually broke, both had sustained injuries, serrations that glistened in the Persian sun, but Sinbad had clearly fared worse. He was royalty, and though he was courageous and had faced battle many times before, he was used to a pampered life. The duel was beginning to take its toll. He panted, wiping a trace of blood from his mouth, feeling every sinew ache.

"What's wrong, puny youngster?" said Ecrasis, licking his own lips slyly. "Too much for you?"

"Never," gasped Sinbad, just as he had to repel another blow from the creature. Sinbad struggled to hold the monster off, Ecrasis pressing home his advantage, pushing Sinbad onto one knee. A sudden crack sounded out and Sinbad's sword snapped in twain, Ecrasis falling forward and Sinbad dodging back in the nick of time. Ecrasis collapsed and Sinbad brought the broken half of his sword up against his throat. Though jagged, the sword-half would certainly rip a hole in the beast's exposed larynx, one from which even it would not recover.

"You have lost, Ecrasis," Sinbad hissed. "I will marry my Ashanti."

"Kill me," mocked the creature, its eyes darting toward the people watching from every nook, from the roofs of houses and from behind smashed market stalls. "Show your people the man you are. Ruthless and determined. Without mercy."

"I would do it," said Sinbad through gritted teeth, pushing the broken blade ever closer to Ecrasis' throat, its uneven teeth pressing against the monster's gullet.

"Show them, then," insisted Ecrasis. "They will *fear* you forever, Sinbad. The Butcher of Baghad."

Sinbad continued to press the fractured blade, then abruptly pulled it away, in the process standing back. "By order of the Sultan you are expelled from Persia," he announced. "Leave now, while I am minded to spare your life."

The creature emitted a rumbling laugh before silkily replying, "Aye, Prince. I will do as you decree."

"Good," said Sinbad, gesturing toward the city gates. He watched as Ecrasis staggered to its feet and headed across the city square, head down, a trail of dark blood in its wake. Sinbad's eyes flitted to the watching people. He attempted a brave smile at them, but they only stared back incredulously.

"You will be my husband," said a familiar voice close to him. Sinbad turned to see Ashanti emerging from her hiding place amongst a pile of rubble.

"I told you to run," he chided, though he couldn't hide the delight on his face. The two embraced and passionately kissed. "What if I had lost? You would be married to that monstrosity."

"I would rather die," she said.

The thunderous roar made them wheel around in time to see the fireball arcing upward and then down, inevitably, toward them. In an instant the world slowed, as Sinbad tried to pull Ashanti toward him, just too late to completely avoid the blazing sphere. The speeding orb winged her before smashing spectacularly into the abandoned market stall, flinging splinters of flaming wood and fire in multiple directions. Holding his beloved with one arm Sinbad instinctively whirled around, sending the tip of his broken sword sailing through the air, toward the laughing Ecrasis. The broken blade arced upward before thudding into the creature's forehead, pitching it backward with a final, guttural cry of surprise.

The monster dead, a panic-stricken Sinbad turned his attention to the woman in his arms. The whole left side of her body had been scorched by the fireball. She looked at him in a mixture of confusion and pain.

"No," whispered Sinbad, "it cannot be."

"My love," his beautiful Nymph murmured, her light blue dress rendered indigo by her rapidly spreading blood. "We will meet again. For now, Allah beckons us on different journeys. Remember me, my love. *Remember me, Sinbad …*"

"*…Sinbad.*" The woman's voice was measured, but its urgency was nonetheless palpable. "You must awaken. Please, I beg you. *Sinbad.*"

"What?" Illia's features resolved themselves. "What..?"

"I'm holding them off," came Illia's breathless reply, her pale eyes swirling. "But I need you."

"What are you?" came a snarling man's voice. Sinbad recognized it as Ik

Numari. Sinbad struggled to pull himself upright. He saw that the Scholar who had been writing his story was bathed in a white glow emanating from Illia's hand, and that this light had frozen him. Her other hand, from which a white beam of light also emerged, was directed at her own Scholar, also rendered inert. Ik Numari was advancing upon her, his eyes flashing with malicious intent.

"You are not virtuous," spat Ik Numari. "How did you enter this place?"

Illia ignored the Scholar and directed her attention at Sinbad. "Listen to me, Sinbad. They're transforming us into pure knowledge so they can archive us, so they can turn us into books and scrolls."

"Captain Sinbad, this woman is a fool," interjected Ik Numari. "You are adventurers. Your knowledge, your experiences, your memories, are invaluable. We can turn you into words and images, we can make sure you're remembered throughout eternity. Forget your gods and churches. Only through us can you gain true immortality."

Sinbad focused on Ik Numari, a smile creeping across his face. "If I'm as virtuous as you say, my immortality will be guaranteed. But not by you. And not this way." Abruptly he launched himself at the Scholar, landing a punch in the centre of the man's face with such force that it knocked him clean off his feet. Ik Numari landed in a heap in the centre of the room.

Sinbad turned his attention to his fellows. Each of them lolled where they sat, eyes tight shut as they dreamt, some of them muttering, some reaching fitfully into the air, their strained faces mirrored in the cowls of the Scholars they sat opposite.

He knew that before anything else he would have to deal with Illia's Scholar. Sinbad socked the individual with the same ferocity he'd hit Ik Numari, the hooded figure skittering across the smooth floor. Illia, relieved of having to stave off her own Scholar, turned urgently to Sinbad.

"Gunarson," said Sinbad, as she directed a beam of light toward the Viking's Scholar. Sinbad dropped to a crouch beside him and proceeded to shake him into wakefulness.

"What?" Gunarson demanded as he came round. "By Odin's hammer, why did you wake me? I was fighting a mighty, heroic battle against…"

"No time," muttered Sinbad grimly, gesturing towards his Scholar. "Can you oblige?"

"Aye, Cap'n," affirmed Gunarson, rapidly grasping the situation. As he dealt with his Scholar, Illia and Sinbad were able to turn their attention to the others. Within minutes everyone had been released from their coma and the various Scholars lay inert.

"Gunarson, Delacrois, go and find the others," instructed Sinbad.

"And you, Captain?" enquired Delacrois, yawning and stretching his arms.

"Our mission still holds. We still need to discover how Al-Izrikel the Scarlet imprisoned the Warriors of Forever," said Sinbad. "You, on your feet." He pitched Ik Numari into a standing position. The Scholar looked to him drunkenly, his nose a bloodied, crunched mess. "No more games," said Sinbad determinedly. "Give us what we came for."

They negotiated their way along a further series of circuitous passages before emerging into another archive space even larger than the one they had originally encountered. Ik Numari's former geniality had, unsurprisingly, vanished, to be replaced by a reproachful, simmering disdain for the group.

"The books and scrolls and parchments," Delacrois said, as they ventured into the library. "They are made from people."

"Of course," responded Ik Numari, as though this were the most natural thing in the world. "We transform people into words that they might live forever." His previously precise diction was now muffled by the broken nose Sinbad had given him.

"That you might have eternal access to them," snapped Illia, unexpectedly. As usual she had replaced her sari hood.

"We are the keepers of knowledge," answered Ik Numari icily. "That has always been our role, and that remains our role."

"Little wonder your ancestors were attacked," interjected Gunarson in an angry whisper. "You were killing their people."

"*Transforming* them," snapped back the Scholar. "Do you not listen, barbarian? Why we ever thought we could learn from you is beyond me ..."

"Despicable mongrel!" roared Gunarson, grabbing the elderly man by the hood of his cloak and lifting him off his feet. "Barbarian? We Vikings are no such thing. We possess writing and law. We are craftsmen and artisans, as well as explorers. Listen to me, little man. Knowledge unhinged from the world has no meaning!"

Sinbad had placed a gentle hand on Gunarson's arm. "Ralf," he said. "I understand your anger with this man, with these people. I share it. But we need him."

"Aye," said Gunarson momentarily, still glowering at the quaking figure. Then he very carefully lowered him to the ground, straightening the
Scholar's cloak as he did so.

"I apologize for the impetuosity of my crewman," said Sinbad quietly.
"But you see, Scholar, each of us grows mightily impatient. I say again to
you, give us the knowledge we seek." His eyes flashed, "Otherwise we will
be forced to take it."

"It is here," said Ik Numari, reaching up the to the book shelf behind
them and pulling out a large tome bound in red leather. He proffered it to
Sinbad. The title, embossed in spidery gold lettering that glittered in the
scant light of myriad torches, said simply *The Life of Al-Izrikel the Scarlet.*

Chapter Eleven

The reading room was a circular, elevated space adjacent to this particular section of the library, accessible via a series of ancient wooden steps which creaked mournfully as they ascended them. The group crowded in, Sinbad invited to seat himself at a lower circular dais by Ik Numari, whose violent encounter with Gunarson seemed to have rekindled a nervous politeness, if not the genial persona they had originally encountered. Sinbad, eager not to fall for any other tricks, looked meaningfully to Gunarson, who understood immediately and made sure he remained next to the Scholar, towering above him in suitably intimidating fashion.

Ik Numari carefully laid the book before Sinbad, then stepped away, bowing reverentially.

"What must I do?" asked Sinbad.

"Read," said Ik Numari simply. "Read aloud."

Sinbad held the Scholar's gaze momentarily, then very carefully opened the cover and began to read the ornate, spiraling script contained within.

For my name is Al-Izrikel the Scarlet, sorcerer of magnitude, seer of future millennia, walker of time. For my name is Al-Izrikel the Scarlet, discoverer of secrets, changer of destinies, piercer of souls. It is I who found the Tomb of Kytaei, who journeyed to the core of the universe. It is I who fathomed the runes of Estrulico, who returned the Axis of Noxor to its place in the Firmanent. It is I, Al-Izrikel the Scarlet, Al-Izrikel Most Powerful, who imprisoned the Warriors of Forever...

And as Sinbad spoke the ancient words they began to lift off the page and to twirl and chase through the air, then to cluster together above the dais, gradually forming an outline of a figure. As Sinbad continued reading, the words bound themselves to one another, giving form and flesh to a kneeling, cloaked man, who raised himself to his feet and then turned to them with something approaching amusement.

"I am but a memory. Why do you disturb my slumber?"

"O wise sorcerer," said Sinbad, clasping his hands together and bowing deeply. "We seek your knowledge concerning the Warriors of Forever."

Al-Izrikel chuckled, then straightened. "Of course. Their imprisonment is at an end."

A look of concern troubled Sinbad's features. "Pray, wise sorcerer, forgive our ignorance. How do you know such a thing? Please explain."

"Isn't it obvious?" said the figure, chuckling. "They must have escaped. Otherwise why would you be here?"

Sinbad smiled and nodded in return. "Yes, of course. Forgive me my foolishness."

Al-Izrikel looked at him quizzically, "You are Sinbad El Ari."

Sinbad could not mask his surprise, "You have heard of me?"

The sorcerer continued unabashed, his excitement obvious in his glittering eyes. "Sinbad the Sailor. Sinbad the Adventurer."

Sinbad shook his head in confusion, "But wise sorcerer, you yourself said you are a memory."

"A memory who remembers," said Al-Izrikel abruptly. "I was a seer. I foresaw you, Sinbad. Millennia ago. A grieving, spoilt young man who would by turns become a hero. An adventurer who would oft save people and lands from the forces of darkness and fury. And perhaps even the world itself." The sorcerer's eyes flashed. "But only if he chooses wisely."

"You are correct, wise sorcerer. Someone has unleashed the Warriors," said Sinbad. "We need to know how in order to imprison them once more."

Al-Izrikel gave an appearance of inhaling deeply, of closing his eyes and thinking. Momentarily he said, "It is clear. There is no other way. Someone must have discovered the Horn of Ostiah."

Sinbad nodded, "Again we are but ignorant fools, Al-Izrikel. Please explain."

Al-Izrikel shook his head vigorously, "To not know of something does not make you a fool, Sinbad. The Horn of Ostiah is the only method of opening and closing the Warriors' prison. Whoever has unleashed them must have found it."

"Pray, where is the prison?"

Al-Izrikel said darkly, motioning about himself, "Why, 'tis all around you, Sinbad."

"I do not understand, wise sorcerer."

"You don't need to, Captain. It will be obvious to you when the time comes. All you need to do is put the Warriors in the prison and be sure to lock the door."

"Aye," nodded Sinbad slowly. "To where should we travel?"

"You must journey to Mount Luicanus. There you will find answers. You are aware of it?"

Sinbad shook his head, "Its whereabouts are not known to us."

"That you are present at this Library suggests the Arlegon of the Moon

Peninsula gave you a map. Am I correct?"

"Yes, Al-Izrikel san," said Tishimi, stepping forward with a bow. "A living map. It inhabits one of our number. The old man Rafi."

"Very good," nodded Al-Izrikel. "The map shall remain in place until you no longer have need of its powers. It will show you the way to Mount Luicanus."

Sinbad bowed deeply, "Al-Izrikel, I thank you for your help."

The sorcerer smiled broadly, "I imprisoned the Warriors because they threatened the world. And talking of prison..." Al-Izrikel's features changed in expression, becoming suddenly dark, his cheerful eyes abruptly menacing. He thrust a gnarled hand toward the quivering Ik Numari. "Scholar Ik Numari, present yourself."

Gunarson pushed the aged Scholar forward that Al-Izrikel might look upon him.

"'Tis I, O Sorcerer," said the man meekly.

Al-Izrikel regarded the quivering Scholar severely. "Thousands of years ago your ancestors transformed me to words. Then they locked me within this tome. This is the first time my book has been opened. I have been alone for so very long."

Ik Numari floundered, "But great sorcerer, we gave you immortality."

"Pah!" snapped Al-Izrikel. "Immortality? A living death seems a better approximation to me." He stepped forward, his form shivering and warping the further he came from the book. "Look at me. I am bound by this book." He reached down, and though incorporeal was somehow able to pick the tome up, examining it with curiosity. "Trapped between its covers."

"We sought only knowledge," babbled Ik Numari, clasping his hands together.

"Your people sought to trap me, Scholar, and they succeeded," said the sorcerer. "I can never escape. But now I need not be alone." Very carefully he placed the cowl of his cloak over his head so that his face vanished into shadow, and then with a flourish of his hand produced a quill from the air itself. "Tell me your story, Ik Numari. I long to hear it."

Sinbad looked to Ik Numari and saw that the elderly Scholar was attempting to back away, but that some supernatural force was compelling him to remain where he stood. His eyes kept flickering shut, seemingly involuntarily. "Please, Al-Izrikel," murmured the Scholar. "*Please...*"

"Tell me your story, Ik Numari," said Al-Izrikel, gently but firmly. He had begun to scratch the parchment of the book with the quill.

"I... I remember a beautiful day..." breathed the Scholar. Sinbad and the others watched in horrified fascination as Ik Numari's hands began to judder, the skin transforming to words, which in turn floated toward the open pages…

Sudden sounds of chaotic activity reached them from the archive area below. Amidst the shrieking Sinbad recognized Omar's distinctive baritone.

"Quickly!" cried Sinbad, unsheathing Grachene. "We have the information that we need and now our fellows need us!"

They descended into a battle. All around the Scholars were approaching the rest of Sinbad's crew and the Xubanthali with open books, their hoods full of nothing but shadow, quills poised, urging their victims to tell them stories that they might be rendered immortal. Several of the Xubanthali stood swaying, eyes shut, mouths murmuring, while their essences were transformed to words and sucked into the pages of the Scholars' books. Omar was efficiently organizing the crew of the Blue Nymph to help defend against the onslaught but the Scholars, possessed by magical forces the crew could not hope to understand, were proving harder to ward off than Omar had anticipated. He turned in relief to Sinbad and the others as they appeared.

"They means to suck out our souls, Cap'n!" he shouted, pushing back one of the Scholars with a well-aimed kick. "Such sorcery I have never seen afore!"

The Scholar, in response, let out a hideous, screeching noise and renewed its approach.

Around the archive the same phenomenon was occurring: Scholars, books proffered, quills quivering in anticipation, relentlessly stalking Sinbad's crew-mates and the wild-eyed Xubanthali islanders. Many had escaped their supernatural pursuers and headed for the chamber's exit and corridor beyond, but there were simply too many of the creatures for everyone to escape.

Gunarson swung his battleaxe at one of the approaching figures, the impact crumpling the creature and the blade continuing its momentum so it crashed haphazardly into a nearby bookshelf. Yet the Scholar's advance was only momentarily stalled. It hissed, then immediately re-coalesced into its previous humanoid shape before resuming its approach.

Gunarson unleashed his red cloak, whirling it at his would-be assailant in the interests of misdirection, then bringing his axe to bear a second time. The effect was the same as before, the Scholar only temporarily hindered, then continuing to advance on the Viking. Gunarson bellowed, "These creatures will not be thwarted by corporeal methods!"

"'Tis true," answered Delacrois, using a book shelf to leverage himself out of the path of two Scholars seemingly working in tandem. "This time only sorcery will demolish sorcery!"

Sinbad did not speak but he concurred with his shipmates' assessment of the situation. He turned to see Illia fighting off a cluster of Scholars bearing down on a group of terrified Xubanthali, some of which were already in the process of being transformed into words.

"Illia," he said, "we need your sorcery!"

"I'm doing my best, Captain Sinbad," she riposted. "Do not overestimate my powers; it is all I can do to hold off three or four at once..!"

Sinbad muttered a silent curse under his breath. The Arlegon seemed convinced that Illia's powers were considerable, yet the young woman herself did not believe this to be true. He called back to her, "What if you could amplify your power somehow?"

"Aye," she responded, aiming her beam at another of the approaching figures to protect Byrne, who had become transfixed. The Celt was woken by Tishimi, who thrust a sword into the dazed man's hands.

"But how, Sinbad?" Illia called, still desperately fighting off Scholars. "Tell me how we would magnify my powers."

Sinbad had been seized by a sudden notion. He could see Al-Bulcar struggling to pull a Xubanthali male from out of the path of a Scholar but his efforts were in vain: as he pulled at his arm it started to dissolve into words in his grasp, which then floated into the waiting pages of the Scholar's book.

Upon seeing Sinbad racing toward him Al-Bulcar shrieked, "I must protect my people... But the demons are too many!"

To Al-Bulcar's surprise Sinbad didn't respond but instead leapt for his neck, snatching at the piece of lens dangling from it. Sinbad ripped it away so that the string flailed in the air, then thrust the lens aloft and shouted at Illia, "Sorceress! Aim at this!"

Illia looked to him hesitantly, then grasped his intention. She wheeled gracefully about, channeling her two beams of light toward the lens, which immediately magnified and refracted them multiple times over, creating numerous, searing lances of light. From all across the library a terrible paean of shrieking went up as the Scholars' advances were abruptly halted.

"Tell everyone to make for the exit!" roared Sinbad, struggling to keep the lens static under the combined force of Illia's magical beams of light.

"Aye, brave Cap'n," responded Al-Bulcar. "But what of you and Illia?"

"Get everyone out!" urged Sinbad. "Get them to the ships!"

Al-Bulcar held his gaze momentarily, looking like he would continue to protest, but then evidently decided otherwise. He whirled around, shouting at the top of his voice and ushering all before him towards the chamber's exit.

Sinbad looked toward Illia. The young woman continued to hold up her hands, her whole body straining to maintain the projection of such phenomenal amounts of energy. Sinbad wondered how long she could keep up such a stance. Ultimately, though, such concerns proved not to be relevant. He felt a sudden wetness and pain in his hands and looked up to see the lens cracking under the pressure of the energy flow, the shards ripping apart his fingers. The lens abruptly shattered and the beams contracted back down to two single shafts, which vanished soon after. Sinbad turned back to see Illia collapsing forward, exhausted.

Sinbad ran to her, cradling the fallen woman in his arms.

They were trapped in an aisle between two mammoth book shelves that disappeared in shadow far above. All around, with no-one else to hunt, the Scholars bore down on them. Everyone apart from them had managed to get through the exit.

"We have to climb," Sinbad urged.

Illia nodded, her pale eyes glassy, and let Sinbad help her to her feet.

"Keep looking up," he said, as she placed a foot onto the book shelf and leveraged herself up.

Again she nodded, and continued upward. When she was far enough up Sinbad began his own ascent. At points a dazed Illia would accidentally grab at books, sending them tumbling downward so that Sinbad had to dodge to avoid them. He looked down to see the Scholars were following, seeming to see in their otherwise vacant hoods glimpses of leering, malformed faces. Taking his inspiration from Illia, Sinbad pulled at the nearest section of books and sent an entire shelf cascading down onto their pursuers. This time he didn't need to look down: the outraged shrieking that ensued suggested the tomes had found their target.

The shelves creaked and rocked as they climbed. Very quickly they found themselves in shadow, though it was some time more before they reached the top of the shelf and encountered the actual ceiling. Searching with his hands revealed the stepped, rough limestone interior, but no sign of a possible exit.

"Do you possess any more power?" he asked Illia urgently.

"No," she replied weakly, shaking her head. "I am not yet recovered. We need some other method through."

Sinbad nodded, "Aye." He could hear hissing and clambering. Their pursuers were near. "If we cannot go up then we must go sideways. You understand?"

"Yes, I think so," she said, her voice resigned.

"We must wait for an apposite moment," Sinbad said, casting his eyes down into the dark void below. "If we do not survive, then we must at least ensure we cause suitable damage that our friends can manage their escape."

"Of course," Illia said. "Sinbad…"

"Aye, fair maiden?"

Her eyes looked to him meaningfully. "Who is Ashanti? Back in the chamber, when the Scholars were writing your story, you kept talking about her, calling for her…"

Sinbad shook his head, "'Tis not the time."

"No," she said, "of course. I just wished to say something to you…"

"I do not think it is the time for that either," replied Sinbad, grinning.

"There will never be a time," she said, and suddenly reached forward, placing a tender, loving kiss on his surprised lips.

"Thank you," he said, gently pushing her away and holding her face in his hands. "Now we must run." And with this Sinbad began to rock on the shelf, the enormous edifice creaking with each backward and forward motion. Though he couldn't see her, Sinbad knew Illia was doing the same thing. They both knew from the loud scrabbling and hissing below them that their hunters were almost upon them, and that they were rising toward them in great numbers. Sinbad looked down to see movement in the shadow. A Scholar's hand reached up out of the darkness.

Then suddenly the momentum of the shelf was all in one direction and it was toppling to one side. Sinbad and Illia grabbed each others hands in the darkness and leapt, smashing into the next shelf as the original shelf collided with it and sent the next one toppling too. The domino effect continued across the library, as Sinbad and Illia sought to outpace the falling shelves against a cacophony of shattering wood and tumbling books. A final, explosive splintering was coupled with a tremendous cracking, and the pair found themselves freewheeling in space towards a fissure caused by the collapsing bookcases. Sinbad managed to grab hold of the crack, Illia swinging free below him, her hand clasped in his.

She looked up at him, imploring, her grasp slipping. "Let me fall," she urged. "Save yourself."

"Never," he said simply, and with one hand pulled himself hard against the crack so that it crumbled sufficiently to allow him to fall through, Illia following. They collapsed on the outside of the pyramid, atop one of the colossal limestone steps, into the morning air. All around them the wind whistled. Sinbad saw that the rising sun was moving exceptionally quickly, haphazardly whipping through space. And then he realized it was not the sun that was moving, but them.

"The Library is falling," Illia said, anticipating him. "Al-Izrikel must have disrupted the Scholars' sorcery when he began writing Ik Numari's story."

"Then we must get to the ships," said Sinbad quickly. "Afore it's too late."

They saw Omar standing beside the Blue Nymph, frantically scanning the pyramid for something, while the rest of the crew urged him to come aboard. The First Mate's palpable look of relief upon seeing Sinbad instantly explained what he had been looking for.

"Praise be to Allah!" exclaimed Omar, clapping his Captain on the back as Sinbad and Illia skittered toward the boarding plank. "We feared the worst!" His eyes played on Sinbad and Illia's clasped hands, and he raised a querulous eyebrow.

Sinbad and Illia followed Omar's gaze, then immediately detached themselves from one another.

"It was a close run thing, old friend," cried Sinbad, as he motioned for Illia to race up the plank to the Blue Nymph.

"Always said no good could come from book learnin'," muttered Omar, following his Captain up the swinging board.

"We're fallin', Cap'n!" yelled Byrne as Sinbad clambered onto the deck. "The sea will smash us t'pieces!"

"Where there's life there's hope," responded Sinbad. He was looking to the other two Xubanthali ships to see if their crews were also aboard. This looked to be the case, but he could see from the panic-stricken faces on deck that the Xubanthalis' usual measured nature had disappeared in the shadow of what looked to be sure and certain disaster. As they span through space, tethered to a gigantic, plummeting pyramid, he could hardly blame them. He hoped their faith in Xuba was as strong as his faith in Allah.

"I want the strongest men with knives and swords positioned by the ropes," cried Sinbad. "Everyone else, down below."

"Aye, Cap'n!" came Omar's reply, the First Mate having finished detaching the boarding plank.

...tethered to a...plummeting pyramid they fell...

"Signal to the other two ships to do the same," continued Sinbad. "Tell 'em to await my signal."

"Aye, Cap'n!" Omar turned on heel and began to shout instructions to the crew.

Sinbad lent over the side of the Blue Nymph in an effort to ascertain their velocity and position relative to the sea. Their descent was gaining momentum but by the grace of the Almighty, things could have been very much worse. Clearly the spell that kept the pyramid suspended in the sky was diminishing gradually, otherwise they would have plummeted like a stone and either been dashed to fragments or consigned to a watery grave beneath the surface. Sinbad surmised that Ik Numari was key to maintaining the sorcery that afforded the pyramid the ability to float. As his essence was transformed to words and imprisoned in the book by the vengeful Al-Izrikel, the spell was becoming less and less powerful. Once Ik Numari was completely consumed they would likely crash into the waves. He turned to Illia to confirm his assessment.

"Yes," she said, nodding. "We had best hope Al-Izrikel does not devour him too quickly, otherwise disaster will befall us."

Sinbad rapidly considered this, "If the spell fails, would you be able to halt our descent?"

She shook her head, almost laughing. "You overestimate my powers constantly, Sinbad. I cannot stop this colossal pyramid from falling into the sea. Such sorcery is well beyond my means."

"Not the pyramid," said Sinbad, gesturing. "But the ships; the Blue Nymph and the two Xubanthali vessels. Could you save us from being dashed into the sea? Could you slow our descent sufficiently to save us?"

"Even then," she responded, sighing. "The power it would require…"

"Even a few seconds might save us," said Sinbad, wheeling around without waiting for an answer. "Omar!" he yelled above the cacophony of the shrieking wind.

Omar turned around, his torn shirt billowing. Their velocity had clearly increased markedly – less heavy objects that hadn't been secured began to shoot into the air, disappearing into the ether. The Blue Nymph's sail rippled like an angry animal.

"Cap'n!" the Master responded.

Sinbad leapt nimbly forward, using the rigging to propel himself. He grabbed Omar by the shoulder and yelled into his ear, gesturing emphatically as he did so.

"When I give the signal cut the ropes!"

"Aye, Cap'n!"

"And make sure everyone secures themselves!"

"Aye!" Omar leant into him, eyes glinting. "Will this work, Cap'n?"

"Trust in Allah," replied Sinbad, clasping his old friend firmly on the shoulder.

Without another word Sinbad rushed back to Illia. He could see she had fashioned for herself a makeshift harness from some spare sections of rope. Reaching her side he gestured toward the harness, his meaning clear, and went to begin securing the rope more effectively. Illia, though, grabbed his hand with astonishing force, holding it firmly, indicating that she would attend to the matter himself. He nodded, at pains to hide his incredulity, then began wrapping his own hands and feet around portions of the exposed rigging.

The pyramid to which the three ships were tethered had begun to spin more rapidly so that the rising sun was only fleetingly visible before disappearing and rapidly reappearing. Sinbad turned to see the remainder of his crew and a few of the more muscular Xubanthali positioned by the ropes. Gunarson was among them, and he and Omar seemed to be the only ones not fighting back the nausea associated with the spinning. The ever increasing speed of their descent was now causing the looser timbers on the Blue Nymph to begin straining, and even a few of them to flip up and start flapping. Each of the men was struggling to stay in position, constantly buffeted by the momentous wind.

His face a grimace, Sinbad turned toward a sudden yelling. One of the Xubanthali men hadn't secured himself adequately and was clutching at the rigging, his massive body flailing up into the air. Before any of the others could detach themselves to go and help him the force of the wind took hold of the unfortunate, wrenching him away from the Blue Nymph and shrieking upward into the sky. The others watched in horror as the flailing figure dwindled from view, them immediately took to checking their own bonds.

Sinbad looked to Illia. Her sari hood flapped away from the upper portion of her face, revealing a brow furrowed in furious concentration, her delicate blue eyes suddenly intense and swirling. Her slender lips formed and reformed into a relentless succession of silent, indiscernible words. As the pyramid span Sinbad caught sight of the raging ocean below them, and he knew this was the time to act.

"Now!" he yelled, signaling emphatically to Omar.

Chapter Twelve

The crew's cutlasses and knives fell again and again, hacking away at the ropes until eventually all of the tethers were severed. Suddenly the Blue Nymph was on her own in the air, flying once more, her single indigo sail blooming, the mermaid on her prow piercing not the sea but the clouds. Sinbad whirled around to see the spinning pyramid behind them now, and saw too that the Xubanthali vessels were also free of its cloying embrace. The three ships soared with joy at their release, an extraordinary spectacle, like something out of legend.

Sinbad could see Illia, her head raised, brow still corrugated in furious concentration, eyes glowing, silent incantations on her lips. Flares of brilliant white energy and wisps of smoke had begun to emanate from her straining body. Sinbad struggled to see over the edge of the Blue Nymph, catching sight of the ocean roaring toward them. Illia was struggling to manage them into a controlled glide. Desperate for a better view, Sinbad fought to detach himself from his moorings. Eventually he succeeded in freeing himself and ran to the ship's side, the buffeting wind no longer coming up from below but along and across the ship. He could see the shadow of the ship falling across the roiling waves.

"Lift the prow!" he yelled to Illia, and she inclined her head ever so slightly in understanding, her face still rapt with concentration.

Sinbad gripped tight, bracing himself for the impact, looking to his fellow sailors and seeing that they were emulating him, their faces masks of astonished anticipation. All except Gunarson, who looked to Sinbad with a tremendous grin, his body rocking with thunderous, jubilant laughter. The Viking was clearly loving the experience.

And then the Blue Nymph hit the ocean, dipping down and creating a wall of water that cascaded over Sinbad, Illia and the rest of the crew, then roaring upward again. Sinbad, soaked with seawater, looked to their aft and saw not only the tumultuous white path they had left in their wake, but the other two Xubanthali craft accomplishing similar maneuvers. First one and then the other came crashing down onto the sea. Illia seemed to have learnt from her experience with the Blue Nymph and this time kept their noses held high, but even then the resulting walls of water were astonishing to witness.

Illia had slumped where she stood, kept upright only by the makeshift harness. Sinbad ran to her, releasing her from her bonds. A trail of blood was making its way down her face from her temple. He lowered her to the drenched deck, beckoning to Delacrois and Byrne to carry her below.

The crew of the Blue Nymph looked to one another in breathless disbelief, but Sinbad knew their difficulties were yet to end. Omar turned to him, a broad grin on his features.

"Today at least Allah watches over us!" cried the First Mate.

"Always!" agreed Sinbad, his gaze travelling past Omar to the sky above them and the tumbling pyramid. "Though we'd best not be premature in our celebrations. Look to the heavens!"

Omar turned and followed Sinbad's gaze, the grin suddenly frozen, eyes wide in horror.

"Heave ho, look lively!" bellowed Omar, swiftly gathering his wits. "To the oars with you, dammit! *To the oars!*"

Those above deck skittered to and fro in their efforts to oblige the First Mate while Sinbad took his position at the ship's wheel. Sinbad turned back, shielding his eyes against the ferocious morning sun, watching the silhouette of the spinning pyramid rapidly increasing in size. Judging by its velocity Ik Numari must have been almost entirely consumed. There was nothing preventing the edifice's rapid descent.

Sinbad turned his attention to the two other ships and saw approvingly that they had realized they were in the path of the gigantic, plummeting object. Unlike the Blue Nymph, neither of the ships possessed the ability to row as well as sail, so they would have to count on the wind to help power them out of the way in time. Sinbad could no longer call on the services of Illia to slow the pyramid's progress, that was clear. From his standpoint on the upper deck he could see her unconscious form being tended to by Tishimi and several of the Xubanthali women below deck.

By now he could hear Omar's beating of the drum, and the Blue Nymph began to plough energetically through the water. Craning behind him he saw the two other vessels were making good progress, though as usual they could not hope to match the pace of the Blue Nymph, especially with her oarsmen hard at work. It was enough for the Xubanthali ships to avoid being struck by the pyramid, but he doubted they would avoid the subsequent waves. Even the Blue Nymph, with her army of muscular, practiced rowers, would struggle to evade the coming onslaught.

In that moment he made a decision, and beckoned for Gunarson to take the ship's tiller. Sinbad skittered across the ship's floor, heading for the First Mate. He bellowed toward Omar, "Lower the sail! Oars on portside only, Master!"

Omar looked to Sinbad in confusion, "Cap'n?"

"Turn us about, Omar!" shouted Sinbad, his voice tinged with anger. Omar could evidently detect the determination in Sinbad's eyes and did not present any further obstruction, turning instead to the oar master and drummer and yelling Sinbad's instructions, before directing other of the crew to the lowering of the ship's sail.

The sky was suddenly black above them. The pyramid's scale was such that it had plunged a mammoth area of the sea below back into night-time. The sea around rose and curled, enormous white-tipped waves crashing in upon themselves, lifting the Blue Nymph and the other ships high into the sky before letting them drop. Sinbad knew the surrounding ocean's sudden tempestuous character to be the result of the pyramid's haphazard spinning.

Sinbad stood and watched the mammoth object hurtling toward them, unable to undertake any other action. He found himself wondering if it was Allah's will that the pyramid should smash him, his brave crew and the two Xubanthali ships to smithereens. Perhaps everything they had achieved thus far in their efforts to discover how the Warriors could be once again imprisoned was all for naught. Perhaps Allah *wanted* the stolen Xubanthali children to be fed to the Warriors of Forever so that these newly energized abominations could tyrannize the world. Perhaps there was some divine purpose to their impending destruction that he, as a mere mortal, could not fathom. Perhaps...

It was abruptly apparent, as the Library came close to finishing its downward descent, that all three ships would just about avoid being squashed by the monstrosity. Allah evidently did not want them destroyed after all. At least not yet, not this way. Moments later the Library smashed spectacularly into the sea in the portion of ocean the three ships had occupied mere minutes earlier, its collision sending an immense explosion of sea water high into the sky.

Just as Sinbad had anticipated, the Xubanthali ships' attempts to avoid the path of the pyramid were not sufficient for them to avoid the result of the pyramid's impact, which emanated outward in a colossal circular curtain of water. The Xubanthali ships were picked up and carried by an ever growing tidal wave which threatened to capsize both vessels.

The Blue Nymph had meanwhile turned in a dramatic arc and was heading toward the tidal wave. Those of the crew who remained on the upper deck looked incredulously to their Captain, wondering if his experiences with the Scholars of Bethshea had rendered him insane. Only Omar and Gunarson, the latter still controlling the ship's tiller, seemed to truly understand Sinbad's intentions.

Sinbad shouted back to Omar, "Now, all oarsmen together!"

"Aye, Cap'n!" came his First Mate's cry, and Sinbad heard him distantly relaying his instructions to the master oarsman and drummer.

The renewed attentions of both sets of oarsmen on port and starboard meant that the Blue Nymph leapt forward, rushing to meet its apparent doom.

"Through the middle of the ships!" yelled Sinbad, and Gunarson grunted his agreement, as he battled with the ship's tiller.

The vast wave bore down on the Blue Nymph, carrying the other two ships before it like trophies. Sinbad no longer looked to any of his crew, no longer heard the roaring of the sea, the shouts of his terrified crewmen or the relentless beating of the ship's drums. He remembered the first time he had seen the Blue Nymph, how he had recognized a kindred spirit in the eyes of the beautiful curving mermaid that emerged majestically from her prow. She was a baghlah, a large deep sea dhow, whose distinctive, sharp bow made her fast beyond compare. But the Blue Nymph was something more, changed beyond recognition by Sinbad and Omar's careful, loving ministrations. That first day in port Sinbad had understood her potential; and that she in her turn would allow him to fulfill *his* potential. In her Ethiopian teakwood he felt the energies of a lost love. Hence his insistence on the indigo sail.

Sinbad snapped back to the here and now as the Blue Nymph ploughed headlong into the tidal wave, the curtain of water parting fleetingly around it, then immediately engulfing it. But the Blue Nymph's unerring path had pierced the wave in its heart, breaking it asunder and causing the two sides to collapse it in upon themselves, their momentum not quite halted but at least dissipated. The two Xubanthali ships passed high above the Blue Nymph in the opposite direction, struggling to ride the wave's remnants into rumbling submission.

The Blue Nymph roared triumphantly out the other side of the tidal wave, battling smaller but still ferocious waves that struggled to keep up with its parents. Sinbad strained to perceive the pyramid through the sea spray, then caught sight of its massive form protruding from the water, waves crashing repeatedly against its hulk, desperate to drag the Library down. He saw the Library shifting position once, then twice, and then a third time before finally vanishing from view.

Sinbad struggled toward the lower deck through the knee-high water, as his shipmates raced to evacuate the upper deck using buckets and barrels and whatever they could lay their hands on. Locating Omar, he indicated that portside should cease their oaring and allow the ship to turn once more, before raising the sail once more. The First Mate nodded and communicated the Captain's instructions to the crew.

Understanding Sinbad's intentions, Gunarson forced the tiller hard to starboard, and the Blue Nymph turned once more in a tight arc. Ahead the two Xubanthali ships had just about recovered control of themselves, and the Blue Nymph raced to catch them.

Al-Bulcar sat back on his haunches, a look of satisfaction on his ruddy features, placing the needle and thread carefully on a piece of cloth at his side. Gunarson approached, wiping his enormous hands on a ragged cloth, grinning heartily.

"Good work," said the Viking, casting his eye over the patch the Xubanthali leader had sewn in the sail. "It must have ripped when we fell from the pyramid."

Al-Bulcar nodded, "Aye, most likely."

"You'd make someone a fine wife, I'd wager."

Al-Bulcar looked to him in surprise. "I apologize, mighty Gunarson," he responded, curling an eyebrow, "but I do not understand your reasoning."

Gunarson let out a low, ringing laugh. "In my land, such work is for women."

Al-Bulcar's confusion deepened. "The men do not repair their clothes?"

Gunarson held up his huge, calloused hands palm outwards for Al-Bulcar to see them. "Can you imagine sewing with such meat hooks?"

The Xubanthali lifted up his own podgy hands and examined them similarly. "My hands are no more delicate," he said reflectively.

"Yet you can sew," said Delacrois, who had appeared from the aft of the vessel, fishing rod slung across his shoulder. "'Tis a good thing, methinks."

"Is that so?" responded Gunarson, gesturing toward the sail. "Then pray tell me, why don't you assist our friend?"

"Mine are the hands of an artist," responded Delacrois, holding them up for Gunarson to regard, "and that of a lover." He laughingly transformed his hands to fists and sent a playful punch flying toward Gunarson, the Viking immediately responding by holding up one of his huge mitts. He easily deflected the blow.

This horseplay proved to be too much for Al-Bulcar, who had breathlessly pulled himself to his feet, simultaneously sweeping up the cloth and his needle and thread. "Forgive me, gentlemen, I must inform Captain Sinbad that my work is complete."

"Aye," nodded Gunarson, picking up a pouch of water from which he lustily drank, watching the Xubanthali leader scurry away. "You'd best keep your libido in check, Frenchie. A mountain stands 'tween you and your next kiss, methinks. You should have worked your magic with the Arlegon." He proffered the pouch to Delacrois.

Delacrois made a disgusted face as he accepted the water, "The Arlegon had their own magic. Witches are best avoided in my opinion."

Gunarson nodded toward Illia, who had resumed her place on the prow, sari once more wrapped around her, eyes obscured from view. "So you have no truck with our pet sorceress?"

Delacrois wiped water from his grizzled cheeks, "Even if I did, I think the Captain is entranced."

Gunarson followed his line of sight to Sinbad, who stood watching Illia impassively from the other end of the poop deck. "Aye, I think you might be correct in your judgment. When they made their escape from the dastardly Scholars they were holding hands, so says the First Mate."

"Omar? The man's as much a flibberty-gibbert as any old washerwoman," said the Frenchman with a wide smirk.

"Yet methinks he's right."

"Oui. But more importantly, what will you do with your share of the treasure?"

Gunarson looked surprised at the question. "Why, I will take it to my family vault."

Delacrois, in return, looked flabbergasted, "You'll lock it away? For your heirs, presumably?"

"For my heirs, yes," acknowledged Gunarson solemnly. "But for my ancestors too."

"Huh?"

"We must honor those that came before us, those that died in battle. The treasure is theirs as much as mine."

"Treasure?" rasped a familiar, low voice. "What treasure is that?"

"Mon ami. The treasure we seek," said Delacrois, turning to Omar. "The treasure that will be ours once we have defeated the Warriors."

Omar puffed his cheeks skeptically, "Aye, if you say so." He lent over and inspected Al-Bulcar's needlework, his eye roving the patch. "'Tis fine work," he observed, thrusting a podgy finger toward the sail.

"'Tis Al-Bulcar's work," responded Gunarson.

"Then we must cease our meaningless gabbing and do 'im tribute by getting it back into position," said Omar icily. "Aye, lads?"

"Aye," said Gunarson and Delacrois with mock weariness.

"I must offer you my apologies," said Sinbad, bowing his head.

"Your... *apologies*?" replied Rafi, his lined, pulsating hands rubbing the cloth of his sleeves distractedly. His attention, as before, was directed to the unfolding ocean.

Sinbad watched him intently. The fibrous lines crisscrossing the old man's skin had become denser since they had escaped the Library and throbbed more slowly but also more intensely. Unlike before, the blood vessels in his hooded eyes were also pronounced. "Al-Izrikel the Scarlet, or at least his memory, said he would maintain the map until we had reached our destination. But you were not with us, so I could not ask you your permission. I am sorry for that."

Rafi nodded, but his features had assumed a surprised disposition. "I assure you, Captain," said Rafi, his tongue delicately licking his lips, "there is nothing to apologize for."

"So you will take us to Mount Luicanus?"

"Aye, Cap'n," acknowledged Rafi. "As Allah is my judge, I shall do as I am bidden."

"Thank you, old friend," said Sinbad, squeezing Rafi on the shoulder. Rafi attempted something approaching a smile, but it seemed to Sinbad forced and unconvincing.

"That was quite a maneuver, Captain," said a fulsome, fruity voice beside Sinbad as he headed to the aft of the ship to relieve Byrne from his duties at the tiller.

Sinbad turned to see Al-Bulcar approaching. "Aye, 'twas the only option in the situation. And your people? Given their travails they seem in good spirits."

Al-Bulcar features became suddenly earnest, "'Tis true we have lost some of our number along the way, Captain, as you know. The ship, of course, that was consumed by the icy vortex. Others too, of course, in our encounters with the Arlegon and the Scholars. But we remain committed to our task, to the return of our children. And we know Xuba smiles down upon us, and that we must therefore smile up to Xuba."

"Good," nodded Sinbad. "That is how it should be. No matter what name you give your god."

Al-Bulcar nodded, his jowls quivering. "You believe we will be success-ful?"

"Successful," echoed Sinbad ruminatively. "Perhaps. Allah affords us the talent and the energy to complete the task, of that I have no doubt. If we afford him our faith we might receive courage in return."

Al-Bulcar licked his lips before saying carefully, "This, uh, *horn* of which the sorcerer Al-Izrikel spoke…"

"The Horn of Ostiah."

"Aye," said Al-Bulcar, forehead furrowing in remembrance. "It's just the woman who controlled the Warriors…"

"I remember what you told me," said Sinbad. "Not more than twenty years old and clad in gold jewelry."

"She wore a horn around her neck. Who knows what strange creature the object heralded from?"

Sinbad clasped Al-Bulcar suddenly by the shoulders. "Then that is it, my friend. That is the Horn of Ostiah. We must seek to retrieve it if we are to return the foul demons to their prison and rescue the stolen Xubanthali children."

"Aye, Cap'n," nodded Al-Bulcar, but his features looked momentarily confused. "The children. Of course."

Sinbad stared at him quizzically but their conversation was interrupted by cheering from elsewhere. The pair of them turned to see the freshly repaired sail flying once more.

As they ploughed ever onward the sky began to drain of all color. It remained like this for the subsequent two weeks, bleached to a bright, ethe-real white that became a translucent canopy at night, concealing the moon and stars along with it. Nor were there any sign of birds as one might or-dinarily expect to encounter, if only occasionally, on such a long journey. The sea, in its turn, became a dull gray, the waves crested only by white when the vessels cut through them and produced a wake. The few fish that they caught during this period were bland, tasteless creatures, even with the application of Delacrois' dried garlic or the many spices brought by the Xubanthali. The wind was similarly disconsolate, as though it could barely be bothered to blow. While it was sufficient to supply the Blue Nymph's sail without necessitating the use of the oars, Sinbad had decreed that each morning everyone should be compelled to row for an hour that they might exercise and ward off a creeping listlessness.

Indeed, the sky's continuing emptiness induced in Sinbad's people an ennui which affected even the most cheerful of crewmembers. It was the case that even the normally relentlessly upbeat Xubanthali were starved of their characteristic bonhomie, becoming downcast and even feeling unable to beat their drums when night-time fell.

"I almost long for a good old-fashioned storm," said Omar bitterly, and Sinbad flashed him a rueful look.

"This weather is unearthly," agreed the Captain, though his mind was elsewhere. His eyes had alighted on the figure of Tishimi. "Might I speak with you?" he asked, towering over her.

The woman inclined her head in agreement and the duo walked to a concealed position behind the rigging.

"This concerns Illia," Tishimi whispered.

"Aye," nodded Sinbad. "Is it that obvious?"

"Your eyes betray you. You have feelings for the woman."

"She intrigues me, it is true."

"It is more than that, I think, Sinbad san." Sinbad thought he could see a trace of a smile on her lips. "But in my judgment the Arlegon were correct in their assertion. She is powerful, more powerful than she shows."

"Yet when Al-Bulcar accidentally set himself alight she did not use her powers to assist him," said Sinbad.

"Perhaps she wishes to hide the extent of her sorcery," replied Tishimi thoughtfully.

"I do not believe that."

"Perhaps your feelings for her cloud your judgment," said the Japanese woman levelly.

"I believe there is another explanation," said Sinbad insistently. "Perhaps she is being controlled."

"By whom, Sinbad san?"

Sinbad did not have time to answer, as Haroun's familiar cry intervened before he could speak: "Land ahoy! Land ahoy!" exclaimed the boy from his perch atop the crow's nest.

Those of the crew not caught up with essential activities raced to the prow to get their own view. It was true. Reaching into the distance was a succession of black rocks that emerged like reaching fingers from the watery depths. Beyond these, faintly visible on the horizon, was a thin black line that peaked in the middle into a prominent hump.

"Mount Luicanus," whispered Delacrois in awe.

"Aye," said Gunarson.

Chapter Thirteen

"That's some mountain," declared Delacrois.

"It's not a mountain," responded a voice with quiet authority. The cluster of men turned to see Tishimi padding toward them. "It's a volcano."

"She's right," acknowledged Rafi, also approaching, his footsteps strangely buoyant, like those of a far younger man. "I can feel the volcano's power," he said delicately. "It speaks to me."

"And what does it say, mon ami?" inquired Delacrois, though his laughing tone sounded forced. The elderly man's curious appearance was such that it did not lend itself naturally to humor.

"It says 'I am hungry,'" replied Rafi, before smiling archly.

"But of course," responded Gunarson. "Odin likes to challenge us, and we like to accept his challenges."

"That's the spirit," said Al-Bulcar, patting the Viking affectionately on his enormous arm. Gunarson flashed him a scowl, and the portly Xubanthali swiftly removed his hand, uncertain as to whether the Viking was joking or not.

Sinbad looked to the worried faces of his crew. Their unease was palpable.

The Blue Nymph had deftly negotiated several of the finger-like rocks, the Xubanthali ships swinging themselves about the obstacles with less precision but nevertheless keeping good pace with the more maneuverable lead vessel. As a consequence the flotilla was much nearer the island now. From this vantage point it was possible to discern a good level of detail, aside from the vast and foreboding volcano, which was cast in silhouette by the bright white sky. Though the terrain immediately surrounding the volcano seemed formed of the same jet black rock, foliage was evident on the escarpments leading up to it. These in turn spread into more densely populated forests that led to the winding gray beaches marking the outskirts of the island.

"Ships," said Sinbad, his eyes narrowing. "Over there."

The others followed the Captain's train of sight. The nearest discernible vessel bobbing in the bay was of a design none of them had ever seen before. Its timber was translucent white and glistened in the watery sunlight, its collection of tattered off-white sails billowing fitfully in the inconstant breeze. This, Sinbad realized, must be the ship of bone described by Al-Bulcar. "Aye, 'tis them," confirmed Al-Bulcar woodenly, his bulbous, fear-filled eyes playing on the white ship. "The devil's soldiers."

Other more conventional designs, seemingly drawn from across the globe, floated beyond the nearer vessel: a much lower slung ship that looked to be a modified dhow, the Viking long boat Al-Bulcar had mentioned, and assorted freighters and battleships.

"Take us around," instructed Sinbad quickly and urgently to Omar. "Find some cover."

"The rocks," suggested Gunarson.

"Aye, but try not to ground us," added Delacrois.

Omar flashed the Gaul a withering glance before erupting into life, "Hard to port! *Now!*" The crew scattered in response.

Sinbad found himself standing next to Illia. "Can you sense anything?" he asked gently.

"The same thing we can all sense," she said simply. "The Warriors are here. Waiting for us."

Sinbad turned away from her to see the island moving away from them as Omar tacked course, back toward the cover of the largest black finger of rock. "Good," he responded.

The sand shifted beneath his feet as they strode through the water. Sinbad could feel Grachene at his side, pulsing, as though his magical blade somehow sensed what was waiting for them. The procession from the Blue Nymph gradually merged with processions from the other two vessels. Though few of the Xubanthali were capable, let alone *adept,* at fighting he had taken the decision to disembark everyone on the basis that sheer weight of numbers might ultimately prove crucial in the inevitable battle that was to come. Besides, the Xubanthali had travelled with them to help rescue their children from the Warriors. How could he possibly deny them the opportunity to play their role in recovering their offspring, or indeed in exacting revenge on the perfidious creatures who had stolen them?

So it was the ragbag collection of seasoned adventurers and blinking, uncertain Xubanthali advanced onto the gray sand of the beach, cutlasses, knives and clubs at the ready. Sinbad had already briefed his crew members, and each of them indicated for groups of Xubanthali to join with them. By attaching one of his trusted crew as leader to each group of Xubanthali, Sinbad hoped to maintain some semblance of strategy in their advance. Unfortunately a single sound very rapidly demolished that intent.

It was the noise of a child laughing.

Sinbad saw the Xubanthali looking to one another in amazement, and then watched as that amazement transformed to expressions of grim determination.

"Our children!" exclaimed one of the men.

"Up there!" cried another, pointing towards a gap in the rocks at the summit of a low, sandy escarpment.

Swathes of the Xubanthali broke forward, awkwardly heading up the slope for the gap. Sinbad lifted his hands to halt their advance. "If you do this, you will endanger your chances of rescuing your children," he said warningly.

"We want our kith and kin, Sinbad," responded a middle-aged Xubanthali woman. "Let us take them and you can take the treasure."

"We must listen to Captain Sinbad," said Al-Bulcar hurriedly, stepping forward. "We have travelled so far. By Xuba, do not let our impetuosity get the better of us, do not let us fail at this final hurdle..!"

"No," snapped one of the men. "We have been patient thus far, Al-Bulcar, but no longer. Xuba is with us and we will have victory!"

And with this the Xubanthali men and women began pushing past Sinbad and into the gap in the rocks.

"Should we stop them?" asked Gunarson, as droves of Xubanthali rushed past him.

Sinbad shook his head, "Fighting amongst ourselves will solve nothing." Grachene was in his hand and he looked to his own people. "Do what you can!" he said, joining the throng as they entered the gap.

They flowed with the Xubanthali along the high-walled fissure in the rocks, eventually emerging into a clearing surrounded by more vaunting, rocky walls. In the centre of the clearing was a foul-smelling swamp of black liquid, from which sprang occasional stubby reeds. Of the child who had laughed, there was no sign. The Xubanthali looked to each other uncertainly.

"This isn't good," whispered Delacrois.

"No," replied Sinbad, his eyes fixed on the swamp. As they watched, a bubble slowly began to form on its otherwise inert surface, its gradual appearance accompanied by a distinctive, long squelch. Another bubble appeared elsewhere on the swamp, also accompanied by the squelching noise. More rose up and settled, rapidly now, so that the entire surface was covered in them, and the air was full of what sounded like flatulence. Appropriately enough, a horrendous stench began to reach the noses of Sinbad's crew and that of the Xubanthali, causing them to recoil in disgust.

"Is that you, Gunarson?" joked Delacrois uncertainly, but no-one laughed.

In the moments that followed silence reigned. Then Sinbad's acute eyesight alighted on something within one of the bubbles trying to break through. The skin of the swamp in this confined area sank marginally, before the tip of a finger, a skeletal finger, began to emerge. The finger rapidly transformed into a skeletal hand, just as another hand began to break through. All across the swamp, skulls and hands and arms were pushing their way through, until leering skeletal forms started to appear, like some hideous, ghoulish mimicry of childbirth. Weapons were appearing now as well: some carried shields, sabers, pikes, while others sported ferocious-looking clubs with spikes and nets. A few carried extraordinary, lethal-looking weapons that neither Sinbad nor any of his crew recognized.

The Warriors of Forever had risen.

"We must go back," said Al-Bulcar in choking horror.

"Too late," said Sinbad simply. "We cannot turn our backs on them. We must stay and fight. Besides, this was always our intent, was it not?" He raised the volume of his voice, "Prepare yourselves for battle!"

The Xubanthali looked to one another in terror, some nodding wordlessly. A couple spontaneously bolted for the gap in the rocks, pushing and pulling past their compatriots in their efforts to escape. One of the Warriors, who like his comrades had until now remained stock still, sprang into life, launching two blades that soared through the air before smacking into the two escapees. The duo fell immediately and without a noise, the blades protruding from between their shoulder blades. The jaw of the Warrior who had killed them swung open, and a rattling laughter emerged from the depths of its undead body.

"We want the children," declared Sinbad. "Give the off-spring of these people back to them and we will leave you in peace!"

At this the rest of the Warriors also began to laugh, the soldiers turning to each other and guffawing, their jaws clacking together hysterically. A Warrior clad in the remnants of what looked to Sinbad like Samurai armor, lifted his hands and the laughter gradually diminished. Unlike the others, his eyes were not empty sockets, but contained glittering rubies.

"We must stay and fight."

"Foolish mortal," hissed the leader. "Even now you do not understand…"

Gunarson and Delacrois exchanged concerned glances, as did the rest of Sinbad's crew and the Xubanthali. Sinbad's gaze, though, remained steadfast.

"Return the children to us," he said quietly. "*Now.*"

The lead Warrior pulled a mammoth Samurai sword from its belt. "You must be shown the error of your ways," he intoned, lifting the sword upward in the pose of a traditional Samurai attack.

Grachene was in Sinbad's hand, and he stood ready to repel the attack. The Samurai Warrior let out a war cry but then wheeled about, bringing the blade up and down at the same time, so that it removed the arm of a Xubanthali male. The man in question reeled but did not collapse, instead looking incredulously to the ground where his limb had fallen. He seemed oddly unmoved by the injury.

Now the air was a flash of blades, nets and clubs as the Warriors attacked. Their attentions, though, were directed not at Sinbad's crew but at the Xubanthali. Some of the Xubanthali repelled the attack with gusto, uttering what they estimated to be war cries, throwing themselves into the midst of the Warriors, thrusting, swinging and flinging their weapons. The Warriors met such courage with gleeful shrieks, parrying each and every thrust, gouge and slice, pressing home their cackling, enthusiastic attack.

Some of the Xubanthali fell back, screaming in horror, trying to hide behind Sinbad's crew, but such a cowardly strategy was equally doomed to failure, the Warriors hunting them out and eviscerating them, despite the best efforts of Sinbad's crew to fight the Warriors off. Still more Xubanthali dropped back but lifted their weapons in an attempt to defend themselves and gain valuable time, perhaps hoping that Sinbad's crew would come to their aid, or that the Warrior in question would demonstrate some hitherto unnoticed weakness. Inevitably, such encounters tended to result in the Xubanthali being hacked to pieces by the snarling undead monsters.

In stark, baffling comparison, Sinbad and his crew found the Warriors would barely engage them in battle unless forced to do so. Sinbad launched himself at the lead Warrior, the one dressed in Samurai armor, aiming to plunge Grachene into its neck. The Warrior, though, was attacking a pair of quivering Xubanthali men, and seemed angry at Sinbad's intervention, thrusting him back with his shield as he continued to assault the men with his blade.

"Our quarrel is not with you!" hissed the Samurai Warrior.

Sinbad turned to see Gunarson experiencing similar problems attracting the attentions of another Warrior. "Fight *me*, cursed creature!" yelled the Viking, struggling to engage an undead soldier in battle, the Warrior more concerned with its attack on a disarmed Xubanthali man who had fallen to his knees and was raising his clasped hands in mercy.

Elsewhere on the battlefield, others of Sinbad's crew, including Tishimi, Byrne and Omar, were also vainly trying to fight with the Warriors, but with little success. Sinbad caught sight of Illia, who stood watching, her face obscured by the sari hood as usual, but her mouth forming soundless words and noises.

Though the Warriors were attacking the Xubanthali, not a single one lay dead. Like the one the Samurai Warrior had earlier relieved of his arm, those with severed limbs or horrendous gashes that would ordinarily have proven fatal to any mortal, continued to move, weirdly unaffected. There was also, he realized, no blood, no sign of injury, none of the horror of the battlefield. Sinbad realized that the noise, too, was quite unlike any battlefield he'd ever encountered. Though the air rang with the clashing of blades against shields and reverberated with the noises of hacking and slashing, there were no screams of pain, none of the moans that ordinarily accompanied the dying.

Abandoning his attempt at engaging the Samurai Warrior in battle, Sinbad grabbed hold of a Xubanthali whose neck had been cut in a manner that would ordinarily have proven lethal. The Xubanthali stared at him in surprise, as Sinbad reached out a hand to the wound, and plunged his fingers in.

When he pulled his hand away, he was clutching at straws.

Sinbad whirled around, looking for another Xubanthali. This time he saw one staggering with an arm missing at the elbow, which Sinbad grabbed at. The Xubanthali stared at him in incomprehension. Where there should have been severed flesh and bone, there was instead straw, and the creature's skin was formed from some kind of weave.

Sinbad realized, with a start, what it meant. The Xubanthali could not die because they were not alive. They were never alive. People-size dolls, given animation and rendered lifelike by some sorcery unknown.

"You," whispered Sinbad, rounding on Illia, the woman still muttering her noiseless incantation. "What are you?" He grabbed her by the arm, Grachene in his hand, the tip poised at her neck. It would be easy to cut her, to discover if she was the same, a creature of straw and fabric given life by devilish magic.

"I'm real," she murmured. "I'm human. *Please.*"

"If you're human," he continued, Grachene still at her neck, "then you're controlling them. Yes?"

"No," said another voice, one he did not recognize. He turned to see a beautiful young woman approaching, her single eye studying him intently, the other masked by a leather patch, her exposed flesh bedecked with complex tattoos. "I control the Warriors." He noticed the horn strung around her neck by a length of twine. He saw, too, that the Warriors ceased their fighting as she passed by them, so that the battle gradually subsided to an eerie stillness.

"Who are you?" Sinbad asked, stepping away from Illia and lowering the knife.

"Does it matter who I am?" she responded tartly, smirking. "Aren't my actions altogether more important?"

"You should be wary of my actions, little waif!" yelled Gunarson from behind as he went to grab her. His intention was halted, though, by the intervention of two of the Warriors, who pulled him back and flung him to the ground. The look of fury on Gunarson's face was matched only by his incredulity at their ability to best him.

The young woman didn't turn around. "Foolish Viking. My Warriors will do everything to protect their Queen Asentua, I assure you. And as you have experienced, they are very, very powerful indeed."

"But not quite powerful enough," said Sinbad, viewing her levelly.

The young woman placed a hand on his exposed chest where his shirt had fallen open, pressing her slender fingers against it, smiling coquettishly. "Power isn't everything," said Asentua, licking her lips. "Sometimes other skills are required."

"You control the Warriors," said Sinbad, grabbing her by the wrist and pulling her hand away. "And the Xubanthali. Why?"

Asentua extricated her hand from his grasp with a sneer. "The Xubanthali are mere puppets."

Sinbad glowered, "To what end? Why have you manipulated these poor creatures? They think they are mortals, formed from flesh and blood like you and are. You have planted memories of lives in their minds, of children being stolen. To what end?"

"To what end?" Asentua said in surprise. "Have you still not guessed? I thought the clever, wily Sinbad El Ari would have divined my scheme by now. Isn't it obvious? I created and manipulated the Xubanthali in order to bring you and your crew here, to Mount Luicanus."

"I understand that," said Sinbad in measured tones, controlling his composure. "You manipulated the Xubanthali into thinking their children had been taken in order to manipulate me and my crew into coming here. But

I say again to you, woman, *why*?"

Asentua chuckled. "I'm not going to tell you, Sinbad El Ari. I'm going to make you wait." She turned abruptly to address the Warriors, who stood awaiting her word. "Take them, bind their hands."

The Warriors acted immediately, grabbing Sinbad's crew roughly by their wrists and proceeding to expertly clamp them with manacles strung from their belts. The Xubanthali puppets, their role in Asentua's scheme evidently at an end, huddled into small groups, some gazing into the middle distance, others examining their wounds, looks of perplexity etched into their faces. Sinbad reflected grimly that if they were real people they would have been howling with pain, or sobbing, perhaps even praying for their god. Any or all of those things would have been preferable to their looks of silent incomprehension. Recalling their deity Xuba made him think of Al-Bulcar, and he wondered where their leader had disappeared to, as he could not see his sizeable frame anywhere in the vicinity.

"And where do you purpose to take us, foul witch?" snapped Delacrois, as his hands were clamped together.

Asentua evinced a look of surprise, "Why, to the volcano, of course."

Handcuffed, Sinbad and his crew trudged up a winding path towards the summit of Mount Luicanus. Asentua strode at the head of the group, head held high, seemingly triumphant. The higher the group went the more the air filled with motes of dust that whorled in their wake. An unmistakable smell of burning reached their nostrils and their throats, making them want to retch. The Warriors pulled them along, occasionally clattering their jaws enthusiastically.

"What do they mean to do to us?" Haroun had voiced the question everyone else was thinking.

"Cook our goose, laddie," responded Byrne gruffly. The temperature rose in tandem with their climb, and the Celt's cheeks were flushed as a result.

"Only if we let 'em," added Delacrois. This evoked a hissing noise from the Warrior nearest to him, who reached over and gently, but firmly, butted his exposed skull up against the Frenchman's. Delacrois responded in kind, letting out his own, Gallic version of the hiss, and pushing his own forehead forcibly back against the monster's.

"Enough," instructed Sinbad, who was walking behind them in the procession and had witnessed the exchange. Foliage had become gradually sparser as they continued upward, and by now their path had narrowed considerably as they wound their way around the higher portions of the volcano. The heat had become intense, and each member of Sinbad's crew was drenched with sweat. Tishimi had even managed to produce a fan from about her person in an effort to retain her composure. Haroun stumbled, and the mighty Gunarson reached down to help him upright. Other members of the crew looked longingly to the cool of the gray sea, and wistfully to the sight of the Blue Nymph, which was fleetingly visible as they continued their winding climb.

Asentua whirled excitedly around as the first members of the procession reached the summit. The Warriors seemed to understand their role in this without being explicitly instructed, and motioned and pulled their captives into place all around the mouth of the volcano. Sinbad, like his fellows, peered down into the depths.

Far below them, bubbling hungrily, was a lake of continually shifting lava. Erratic gushes of molten liquid erupted upward and then fell back down, throwing up flames and plumes of gray-black smoke. The heat was so intense it almost bowled them over. Fascinating though the spectacle was, Sinbad forced himself to assess the state of his crew. Most looked terrified. Some, like Gunarson and Omar, looked resolute. Delacrois, as usual, looked mirthful, as if he somehow understood life to be a joke and presumably death to be the punch-line.

"Brave adventurers," announced Asentua abruptly, marching up and down the ranks as though they were as much a part of her army as the undead creatures that had driven them up here. "Your journey has been arduous. I can only apologize."

"Why these nonsensical lies?" demanded Gunarson. "Why did you not simply capture us in the first place and bring us here?"

The young woman bowed her head with what seemed to Sinbad like synthetic sorrow, "I understand your fury. You would have preferred it if the Warriors had brought you to this place clapped in irons."

"We would never have allowed such a thing," riposted Gunarson. "We would rather have died."

"Exactly!" exclaimed Asentua. "So I concocted a strategy that would bring you to Mount Luicanus willingly, never suspecting a trap."

"Then, madam, your scheme has failed already," mocked Delacrois. He held forth his handcuffs, "For you will find us far from willing."

"We shall see," replied Asentua, smiling archly.

"Explain yourself, damnable woman," rumbled Gunarson.

"Dear Viking. I will explain myself in due course," said Asentua, a trace of impatience flashing in her single eye. "Trust me. There was no other way. You are good and true people. Fearless, as well. I knew if I gave you a suitable mission that you would seek to accomplish it, that no manner of hardship or danger would prevent you. All that was required were suitable goals."

"The rescue of the children," said Sinbad quietly. "But there were none."

"I'm sorry, but yes, the children were a fiction. How could they be anything other, given that the Xubanthali are nothing but straw and cloth?" Asentua smiled. Her eyes played on Gunarson and Delacrois. "Of course, I knew the possibility of treasure might appeal to some of your number, but I also understand too that you, Sinbad, would require something altogether more... *virtuous*. And so I concocted a story about lost children."

"The Xubanthali are your puppets," said Sinbad. "You lied to them, created a world of illusion. Their island, their lives. All a lie."

"The island exists, you visited it yourselves," said Asentua, a touch reproachfully. "But you're right. I contrived my first puppet, Al-Bulcar, from straw and cloth and careful stitching. In fact, I probably used too much straw and cloth on that first poor creature if I am honest. Then I gifted him animation and got him to make another puppet. And so on, until we had populated the island."

"Ingenious," offered Delacrois.

"Thank you. I think so. The spell of animation is such an easy one. Creating their lives, stitching memories and experiences into their brains, that was much more complicated. And the effort of controlling them subsequently, well that was exhausting... But it worked, and here we are."

"You are Xuba," observed Rafi.

"Yes, I suppose I am," said Asentua, turning toward the aged sailor. "To all intents and purposes. How clever of you to observe that, old man."

Rafi hissed at her, the striations on his body pulsating angrily, "You have played god. Allah will punish you."

Asentua nodded, regarding his glowing physique with amusement. "Wise old Rafi. Are you enjoying the power the Arlegon Witches awarded you? None of your crewmates realize quite how much you get pleasure from it, do they now, eh? No wonder you don't want to give it up."

Rafi lowered his head, his forehead knitting together in shame.

"You are a lie, Queen Asentua," said Tishimi quietly. "You do not possess the powers of sorcery you speak of. They are borrowed."

"Hush, Tishimi," said Asentua, rounding on her. She lifted a finger to her lips. "*Hush.*"

"Why have you brought us here?" demanded Omar. "To kill us?"

Asentua cast her hand toward the mouth of the volcano. "Quite the contrary. Mount Luicanus is the giver of life. It is the means by which the Warriors became immortal. They came here thousands of years ago, from all across the world, intent on becoming eternal soldiers. But they knew that to achieve that they must throw themselves, freely and gladly, into its waiting maw." She gestured towards the skeletal Warriors. "So they did. And they received their eternal life."

"Eternal war," intoned Tishimi, looking pointedly from one decaying corpse to another. "Eternal horror."

Now Asentua moved down the line to tower over the small Japanese woman. "Tishimi," said Asentua slowly. "You sense something, don't you?" She reached out and grasped Tishimi tightly by the chin, thrusting her head upright to expose her throat. Asentua ran her slender fingers down her gullet. "Be careful, my beauty. I might have to cut that delicate throat of yours."

"I say again, yours is borrowed power," said Tishimi, her words gurgled.

"You're using Illia," hissed Sinbad.

Asentua looked to him in surprise, letting go Tishimi. "What's that, Captain?"

"You're using Illia," repeated Sinbad. "Release her." He had stepped forward and a nearby Warrior struggled to push him back into line. Asentua waved her hand, and the Warrior stopped in its attempts to manhandle Sinbad.

Illia stood, her head bowed, face hidden. Again her mouth moved in silent incantation.

"She is a conduit," said Asentua delicately. "To a far greater power even she cannot conceive."

"You did the same to her as you did to the Xubanthali. You used that power to contrive her entire world, her life," snapped Sinbad angrily. "Nothing she knows is true."

"She has played her part," responded Asentua icily, "as have you. Now she will receive her reward." Asentua motioned toward two of the Warriors, who grabbed Illia by the arms. She presented no opposition as the Warriors led her stumbling toward the lip of the volcano…

Chapter fourteen

"Hold!" snarled Sinbad. "Hold, I say!"

The Warriors held Illia between them, forcing her to teeter on the edge of the volcano, their jaws clacking in lustful anticipation.

"Hold!" bellowed Sinbad.

Asentua's eyes flashed and she motioned curtly toward the two Warriors. They stepped back from the edge, pulling Illia with them, their disappointment palpable.

Asentua wheeled around to face Sinbad. "Speak," she commanded.

"She has been your pawn," said Sinbad through gritted teeth. "Enough. If you require a sacrifice, let it be me."

Asentua smiled. "If you give of yourself willingly, you will become like them. You will become a Warrior of Forever."

"I understand that."

"I am honor bound to you, Sinbad, as my Captain, as my leader, and as my friend," intoned Gunarson. "If you step into the volcano I will surely follow."

"I will do similar," said Rafi, his head still bowed, the striations on his body pulsating with each word.

"Ach, me too," said Byrne. Others signaled their fealty to their Captain in similar fashion.

"Really?" Delacrois looked to the others, perplexed, before a look of pained resignation creased his features. "I mean *oui*, yes of course."

Asentua regarded Sinbad and his crew with something that might have been admiration. "Very well. Sinbad El Ari will go first, and then his crew."

Tishimi suddenly broke away from her captor to approach her Captain. "Sinbad san, this is what Asentua desires," she whispered urgently. "This is why we were brought to this place. To give ourselves *willingly* so that she might have an army of intelligence, capable of strategy…"

"Rather than these brain-dead zombies," said Sinbad, casting his glance to the Warriors surrounding them.

"Yes, Sinbad san," urged Tishimi. "The volcano grants immortality but only if you give of yourself freely. Yet think of what immortality really means, what it does to the mind and body. The Warriors of Forever are *imbeciles*, an army incapable of strategy, of guile, of anything other than brute force. Life everlasting has turned them to fools."

"You are correct, Tishimi," called Asentua, smiling. "But that process takes thousands of years. Sinbad and his crew will retain their keen intellects for many centuries, believe me. Enough until I need to replace them once more."

Tishimi did not look to Asentua, but continued gazing up at her Captain. "If you do this, you will give her what she wants. You will doom the world to the tyranny of an undead army led by *you*, Sinbad!"

Sinbad sighed, "Dear Tishimi. I understand. But believe me, I cannot hesitate. Not this time. I hesitated once before and it cost me the woman I love. I will not do that again."

At this Illia looked up to him, tears apparent in her pale eyes.

Tishimi nodded, bowing her head. "All is not what it seems," she said, *sotto voce*, as the Warriors dragged her back into line.

"I understand that too," whispered Sinbad. He turned and addressed his crew, his voice characteristically resolute. "What I do now I do freely, and without regret. I know you, brave adventurers, will follow suit and for that I thank you from the furthermost reaches of my heart."

"Aye, Cap'n," said first Gunarson and then Omar, and then quickly the others chorused their agreement.

"Release his bonds," said Asentua.

"Aye, Your Majesty," clacked one of the undead Warriors, pulling a key on a chain from the midst of its rusting armor. He proceeded to unlock the cuffs binding Sinbad's hands.

Sinbad turned, his face a mask of grim determination, and began a steadfast walk towards the lip of the volcano. He could feel the heat, already ferocious, beginning to singe the hairs of his beard and arms. In a moment he stood on the very cusp of the volcano, head bowed, staring into the bubbling, crackling depths. He closed his eyes and issued a small prayer to Allah.

And then Sinbad jumped, not forward but instead executing a graceful back-flip, so that he landed expertly beside Asentua. The young woman looked at him incredulously, but before she or any of the Warriors could react he grabbed at the horn around her neck and ripped it away.

Asentua grasped at him but Sinbad was again too nimble for her, lithely jumping backwards. He lifted the Horn of Ostiah to his pursed lips and blew, producing a low, sonorous note. All around the Warriors lifted their skeletal hands to their heads, some collapsing to their knees, all of them in apparent agony. Sinbad continued to sound the note, his lungs rapidly emptying, until finally he could blow no more. He pulled the horn from his lips, and stood gasping.

For a moment all was still, the only noise the bubbling of the volcano and the distant lapping of the waves. But then the laughing began. It was the same noise as before only more intense, more hysterical. A horrible clacking noise that began with one Warrior but quickly spread. Those that had dropped to the ground suddenly rose, looking jubilantly to their comrades-in-arms. Amidst it all, unmistakable, was the sound of a young woman laughing too, and Sinbad turned to see Queen Asentua shaking with mirth.

"Impressive," she said delightedly, "if misguided in the extreme."

And in that second Sinbad realized his mistake. Grachene seemed to know, too, for it was in his hand, and in a fluid movement flying from his grasp. Asentua's smiling face became suddenly fixed, and she reached a tentative, fluttering hand to her good eye, to find the blade embedded there. A gurgle emerged from her lips, her ability to form words suddenly stolen from her.

Then a look of determination crossed her face and she defiantly began to pull at the knife. But Grachene was stubborn, and seemed determined not to be extracted easily. She pulled and pulled at the blade, in the process ripping herself still further. Abruptly it was free and she held it up in triumph. But her good eye dangled from her face, little more than a colored, ornately crafted glass bead, attached by a series of threads.

Asentua staggered where she stood, still gurgling furiously. Sinbad darted forward, extracting Grachene from the Queen's quivering grasp. He thrust at her with the blade, ripping a long jagged hole down the length of her body, the torn fabric of her fake skin exposing a chest full of straw. There was no evidence of blood or tissue or bone. She was as much a puppet as the Xubanthali, animated by direst sorcery. In fury Sinbad tore and tore at the body until she was little more than ripped cloth, threads, buttons and straw. Even then the straw dolly continued to move. Sinbad staggered back, wiping the sweat from his brow, when he heard a nearby sound.

The Samurai Warrior was upon him now, whirling its sword so that Sinbad was forced to parry. As he forced his assailant back, Sinbad caught sight of Gunarson, hands still clasped together, crashing into a whole group of the Warriors. The other members of the crew immediately launched themselves onto the fallen, flailing Warriors, struggling to extract keys and release each other. Gunarson meanwhile launched himself into more of the Warriors, sending three of them stumbling headlong over the lip of the volcano and into its fiery depths, their screeching cries audible even above the cacophony of battle.

Delacrois had extracted a set of keys and struggled to release himself, heaving a kick at an advancing Warrior that sent him tumbling into a group of his comrades. The cuffs clicked open and the Gaul pulled his bow and arrows from across his back, launching arrow after arrow into the midst of the Warriors, the impact removing limbs or sending Warriors wheeling backward into the volcano. Delacrois shouted to Haroun, who snatched the set of keys up from where they had fallen amidst the rocks and rapidly released himself before setting about helping his fellows shed their bonds.

Tishimi, her wrists still bound, saw that a group of Warriors had evidently singled out Gunarson as one of the main threats to be dealt with and had set about harrying him with blades and axes. She launched herself at the rear of one of the Warriors clutching a cudgel, pulling the handcuffs up and over its throat and wrenching backwards to garrote him. The Warrior staggered with her sudden weight but quickly regained its focus, bucking in an effort to remove her. Tishimi, though, was dogged, tightening and tightening her grip. Suddenly the Warrior's head popped from his body, and Tishimi elegantly slid down his back.

Elsewhere Haroun was backing away from a snarling Warrior who for some reason seemed particularly interested in dispatching him, presumably because he'd succeeded in releasing so many of the Blue Nymph's crew from their cuffs. Haroun staggered backward, landing awkwardly, his blade falling from his grasp. As the triumphant Warrior advanced, the young man's eyes widened in amazement as they caught sight of the extraordinary scimitar the monster clutched, and its distinctive ebony handle...

Gunarson barreled into the remaining Warriors, sending them flying in different directions. He arrived, breathlessly, in front of Delacrois, and the Frenchman obligingly released the Viking. Gunarson instantaneously brought about his broadsword, severing the head of the nearest Warrior, while Delacrois launched a swift volley of arrows that each found targets in the chests of their ghoulish adversaries.

The Samurai Warrior had meanwhile fought Sinbad back toward the mouth of the volcano, continuing a relentless barrage of blows. Sinbad stood, his heels over the edge, no room available in front of him. The Samurai, his skull face leering in anticipation, lifted his sword for the final, decisive blow. As the blade sliced through the air Sinbad danced to one side and the Samurai pitched forward, a surprised shriek emanating from its rattling maw, its body flailing uselessly into the fiery depths of Mount Luicanus.

The battle raging around, Haroun continued backing away from the figure with the distinctive scimitar.

"Father?" he croaked, and the figure stopped in its tracks, his blade poised to deliver the killing blow.

"Haroun," came a noise from deep within the skeletal figure, like the roaring of the wind.

The creature's delay was enough for Delacrois to launch an arrow which sent the figure wheeling around. The Frenchman leapt forward, helping the dust-covered Haroun to his feet.

"No," muttered Haroun, tears weaving down his face, "it was my father... *My father!*"

Sinbad pushed his way through the melee, intent on finding one person. She stood stock still in the midst of the battle, head lowered.

"It's over," he said as he approached. "You're stuck with your army of fools. Though they might live forever, these soldiers are simpletons."

"You are the fool, Sinbad," replied Illia, not lifting her head. "You could have been my eternal General. You and your crew could have travelled the seas forever, adventuring, conquering. The treasures of the world would have been yours in perpetuity. All you had to do was sacrifice yourself willingly." She cocked her head to one side, still bowing. "You could have been my eternal *lover*, Sinbad El Ari."

"You knew my feelings for you," said Sinbad quietly. "That's why you continued the charade with Queen Asentua."

She inclined her head ever so slightly in agreement, "It is true. For my plan to work I needed a villain, and for that role I chose Asentua." He heard a sigh hiss from her body. "And I needed you to believe I was the victim, that you might sacrifice yourself for me."

"Then I tell you it's over," repeated Sinbad. "Without someone of intelligence to lead them your army of undead fools will never conquer the world. You have lost." He stared at this beautiful, unearthly woman and felt his soul ache. "You have lost everything."

"That remains to be seen," she said abruptly, lifting her head so that Sinbad could see her eyes. The reflected fire of the volcano danced within them, and he knew in an instant the sorceress' plan.

Before he could stop her Illia was running, evading his grasp, and leaping straight over the edge of the volcano. He raced after her in time to see her body tumbling headlong into the bubbling firmament. A roar of tumultuous flames and burning rock shot up in her wake, sending him flailing backward.

The ground beneath him began to rumble, the quake sufficient for Sinbad's crew and the Warriors to halt, at least temporarily, in their battle.

"At last, we have a leader," hissed one of the Warriors, turning gleefully to Sinbad. "The sorceress Illia! She will rise!"

The other Warriors clacked their jaws appreciatively, and the battle abruptly recommenced. Those Warriors apparently dispatched by Sinbad and his crew drew themselves to their feet, grabbing up their lost limbs and fixing them back in position. Even the creature seemingly bested by Tishimi had rediscovered its skull and was busy reattaching it. Haroun's father, apparently dispatched by Delacrois' arrow, pulled himself to his feet, dragging the ebony-handled scimitar with him.

"This battle cannot be won!" yelled Delacrois, determinedly letting off a succession of arrows that again smashed into their targets.

"Every battle can be won!" roared Gunarson, crashing his axe across three encroaching Warriors, flinging bones, rotting skin and armor in all directions.

The volcano shook again, more violently this time, and great jets of fire sprang up.

As he fought, Sinbad maneuvered himself into position next to Gunarson. "We must get to better territory…"

"Aye, Cap'n!" bellowed the Viking, smiting a raft of the Warriors with a succession of well-timed blows of his blade, culminating in a smash with the hilt of his sword that spectacularly fractured a Warrior's skull.

"Gunarson, you, me and Delacrois need to buy us some time," continued Sinbad, parrying a blow from a cudgel-wielding assailant.

"Aye, Cap'n," riposted Delacrois, loosing an arrow that spun a Warrior attacking Tishimi around, in turn allowing her to plunge her katana into its throat. "It will be a pleasure!"

A further rumble of the volcano was enough to knock several of the Warriors and assorted members of Sinbad's crew to the ground. Sinbad barely managed to avoid falling himself, and saw that the rocky terrain beneath them was beginning to crack apart.

"Quickly, now!" he ordered. "Back down the path!"

His crew members nodded and began withdrawing, still battling the undead Warriors as they headed back toward the narrow, winding path that led down the volcano. Rafi, who had witnessed Haroun's encounter with the scimitar-wielding Warrior, used his newfound strength to propel the young man down the path and away from the Warrior in question.

When all but Sinbad, Delacrois and Gunarson remained, Sinbad shouted to Delacrois. "Henri, the volcano might help us make our escape, you follow?"

"Aye, Cap'n!" responded Delacrois, a grin forming on his face. "Perfect-ly!"

With the rest of their shipmates having departed, the Warriors were encroaching on them en masse, forcing Sinbad and Gunarson once more toward the rumbling volcano mouth. Delacrois had engineered himself to be on the other side of the opening. He had loaded a phalanx of arrows into his quiver and dropped to one knee in breathless anticipation.

The volcano roared again, sending up another torrent of fire, billowing smoke and burning rock. Delacrois seized his chance, letting his arrows fly through the surging magma so that they caught alight. Each of the arrows then found their target, causing the Warriors to explode in a morass of flaming bone and armor.

Gunarson yelled triumphantly, "Fine work, Frenchie!"

"Ought to slow 'em down a little," muttered Delacrois, as he joined Sinbad and Gunarson in running helter-skelter for the narrow path off the summit of the volcano.

They emerged, foliage snagging at them, onto the beach at the foot of Mount Luicanus. Omar and the other crew members whirled around, blades at the ready, then lowered them with palpable relief.

"A sight for sore eyes!" exclaimed Omar, patting Sinbad enthusiastically on the shoulder.

But Sinbad was already moving, not glancing back. "Delacrois bought us some time but the Warriors will shortly be upon us, mark my words. And now we have a far bigger problem."

Omar watched Sinbad's departing back, then looked incredulously to Gunarson. "A *bigger* problem? In the name of Allah and all that is holy, what does the Captain mean?"

As if to answer his question, the volcano rumbled, the sand beneath their feet quaking in response. "The volcano?" said Omar, struggling to remain standing. "Pah! The Blue Nymph can outrun it."

"I don't think he means that," suggested Delacrois, looking concern-edly up at to Luicanus' peak at the ascending cloud of gray-black smoke. "There's something else coming."

"What?" said Omar, as the other crew members gathered around him.

"The woman Illia leapt into the volcano's heart," explained Gunarson gravely.

"What matter?" responded Omar. "She was a harpie and she manipulated all of us, not least our Captain. She deserves death. I only regret she will not suffer for her crimes."

"Unlike her puppet Queen Asentua, Illia is a sorceress of tremendous power," said Tishimi quietly. "She has thrown herself willingly into the volcano."

"What're you saying to us, maiden?" demanded Omar.

"It'll transform her," said Delacrois.

"Transform her?" Omar looked at Tishimi in terror. "Into what, for the love of Allah?"

"Into *that*," said Sinbad. He had walked some little distance into the sea to get a better view of the volcano. Now he thrust Grachene's glowing blade toward the summit. The others raced to join him in the shallows, following his train of sight. From here they watched in horrified fascination.

Something was emerging from within the volcano. Huge, tree-like objects were coming into view, flesh colored in appearance but striated with lines of pulsating scarlet. They were fingers, that much was obvious, but their size and composition was unlike anything any of them had ever seen. This was the hand of a colossus, reaching up, grasping the lip of the volcano and using it to lever itself upright.

Now something else appeared, glistening and huge. It possessed what looked like a gargantuan human head, but one partially devoid of flesh, a sweep of singed hair emerging from the rear of the cranium. What little skin it did possess pulsated with the same striations as its enormous hand. As it turned its head it was possible to see its pale blue eyes blinking uncertainly in the watery sunlight. They were blood-shot, crazed portals to a soul in torment. As the creature rose still further, the tattered remnants of her ripped sari revealed still more of the ridged flesh in which lava now flowed, as well as more of her exposed, burning skeleton. The snake bracelet on her hand, now fully visible, was the only part of her that seemed unaffected.

Sinbad was vaguely aware of something occurring on the beach. The Warriors of Forever, still flaming from Delacrois' arrows, had appeared, shrieking, brandishing their weapons with newfound fury, Haroun's father

...something appeared, glistening and huge.

among them. Battle was joined, Sinbad's crew struggling to stave off the renewed onslaught. But Sinbad knew he could not help his crew, not yet.

He task was to destroy the sorceress Illia.

She continued to pull herself from the depths of Mount Luicanus, her head pivoting, as though looking for something. She placed one, then another mammoth foot onto the ground at the base of the volcano, sending shockwaves out that knocked Sinbad's crew and the Warriors to the ground. And then she found what she sought, her expression transforming from a look of bewilderment to one of incalculable rage.

"Sinbad," she hissed, her voice riven with agony, "*you* did this to me."

Sinbad looked up at to the monster. "You did this to yourself!" he riposted. He felt Grachene throbbing with energy.

"I offered you immortality!" she snarled.

"I would rather live in legend than in agony," he answered.

"Then you will not live at all!" Illia shrieked, opening her mouth wide. A torrent of lava issued forth, arcing through the air. Sinbad barely had time to cart-wheel aside, the stream of magma smashing into the shallows where he was standing and transforming the water into molten rock. He stood, panting, searching the creature's body for some weak spot, when she vomited another surge of fiery death in his direction, again forcing him to leap aside, again leaving a pile of molten rock in its wake.

For a third time she bellowed; this time the flow of lava finding its target. The gushing stream glanced him, wheeling him around so that he sank to his knees. The pain seared through Sinbad's shoulder, tearing at his tissue, at the bone beneath. His face a mask of pain, he was aware of a mighty, distended shadow falling across him. He looked up to see Illia bearing down upon him, lava dripping from her lips. Sinbad El Ari closed his eyes, prayed to Allah, and waited for death.

Chapter fifteen

But death did not come. Instead, a bellow of pain reached Sinbad's ears. He opened his eyes to see a figure repeatedly slashing at Illia's leg with an axe. A figure who could barely stand, his bulbous arms and haggard face almost torn beyond recognition. Almost, but not quite. Sinbad knew it to be Al-Bulcar.

The sorceress Illia turned and looked down at the impudent figure swinging the axe repeatedly at her leg, her molten blood spraying outward. Sinbad could see that if he didn't act quickly she would likely spew lava at him. Seizing his chance, and despite the pain coursing through his veins, he launched Grachene at Illia. The blade shot through the air, embedding itself in the monster's shoulder and causing her to reel backward.

Sinbad grabbed Al-Bulcar and pulled him away, heading for the beach, reaching upward as he ran, Grachene returning obediently to his grasp. Al-Bulcar looked up at him, glassy-eyed, as Sinbad pushed him to the ground behind the relative safety of some rocks. Gazing at him now, Sinbad wondered at the power of the perception-altering enchantment Illia must have employed to make a creature so patently constructed from material and straw seem so human. Al-Bulcar's face and exposed upper torso was a mess of rips, the stitching obvious to behold, tufts of straw emerging from where his neck had torn. Sinbad wondered even more, though, what force enabled this puppet to continue when its purpose was so clearly spent.

"Our lives were but lies," Al-Bulcar murmured, gazing up confusedly at Sinbad. "Why did you save me from the she-beast?"

"The same reason you saved me," responded Sinbad. "I value your life."

Before the blinking Al-Bulcar had a chance to properly reply Sinbad had turned on heel and was running back along the beach. Illia, who had temporarily lost sight of him, roared with indignant approval upon seeing him, and sent another stream of lava hurtling in his direction. This time Sinbad leapt the stream, feeling the heat upon the soles of his sandals. He skidded to a halt beside Rafi and Haroun, the oldest and youngest of his crew struggling to fight off a Warrior's snarling advance. Sinbad brought Grachene round in a tight arc and decapitated the creature. It didn't stop it moving but it made its attack much less purposeful.

He ushered Rafi to some cover behind some foliage.

"I need a way of defeating Illia and the Warriors. What is it?"

Rafi shook his head, the blood vessels on his face still glowing fiercely.

"I'm not sure. Al-Izrikel said the Horn of Ostiah was the only way of imprisoning them."

"The horn, the one worn by Asentua that was smashed, was a decoy."

"Aye," said Rafi, his brow creased in concentration. "Which means, if Al-Izrikel spoke the truth, that Illia must have access to the real object."

Sinbad peeked from behind the foliage. He could see Illia making her inevitable way through the shallows, intent on locating him. Sinbad's eyes played on her malformed figure, alighting on her wrist. He dodged back into cover.

"The snake bracelet," said Sinbad rapidly. "It's not a bracelet at all."

It was Rafi's turn to peek from behind cover. "The horn you mean? It could be, I suppose. How would you steal it from her?"

"That's my problem," said Sinbad, clapping the elderly man on the shoulder. "Thank you." He broke from cover, making for Gunarson and Delacrois who were fighting alongside each other. "I need a distraction!" he hissed at them, and the two men nodded their understanding.

Sinbad ran for the pathway leading up the volcano, narrowly avoiding a further torrent of lava from Illia. Two of the Warriors, who happened to be in the path of the onslaught, were transformed into sizzling rock, and stood petrified, their sword arms raised in readiness. Sinbad pelted up the winding path; catching glimpses of the battle below through the increasingly sparse foliage, until eventually he was completely exposed.

Looking down, he saw that Gunarson and Delacrois were being as good as their word. Gunarson was harrying Illia with a series of blows from his broadsword, while Delacrois ran hither and yon loosing arrows at her. She snarled in fury and pain, struggling to bat the men away, launching fire and brimstone at them, but they were both agile, intrepid fighters, and they were used to working in tandem to fulfill their aims.

With Illia distracted and her back turned, Sinbad chose his moment to leap. He landed with a tremendous thump on the neck of the creature, who flailed and screeched as she realized she was under attack from behind. Sinbad brought Grachene down deep into the sorceress' shoulder blade, twisting and turning the weapon, and sending up a fiery jet of liquid that narrowly missed his face. But the searing light of her own blood was too much for Illia's pale, sensitive eyes. The giant sorceress staggered back and forth, blinded and raging.

As Illia bucked and twisted in her efforts to remove Sinbad she sent a ferocious, mammoth stream of lava all about her, forcing Gunarson and Delacrois to dive for cover, the latter spattered with burning liquid. Still clinging to Illia's neck, Sinbad caught fleeting sight of Gunarson helping his friend. Illia's efforts had effectively created a circle of ferocious molten rock around herself, meaning that Sinbad was unlikely to receive any further help from any quarter. Now he was on his own.

He extracted Grachene, only to plunge the blade back into the upper portion of Illia's arm, again throwing up a spray of boiling blood. The monster screamed in agony and frustration, burned and blinded by her own body's secretions. A determined Sinbad grabbed onto the hilt of the weapon, riding it downward as the knife cut deep along her arm. At the final moment he grabbed hold of the snake bracelet, pulling it with him as he fell. The bracelet snagged on Illia's wrist, leaving him suspended, hands straining to hold on, legs flailing in space. Sinbad saw Illia's mammoth head looking down at him furiously, contorted with pain, barely able to see, but sensing he was within her grasp. She reached out her colossal hand and began crushing him.

Sinbad continued to hang from her bracelet, tugging with all his might, hoping that gravity, or Allah, might release it. Illia continued to squeeze, and he felt his ribs begin to crack. Finally, abruptly, the bracelet gave way. Sinbad reached out a desperate hand and then Grachene was back in his palm. He brought the blade ferociously down into one of her gigantic, malformed fingers. Screeching, Illia released her grip and Sinbad, still gripping the bracelet, tumbled through the air.

As he plummeted, the object he clutched shrank in scale, so that when he smacked heavily into the ground it was back to its original size. Winded, he looked up and saw Illia lifting her foot, intent on squashing him beneath her heel. In that second Sinbad had put the bracelet to his mouth, finding it hollow. From somewhere deep within him he tried to find the energy and breath to blow. It came abruptly: a low, long, sonorous note. As he blew he heard first one scream and then another and then another going up all around, until the air was a cacophony of shrieking. He continued blowing, pulling himself to his feet, seeking to look beyond the circular wall of molten rock, his eyes steaming because of the heat haze. The Warriors were collapsing to their knees, skeletal hands holding deformed heads in horror. Above him, Illia was also struggling to remain standing, both feet now planted on the ground, her body racking with pain. Like the bracelet she was shrinking, all the while retching gobbets of lava that Sinbad had to dart to avoid.

A disturbance behind him caused Sinbad to whirl about. Gunarson was using a dead log to smash a way through the circle of molten rock, creating a means for Sinbad to make his escape. Sinbad turned back to Illia. By now the young woman had reduced to her original size. She lay crumpled on the ground, her body still quaking, the striations glowing only intermittently, like dying embers. Flakes of her body were rising like ash into the ether.

"The same thing is happening to the Warriors," said Gunarson, crossing the log to join Sinbad.

"I see it now," explained Rafi breathlessly, joining them, his own body still glowing brightly with the power of the Arlegon map. "I see it all. They are being scattered. That is their imprisonment; to be turned to dust and scattered in the wind. Always conscious, always strewn throughout the world. An eternal torment. That was the prison Al-Izrikel made for them."

"Please," whispered Illia, her wretched body prostrate before them. "I don't want to be this forever... Please help me..."

Sinbad looked to Rafi, wild-eyed. "Is there anything we can do to help her?"

"She chose this willingly," said Rafi, rubbing his hands, his head low. "I do not think so."

Gunarson shook his head, "She was a foul sorceress who became a wicked demon. But I do not wish this upon her."

Tishimi had appeared, her head bowed. In her hands she held her katana, which she proffered to Sinbad. He looked at it incredulously.

"It is my father's blade," she explained. "It contains his chi, his soul. No magic can oppose it."

Sinbad held Tishimi's gaze, comprehension creeping across his features.

With due reverence, Sinbad accepted the sword, weighing it in his hands. He turned back to Illia. Her body had begun to feather, to blur at the edges, the particles rising into the breeze ever more rapidly.

"Please," Illia said again. "If you ever loved me, act now. Do not hesitate."

Without a word, Sinbad plunged the sword into the woman's heart. Her body arched once, then stopped moving. As life left her, Illia's form became clear, its lines absolute, no longer dissipating. Sinbad pulled the sword away, stepping back.

All around them, the Warriors of Forever were whirling into dust. Elsewhere on the beach, Haroun stood and watched a lone figure of a Warrior, a scimitar gripped in its hand, turning toward him.

"Son," rasped the figure. In his empty eyes there seemed to be some kind of understanding, some kind of appreciation. You might even say pride.

And then Haroun's father billowed away to nothing.

"The mountain is angry. It cherishes what it creates and in killing Illia we have taken something from it. We need to leave." Though Tishimi's words were spoken with characteristic softness and despite the quaking of the ground, they all heard her. They followed her gaze to the trembling summit of the mountain and saw the fire and sparks emerging from its maw. Each time it rumbled a great cloud of thick, spiraling smoke burst upward.

"The lady's right, Cap'n, we must away," urged Omar. "There's nothing for us here."

"We made a promise," said Sinbad, rising to his feet. He had been kneeling beside Illia's body, lost in contemplative prayer.

"The Xubanthali?" said Omar in surprise. "They aren't people. They're fabric and straw. Puppets."

"Al-Bulcar saved my life," responded Sinbad angrily. "It is for Allah and Allah alone to decide what is life and what is not. Not us."

"Aye, Cap'n," said Omar, bowing his head in shame. "What would you have us do?"

"Find them, get them to their ships," instructed Sinbad. "With all due haste."

A sudden explosion shot up from the midst of the volcano, sending lumps of burning rock cascading down on the beach, forcing several of the crew to dart out of the way or cover themselves with items of clothing.

"*Quickly!*" cried Sinbad. The crew did not need telling twice. They plunged back into the narrow crack in the rocks, heading for the clearing and the swamp where they'd first encountered the Warriors and discovered the true nature of the Xubanthali.

Sinbad, meanwhile, headed up the shore, back to where he'd left Al-Bulcar. The portly man was still cowering behind the rock.

"Is it over?"

"The sorceress Illia is defeated," said Sinbad. "But you can see for yourself the volcano is angry. It made her immortal and in killing her we defied it. We must leave this place as quickly as we can."

Al-Bulcar shook his head, "We are not worthy, Sinbad. We are not real people. We are but puppets, formed from straw and material, and animated by the evil sorceress Illia. When we are cut, we do not bleed. We do not cry. We do not holler."

Sinbad sighed, "Don't you see, Al-Bulcar? Blood does not run in your veins, I agree. But are you not talking with me? Can you not walk of your own volition? In fact, you can swing an axe and praise be to Allah that you did, because your intervention saved me from the sorceress. Illia may have created you and controlled you, but it is no longer so. You control your own destiny."

"I say again, honorable Sinbad. We are not real people. We are not flesh and blood. Not like you." He cast a hand toward Sinbad's crew. "Not like your people."

"From what I have seen of you and your people, the Xubanthali are no worse or better than those of us formed from flesh and blood, from tissue and bone. We are defined by our actions in this world, not by who we are."

Al-Bulcar, still frowning, inclined his head in nodding agreement. "Aye, perhaps. You are a good man, Sinbad."

Sinbad couldn't help but smile, as he helped Al-Bulcar to his feet. "We will get you home, as Allah is my judge. Come, I say. *Come.*"

A pensive Al-Bulcar accepted Sinbad's outstretched hand and rose to his feet. By now a stream of confused Xubanthali was being led back from the narrow gap and out onto the beach. The volcano thundered in fury once again, sending out still more lumps of flaming rock. Lava was cascading ferociously down its surface.

"We must hurry," instructed Sinbad. As they ran another eruption flung molten debris outward in a wide circle, spinning rock arcing through the air and impacting violently on the beach and into the sea. Lava was advancing rapidly down the surface of the volcano. Any foliage or trees caught in its way flared into sparking life before being consumed amidst the creeping liquid.

"Is that everyone?" demanded Sinbad as he approached Gunarson. The Viking stood on the beach, directing the fleeing Xubanthali towards their ships. Crew-members escorted them, glancing behind themselves worriedly.

"Aye, I think so," nodded Gunarson. He took Al-Bulcar firmly by the arm and pulled him through the shallows towards the ships.

Sinbad stood on the empty beach. The lava had reached Illia's corpse, and he watched as it began to consume her, transforming her corpse to molten rock. The ornate snake bracelet, the real Horn of Ostiah, lay atop her and he watched it cracking apart as the insatiable red liquid ate that too. In a moment more Illia's body and the Horn had been completely covered.

The sorceress Illia and the Horn of Ostiah were gone forever.

And so were the Warriors.

The sea bubbled and boiled in their wake, transforming to a blood red. Sinbad had necessarily dispatched Omar and Gunarson each to captain the two Xubanthali vessels, as none of the Xubanthali seemed in a capable state of mind. Even amidst the roar of the volcano and crashing of the waves Sinbad could hear both men shouting their crews into action. That both vessels managed to turn themselves and make up distance with the Blue Nymph suggested that this approach had been a shrewd one on Sinbad's part. It was Sinbad's feeling that with Illia no longer controlling them, the Xubanthali needed a sense of purpose, and that this was a good way of furnishing them with one.

Mount Luicanus rumbled its disapproval as the three ships plowed away. Sinbad and his crew-mates watched the volcano receding into the distance, its crown enveloped in a trail of fearsome, heavy smoke, its otherwise pitch black crust striated with scarlet. Sinbad turned his attention back to their course. They were negotiating their way around the crooked rock fingers they had encountered on their inward journey.

Luicanus rumbled again, and suddenly sprays of lava burst forth from the fingers. Byrne staggered backwards, bellowing with pain, his body studded with molten rock. Tishimi and Delacrois rushed to his assistance, while all across the Blue Nymph crew-members fought to put out fires. Sinbad saw the problem was even worse on the Xubanthali ships, the crews' composition of straw and cloth making them more likely to burn if any of the flaming debris hit them. He saw Omar and Gunarson racing to instruct them. The sail of one of the ships had caught alight, and needed the attentions of several Xubanthali before it was extinguished.

They were through the rocky fingers now, the fires on all three ships dealt with. Of the two Xubanthali craft, one seemed largely unscathed. The other ship, though, the one whose sail had ignited, now suffered from a tremendous burn mark in the centre of one of its sails.

"That'll need to be repaired afore we can continue," observed Rafi.

"Aye," said Sinbad.

Once they were far enough away, the ships dropped anchor in order that repairs could be made ahead of their long journey back to Xubanthali. Al-Bulcar boarded the most damaged of the Xubanthali vessels that he might oversee the mending of its sails. By the time he had finished, it seemed to

Sinbad's trained eye that he had made several considerable improvements to their design, reducing them in size and attenuating their appearance in many appealing ways. The following night, when they were underway once more, the faint sound of drums reached Sinbad's ears. He looked across to see the crew of Gunarson's craft beginning to celebrate in their traditional fashion. The merriment quickly spread, first to the Xubanthali vessel captained by Omar, and then to the Blue Nymph itself, the Xubanthali aboard encouraging Sinbad's crew to join them in festivities.

Sinbad gazed to the heavens, at the spread of twinkling stars, at the moon bisected by gently drifting clouds.

"I am sorry your crew did not get their treasure," said a voice close by.

Sinbad turned to see Al-Bulcar, newly returned to the Blue Nymph. He seemed in fine fettle, the cuts on his face and arms seeming to have healed, or rather to have been mended. He also seemed appreciably thinner. In addition, something of Illia's spell appeared to have returned: he looked to be a man once more.

"That is of no matter," observed Sinbad. "Our adventure was our reward. I am glad to see you look better."

"Aye," nodded Al-Bulcar. "We have been diligent with needle and thread. We have repaired most injuries admirably, I believe."

"And yet?"

Al-Bulcar sighed, "We were the sorceress' creations, her puppets, designed to deceive you and your crew into travelling to Mount Luicanus. Her actions were evil, of course, or at least misguided. But now she is gone we lack a sense of…"

"Purpose."

"Yes, purpose. That is the word. What are we for? What is our point in life, in the world?" He looked to Sinbad earnestly, inquiringly.

Sinbad smiled, "That I cannot tell you."

Al-Bulcar hunched over the side of the vessel, his hands straining against the Blue Nymph's wooden side. They were no longer bulbous, and his gut seemed much reduced.

"The future is terrifying."

"Aye," nodded Sinbad. "And exciting too."

The pair lapsed into silence, looking out to sea, the sounds of celebration echoing across the lapping waves. "And is adventure reward enough for you and your men?"

"Perhaps," reflected Sinbad. "Is liberty from Illia reward enough for you?"

"No," said Al-Bulcar sadly, shaking his head. "I fear it is not."

Sinbad nodded. "Your children."

"Our memories of their laughter, of drying their tears, teaching them to walk, to swim. All lies. There were no children. There can never be any Xubanthali children. How could there be? Though we are created we cannot ourselves create."

Sinbad pursed his lips, "Unless…"

Al-Bulcar creased his features, "Unless what, Captain?"

"Illia animated you. She was able to animate the statue of Xuba as well."

"But she was a powerful sorceress," protested Al-Bulcar, shaking his head.

"I know little of sorcery but I understand that particular enchantment is straightforwardly grasped."

"Yes," nodded Al-Bulcar slowly. "I see what you propose. But it's… well, it's extraordinary, Captain."

"Is it?" asked Sinbad levelly. "You could create children from the same substances from which you were yourselves wrought: cloth, straw…"

"And then give them animation." Al-Bulcar's hand flittered excitedly to his mouth. "Is it possible, what you suggest?"

"You would need a source of magical energy, I think. That will be your biggest challenge. But if you overcame that… Who knows?"

"Thank you, Captain," said Al-Bulcar warmly, grasping Sinbad by the hands. "I will think on it." He turned, and disappeared into the celebrations.

Sinbad watched him go, a thoughtful expression playing on his chiseled features.

Chapter Sixteen

The journey back to the Xubanthali island was as uneventful as any sea journey could hope to be. Omar got his desire for a storm to break the bleak, unchanging weather when a particularly taxing tempest materialized. The monstrous weather front sought with all its might to capsize the trio of ships, and in the case of one of the Xubanthali vessels very nearly succeeded. The Xubanthali, though, had learned immensely during their time on the sea, and obeyed the instructions of Omar and Gunarson, still at that stage their temporary captains, with unquestioning efficiency. Such skills were also evident weeks later when the ships encountered pirates intent on seizing the Blue Nymph and scuppering the Xubanthali vessels. With the Xubanthalis' help the threat was repelled, as was a tentacled sea creature that attempted to drag the Blue Nymph to its underwater cave a month later.

With each experience the Xubanthali grew still more in confidence, and Sinbad began to hear excited chatter about what they might achieve once they had returned to the island. The conversation with Al-Bulcar played on his mind though, and he noticed in some of the Xubanthalis' bonhomie a trace of regret at something that never was, and as far as they could see, never could be.

Part of the reason for the flotilla's swift progress undoubtedly lay with Rafi. The Arlegon's living map had demonstrated no indication of leaving him. If anything Rafi had shown signs of *assimilating* the sorcery. He no longer stood at the prow, watching the horizon and dictating to Sinbad and Omar their trajectory, scolding them when the Blue Nymph veered from the correct path. Instead, he bounded around the deck, engaging in the activities of the crew, discussing Gaul literature with Delacrois, explaining history to Al-Bulcar. His body seemed to change at the same time, Rafi's elderly physique subtly altering, the mottles on his hands dissipating, his posture becoming altogether straighter. In short, he was becoming young again.

It was some time before the crew would find out what this really meant. Rafi, taller than ever because of his straightened posture, was illustrating a particular point with some expansive gesturing of his arms, while the diminutive Tishimi listened with characteristic politeness. Sinbad could see that the spidery lines on Rafi's skin were pulsating even more than normal, and that the rate of their glowing had increased significantly. The old man had stopped talking, his face an expression of alarm, and suddenly he began to jerk uncontrollably. The veins on his body were no longer pulsing, but had become a constant glow, so that his entire body seemed to be consumed by the red light. Tishimi went to help him but recoiled, presumably from the heat he was now giving off. The rest of the crew turned from their tasks in horror, but there was nothing any of them could do, the heat was so intense.

"Enough," said Sinbad, as he approached Rafi, shielding the light from his eyes. "The power is too much for you, Rafi. You are wise enough to know that."

"Such power, Sinbad," said a rasping voice from deep within Rafi's body. "I can see everything. I can map all futures, all pasts. I can live forever, for always, if I so choose. I will no longer be old, frail…"

"Nobody can truly live forever. Not really, not in this world, though perhaps in the next, if Allah decrees it," replied Sinbad, Grachene at his side. "The price is too high. The Scholars of Bethshea could only manage it through words. The Warriors lost their minds. It is not living, Rafi. Not really. Search inside yourself. You know it to be true."

"The power of the Arlegon courses through me," hissed Rafi. "It is immense. It is… *beautiful..!*"

Tishimi was at Sinbad's side. "He will destroy himself and us if he is not stopped," she whispered urgently.

"Yes, but how?" responded Sinbad.

"I have such power!" cried Rafi, his eyes burning the brightest red. "But I don't know what to do with it."

"Give it to us," said Al-Bulcar. The Xubanthali leader had appeared, holding something in his hands. Sinbad struggled to see what it was. It looked to be a bundle of clothes, but on closer inspection Sinbad thought he could discern arms and legs, and a sphere that might be a head. A jolt of realization hit him. It was the body of a child. No, wait, it was a dummy, fashioned to look like a child.

"Please," implored Al-Bulcar.

Though Rafi's face was only just visible through the searing light, Sinbad could see a trace of emotion he recognized. Compassion. Rafi beckoned to Al-Bulcar, and the Xubanthali leader stepped toward him, lowering the mannequin to the deck of the Blue Nymph before stepping away.

Despite his height, Rafi stooped and reached out a hand, energy sparking and weaving from his long, slender fingers. A crackle of flame issued from his fingertips, connecting with the pile of cloth and straw. As it did so, the glow of Rafi's body started to wane, ever so slightly. The flame traced around the body of the child, and everything was silence, save for the creaking of the Blue Nymph and the roar of the eternal ocean.

For long moments nothing happened. Then the pile of cloth and straw sat up and stared, bewildered, at the world around him.

The Xubanthali swarmed around the youth, kissing him, cuddling him. Meanwhile, Sinbad and Tishimi rushed to the figure of Rafi, who had fallen back against the side of the ship. While his entire body was no longer a mass of energy, the lines remained, gently pulsating with warmth.

"No treasure. Mon ami, we were duped." Delacrois sat on the golden shore, staring out at the sea. In his hand a smooth pebble, which he continued to absently caress. In the near distance bobbed the Blue Nymph and the two Xubanthali ships. The sky was a paradisical blue.

"We stopped an evil sorceress," observed Gunarson.

"Is that enough?" mused Delacrois.

"For an honorable adventurer, yes," said a gruff voice beside them. It was Omar.

"You never did think we'd find any treasure," replied Delacrois, casting the pebble into the sea. It skipped the water once, twice and then a third time before disappearing into the gently lapping water.

A giggling child's laugh reached them on the breeze. This time there was no deceit. The child's laughter was joined by another, and then another. The three men turned to see a clutch of youngsters running along the beach, skipping and playing in the shallows.

"No treasure, huh?" said Omar ruefully . "Come, the Blue Nymph awaits us. Our time here is at an end."

"Venerable Sinbad," said Al-Bulcar, bowing deep. "Your reputation is deserved. You have given us so much." Sinbad and his crew stood on the jetty, the Blue Nymph bobbing gently beside them. The Xubanthali had gathered in their dozens, and with them the children. Sinbad's eyes played on their innocent faces: newly stitched together, stuffed with straw. As Sinbad looked at Al-Bulcar's slimmer, almost svelte figure, he realized who had provided the straw from which that first child had been wrought. And as his eyes played on the Xubanthali ship with its curtailed sail, he understood where the cloth had heralded from.

"I am glad you are happy and that this island rings with laughter," said Sinbad, himself bowing.

Al-Bulcar smiled, "In return, we can offer you these paltry tokens and our eternal, heartfelt gratitude." The children stepped forward, proffering basket after basket of extraordinary fruits and vegetables, of bread and meat, which the crew warmly accepted. Sinbad's men nodded and grunted approvingly as some of the Xubanthali adults brought forth mammoth kegs of the islanders' distinctive wine.

"I thank you," said Sinbad. "Your generosity will sustain us as we set sail for our next adventure."

The children, having handed over the baskets, now gathered around the figure of Rafi, pulling at his robes and hugging him. All of the energy of the Arlegon's living map had been used to animate the children, and there remained no traces of the extraordinary glowing lines on his body. Instead, his face was once again lined with experience, and his slight stoop had returned. The aged man looked down at the children capering around him with a barely concealed sense of wonderment, and Sinbad thought he saw the trace of a smile on his thin lips.

"Oh, and one last thing," said Al-Bulcar suddenly. "The treasure you were promised. I am sorry you were misled."

"No matter," said Sinbad with a dismissive wave of the hand. "We will find other riches."

One of Al-Bulcar's aides had passed something to him, which the Xubanthali leader in turn passed to Sinbad. As the Captain lifted the object up, he was aware of his crew crowding around him.

"Sacre bleu!" exclaimed Delacrois.

"Impressive," nodded Gunarson approvingly.

It was the statue of Xuba, the one that Sinbad had defeated. It had been bolted back together, and its jeweled eyes glittered up at him, newly polished.

"I am sorry the rubies are not the same size as when you vanquished the beast. But they will be worth a substantial amount, I think," said Al-Bulcar. "And who knows? The object itself might have value too."

Sinbad looked up at Al-Bulcar inquiringly. "You do not have use of this?"

"No, Captain Sinbad," replied Al-Bulcar sagely. "We no longer need Xuba."

The Blue Nymph's indigo sail bowed full in the wind, the ship dipping and rising through the encroaching waves. From his vantage point atop the crow's nest, the young man Haroun watched the crew, his slender hand idly stroking Samson the cat. There was Rafi and Tishimi engaged in heated conversation about some point of philosophy. The mighty Gunarson sharpening his great battleaxe. Delacrois relaxing in his gently swinging hammock, lute in hand, plucking melodies of lost love. Omar at the tiller, a look of quiet satisfaction on his sun-kissed features. Haroun felt a wave of pride course through him: pride at the crew, pride at the ship.

Pride at himself.

And on the prow of the ship stood a man that time would never forget, a man whose deeds and derring-do would live forever in memory. His name was Sinbad El Ari.

Sinbad the Sailor.

Sinbad the legend.

The End

ABOUT OUR CREATORS

WRITER –

CB HARVEY – is a British writer, narrative designer and part-time academic at King's College, London. His novella, *Dead Kelly*, set in the Afterblight shared storyworld, was published by Abaddon Books in 2014. His other forthcoming work includes short stories for Moonstone, a *Commando* comic for DC Thomson and narrative design work for a British game developer. He's also currently writing a book about science fiction and fantasy franchises for Palgrave-Macmillan.

CB Harvey's gothic fiction won the first Pulp Idol award, jointly conferred by *SFX Magazine* and Gollancz. He's the author of 'Love and Hate,' the second episode in the *Highlander* audio series produced by the British company Big Finish under license from MGM and Davis-Panzer and starring Adrian Paul from the *Highlander* television series and movies. CB haa also contributed to Big Finish's *Doctor Who* range, published under license from the BBC. He's written numerous videogame narrative design documents for Sony and written videogame journalism for magazines such as *Edge, RetroGamer, Develop* and *ScriptWriter*. CB has also authored academic papers about *Battlestar Galactica, Doctor Who,* Neil Gaiman's comic work and transmedia storytelling. Oh, and he has a PhD in videogame storytelling. Seriously.

He lives in London with his wife Anna and two kids who think he just spends his time mucking about and getting paid for it. Which just isn't true. *Honestly.*

ARTIST–

JAMES CONAHAN – is a Chicago area resident. He graduated from Art Center College of Design, Los Angeles, CA with a Bachelor of Fine Arts degree. Jim has won several Merit Awards form the New York Society of Illustrators, a Citation of Merit from the Chicago Artists Guild and Print Magazine Award of Design Excellence. He has exhibited at the Daley Center in Chicago, the Pritzker Military Library and his art has been included in a Japanese National touring show.

More Sinbad!

SET SAIL FOR ADVENTURE

The greatest seafaring adventurer of all times returns to the high seas, Sinbad the Sailor!

Born of countless legends and myths, this fearless rogue sets sail across the seven seas aboard his ship, the Blue Nymph, accompanied by an international crew of colorful, larger-than-life characters. Chief among these are the irascible Omar, a veteran seamen and trusted first mate, the blond Viking giant, Ralf Gunarson, the sophisticated archer from Gaul, Henri Delacrois and the mysterious, lovely and deadly female samurai, Tishimi Osara. All of them banded together to follow their famous captain on perilous new voyages across the world's oceans.

So pack up your you traveling bags, bid ado to your loved ones and get ready to sail with the tide as Sinbad El Ari takes the tiller and the Blue Nymph sets sails once more; its destination worlds of wonder, mystery and high adventure.